D0934970

THE
MOONLIT
TRAP

THE
MOONLIT
TRAP
by Ruth Willock

A Martin Dale Book
HAWTHORN BOOKS, INC.
PUBLISHERS / *New York*

THE MOONLIT TRAP

In preparing some of the background for this book, the author
is grateful for the assistance of Edith Knight and Donald Darling
in London; Marion d'Heureuse and John Roggmann in Zurich.

To my mother and father,
Mary and Frederick Willock

1

The sand around us was only now at this late hour growing cool and a little damp in the wind from the Sound. Sheltered by the invisible sandbar, the bay curved darkly away from dwindling shore lights, edged by the faint surge of the tide as it creamed and receded.

Now that the four years are over, I thought, I shall miss this. This north shore of Long Island. The smell of the sea.

Beyond the harbor a tanker signaled long, demandingly, to announce its arrival, and Tony stirred beside me. His cool hand covered mine, but I dared not move, dared not respond. *Not now,* I thought. Not this last night. *Not yet.*

And then he reached across and firmly but gently turned my face toward his. "Constance?"

In the silver beam of moonlight I could see the dark eyes, brooding now, the sensitive lips. They were too close.

"No." I drew away abruptly. I could not add, "Not yet," for I was not sure whether there would ever be a time.

"Don't go tomorrow." His words were sharp. "I don't want you to go." He sprang to his feet, grasped both my hands, and pulled me up, his actions rough, almost angry.

"Please, Tony." My disappointment that he had forgotten our talks, my plea that we wait, was tinged with relief. It was easier to cope with this sort of mood, to reject this sort of behavior. Tenderness would have been another matter, could have complicated my life now. "It will only be a couple of months," I reminded him.

"I wonder." He did not relinquish his hold, although we stood apart and in darkness. Clouds had drifted in the wind, obscured the moon. I could not see the intelligent eyes, the smile that often hovered on his mobile lips.

"Peg will be waiting," I murmured, slipping my fingers from his.

"I'm sure." The bitterness was almost palpable. He turned away, yanked the canvas beach seats toward him, deftly folded them, and stacked them against the small clubhouse.

I glanced round at the darkened cottages behind us, rising from the Long Island shoreline, stabbed with only an occasional rectangle of light.

"Come up for coffee." It was an attempt at reconciliation. And even at this distance I could see the leaf-shadowed glow of our bay windows, Peg Hobart's and mine. The light was faint but there.

We drove in silence around the shallow curve to the pleasant sprawling neo-Tudor garage over which Peg and I had lived during our college years.

And as usual lately, Peg was waiting. Beneath one lighted lamp her half-finished coffee, half-smoked cigarette, half-open book on the low table beside the sofa were clearly indicative of her mood. The romantic strains of a Mozart sonata from the hi-fi apparently had done little to relieve the tension.

"You're late." She swung around and pushed herself up from the stacked cushions. Her cool glance swept past me.

I knew that Peg did not approve of my dating Anthony Jenner, but she had never been so obvious about it. After all, no matter how ambivalent I was about romance, how suspicious about love, I was twenty-one and on my own. Tony was twenty-five and free. And Peg knew we were just friends. At least I had been attempting to preserve that relationship. Especially now. It had been difficult—was still difficult.

I frowned, puzzled by this last-minute display of antagonism. "It isn't midnight yet," I said, and moving into the room, switched on another lamp. Something on the table, an object new to me, rocked and settled. I stared down at it: a tall, carved, medieval wooden figure, a bishop or priest, his deep-creased weathered vestments flowing back in arrested motion. A handsome piece.

Peg did not wait for my question or Anthony's. "Gift." Her voice was dry, flat. "Bon voyage from Father. He is in Mexico selling Hobart's nuts and bolts, I think."

She unfolded herself, and limping slightly from the childhood injury (I could never forget it, for I had witnessed her fall), she crossed the room toward our streamlined kitchenette. Her normal sardonic behavior was returning. "You'll settle for coffee,

2

I suppose," she flung over her shoulder at Tony. "Unless you plan to split."

"Thanks. If you don't mind too much, I will clink cups." His dryness matched hers. "Your last night here." His words could have been for both of us; they were slightly accusing. Accusing Peg perhaps. It was she who had promoted the plans for a summer trip to Europe, had induced me to join her in Switzerland and Austria for a walking tour after six weeks of lectures in London.

Tony was tall, somewhat inclined to be rangy, yet far from awkward, his movements invariably swift, soundless. I was surprised when I started back from the china cupboard to see that he had crossed the room, picked up the new carved piece. He was examining it minutely, the mitre, the chasuble, the pallium, the base.

"This thing come today?" he asked Peg.

"Special delivery, the way the man does everything." She was heaping coffee into a filter machine.

"It's not Mexican."

"No. Came from some antique shop in New York."

Tony whistled.

"I know," Peg said. "*I* scrounge around for my bits and pieces, restoring and repairing. *He* probably told a secretary to order this."

"Not all that easy," Tony muttered. "I think it's an old piece. And very good."

Peg had turned, was watching him. Interest flickered almost reluctantly in her green eyes. "I know." She turned away again, and her long straight mahogany hair hid her expression. "Better than the piece I brought back from Germany last year. This one's eastern European, I think. Hungarian, maybe."

He nodded, not looking up. "You'll likely find more of this sort of thing, even in Austria, if you really dig." He set the figure down carefully but did not move from the spot; in fact, he seemed distracted, distant, until Peg snapped her fingers.

"You're not with it, Tony," she said.

His reaction, his words, were slow, unlike him. *For* is the proper preposition. I'm not *for* this summer plan at all."

"You mean you're not for *Connie's* summer plan," Peg stated flatly.

He ignored her. His eyes were on mine, and I was glad that

3

there were three of us in the room and that I had not seen his face when we had been alone in the cloud-shrouded moonlight. In the warm brown depths there was a lost, drained look I could not understand. He seemed more vulnerable, not truculent as he had been lately. And somehow—I do not think I imagined it—there was a hint of fear—or apprehension.

Not half an hour later I stood in the doorway to our rooms at the top of the single flight of stairs bidding Tony goodnight.

"Stand there," he whispered. "The light, your hair—it's pure gold. The way you wear it suits you so." He reached out, then dropped his hand. "Don't ever change it. Don't ever look like everyone else."

I knew what he meant. My hair was long, but I would not permit it to hang over my face, across my eyes, tangle with collars and scarfs. I wore it brushed back, twisted into one fold on my neck, sometimes the heavy strand caught with a concealed barrette. At least the hair that flowed down my back then was out of my way.

Anthony Jenner was not the only man who had admired my hair. There had been other men who had come close to touching me, loving me. Other men I had turned from. I heard Tony say, "You're beautiful." I could not thrill to such words, could not laugh as Peg might have. The words embarrassed me.

Thrust back in memory I was off guard for the moment until I felt his lips, cool and light on mine, tentative, searching. The sort of touch I did not trust. I stiffened.

"Oh, darling." The words were barely breathed, yet the pressure of his fingers on my shoulders was almost painful.

"Good-bye, Tony." I moved back, held out my hand.

"It's good-*night*, remember. I'll be seeing you." His footsteps were quick and firm on the stairs, on the flagstones outside.

I felt the movement behind me then. "That means he definitely expects to see us off tomorrow night, I suppose," Peg said.

I did not move immediately, controlling the flick of annoyance at her habitual watchdog surveillance, which had seemed too apparent tonight. When finally I slipped into the room and closed the door, I spoke more brusquely than I ever had. "After all, Tony did 'package' our plans, did offer to see us straight through to the plane. I thought you'd actually arranged it?"

"That was weeks ago, before you and—" she paused and looked away. "Yes, I know it's convenient. Trouble is, *you've* been too convenient for him, I think. Living in the village as he does, then using the garage downstairs, he's been too close." The hesitation was brief before she rushed on. "And, Connie, I do wish you'd fall for the right man, just once."

"And Tony's not?" I had not meant to defend him; I suppose it was partly defense of myself.

"Tony's not, believe me."

I started to collect the cups from the table. I had heard some of this before, during these school years, about almost any man I had met. At the kitchenette I looked back. "Why are you so certain this time, Peg? You've always let things drift off before. You've never harassed me."

She was switching off lamps, had reached the last one, and did not look up when she spoke. Her answer was not quick and flip.

"I'm sorry, Connie. I really am. Perhaps it's because I know how you've been pushed around." She was standing by the wooden priest, her hand resting on the shoulders. Very quietly she added, "*We've* been," and blew out her breath.

"We're a fine pair, aren't we?" I was surprised that the bitterness I had so long controlled should surface now. "You and your jet-set family spawning too many brats—those are *your* words, Peg, not mine. Your ecological hang-ups, your religious probing." Remorse overtook me. I stopped, appalled.

"Right," she said tonelessly. "Compensation. You know that. You've indulged."

I said nothing but turned and proceeded to wash the china too vigorously in too-hot water. Yes, I knew.

"Connie, let's face it. Your family irritates me as much as mine bugs you. Two fathers. Two mothers. No wonder you're——"

"Afraid of love?" I whipped a tea towel from the rack, pretending preoccupation with a routine task.

"Listen to me," Peg said. "You're tired. You haven't had a free hour since graduation, since May. Working all day and half the night at that restaurant for two months. While I've been floating from Brooklyn to Montauk collecting things." Her fingers encircled the priest's neck.

5

"I didn't mind, Peg. I thought of London every time I saw a dollar tip. And Austria."

I had never been abroad; the idea had only been a dream until my father—my real father—had offered to match every dollar I saved. The total at the end of July had been surprising.

Though Peg and I had grown up almost next-door neighbors in an upstate city, my father had not inherited a booming engineering supplies business as hers had. And for a while, until my mother married again, he had had two wives to support. And a new son. I was fortunate to have gone to college at all. And now I was starting work on my master's degree with the short course at London University: late eighteenth- and early nineteenth-century literature and the arts—in London.

It was indeed a dream come true. And if Peg had not produced an apartment there for me, I doubt I should have been able to afford to meet her in mid-September in Switzerland. Peg's vast Hobart family connections included a traveling older cousin who was generous with the key to what she called her *pied-à-terre* in London.

And Peg had known Tony, who was in the travel business, since she had gone abroad last year, but she had not introduced him to me until he had moved his car into the garage below our flat a few months ago.

Apparently recalling this now, she groaned, managing a twisted smile. "Trouble is, I feel responsible for this one."

"Tony's been a gem, you know that, Peg. I'm glad you knew him. I'd never have had time for all the details."

Anthony Jenner's Students' Travel Bureau (Overseas) Inc. had handled everything but the London flat: plane tickets, the actual enrollment at the University in London, transportation to Zurich, a tiny apartment there, a small inn at our first Austrian stop, and of course all of Peg's Swiss and Austrian travel plans too.

"That's his business, honey." Peg started for our small study-bedroom, and I followed. "The next six weeks should be a break for all of us. You in London. Me in Zurich. Tony here." At the bathroom door she turned and faced me. "He *is* staying here, isn't he? On Long Island?"

"Staying here?" I repeated, staring at her. "Why shouldn't he?"

6

"I don't know. I just don't know about that lad. And I'm not sure I trust him. He could turn up anywhere. With any encouragement."

Before I answered, I unzipped my sheath and stepped out of it. "Don't worry about me," I said.

"You think he's really got the message, then?"

"Yes."

"Think of it!" she called back from the bath. "Free at last. After tomorrow you'll finally be alone. Couldn't happen to a better pal."

Alone?

When our rooms were dark, the night silent, the first misgivings stirred in some secret chamber of my mind. Perhaps because I *was* tired, because I had not had time to think.

The truth was I had never been truly alone before; for the next six weeks I would be alone among strangers. And yet the alternative was not the answer. I needed the freedom, even freedom from Peg. And a new environment. This summer I had balked for the first time at being subjected to the two emotional bouts I had faced in former years, to being split in half, shared with two families. Father's in upstate New York. Mother's in her native Wisconsin. I needed perspective to be able to cope with all of them eventually, to be able to accept all of them completely.

Peg knew that. She had fought her own battle and conquered in her own way. She dwelt in a brittle shell of bravado that hid her natural warmth. And I knew I must find my own way. But it was not easy.

I tossed, tangled myself in the sheets, punched the pillow, was about to return to the sitting room to read, if I could, when Peg spoke. "Something on your mind, Connie?"

"Can't sleep. Last-minute qualms, I guess. Silly of me. For the first time I'm a little afraid."

"Afraid?" Against the curtains and the pale glow beyond, I saw her sit erect. "Of what?"

"Of . . . myself, maybe. Of the next six weeks. The responsibility of a strange flat. London, alone."

"Oh." I thought she drew a deep breath before she lay back in the darkness again. "Is that all?" It was a moment before she added, "Relax. There's an associate travel setup in London.

7

Name's on the Jenner letterhead. Just in case the flat gets burgled or you lose your money, your passport, your luggage." Her voice trailed off. "Heaven forbid," she mumbled finally.

Tony was shockingly late the next night, and the drive across the Island to the airport wild, especially after we encountered dense traffic on the Southern State Parkway. There was a moment or two when I thought we might actually miss the plane. And sitting between him and Peg, I was constantly aware of her sidelong glances at him, the hostile, once appraising look she sent his way.

Finally, with eleven minutes to spare before plane time, we pulled up at the airlines terminal. Peg snapped open the car's door and muttered to Tony, "Now, see how you can fumble the check-in. We'll aim for that panting monster on the runway."

He managed with professional skill, came straight through with us to the plane's steps. Except for carrying both our tote bags, he ignored Peg until he bid her a brisk "Good luck" with a brisker handshake. Then he turned to me.

An official beside us slapped his pad shut and signaled an all-clear. "Sir," he tapped Tony's arm.

Tony ignored him, too.

"Two months is a long time." He lifted my chin. His expression was difficult to fathom now; there were too many busy lights on the field. "You'll be alone," he paused, "for a while."

Remembering, I raised my hand. I had wanted to ask him about his London affiliate, and now it was too late. The airlines official was repeating, "Sir, I must ask you——"

I had backed up the first step when Tony said, "Don't let anything, anyone touch you." And then he caught me to him, his lips once more cool and light on mine. The whispered words were for me alone. "My love, you don't *have* to go. You don't."

"*Sir!*"

I should have thanked the official, for if there had been more time, if Tony had always been as tender as these last promises, I might—I just might—have turned back.

8

2

The plane roared into the August twilight, sweeping in a wide arc north and east, away from the vast megalopolis spill-over below. I looked down, looked back, imagining that I saw Tony's pumpkin-colored car winding away toward the web of parkways and the north shore village.

But of course that was impossible. Like the chain in a broken necklace, the hundreds of cars glittered in the last rays of the sun, diminishing until they disappeared altogether into the faraway blur of the island. There was nothing but the cold deep blue of the sea; Tony was far behind me.

I did not want to think about him now. He was still too close; his parting kiss still lingered on my lips. I wanted to believe that. it *was* too early to talk of love. And yet I already felt a strange sense of loss, already missed the new warmth I had longed for, the tenderness that had come so late. I shut my eyes for a moment, remembering the months just past.

Peg, of course, had been the catalyst. It had been Peg with her amazing pent-up energy who had conceived and planned the next two months. She had found Tony.

I stirred uneasily, wondering not for the first time whether her censure of him was not the result of a more personal involvement, conscious or not. I stole a glance at her.

"A penny," she said slyly, without turning. "I'll make it a new one, British, worth three of ours. You were thinking of him, weren't you?"

"I was thinking of all of us."

"Well, leave him out of it. This is the perfect time, I told you."

I stared at her profile, smiling in spite of my secret doubts, for I noticed that she was already casting a critical eye at the dinner trays. And, faintly defined with her favorite bronze tint, her parted lips indicated an eager interest.

9

"Buy you a split of champagne," she offered somberly.

"Save your money for your wooden angels in Austria."

"Forget that now. We're celebrating the end of an era."

Are we, I thought. But I said nothing.

After dinner, when most of the lights had been dimmed and the plane droned into the night, the thoughts crept back, fragments of memories of my hours with Tony. I wished I could dismiss him for the time, at least, as part of the college "era," but I could not forget the last hours, could not comprehend his strange new tenderness any more than I could Peg's curious antagonism. All the qualms that had upset me last night and had recurred during this last day persisted through the Atlantic darkness while Peg dozed restively beside me.

Maybe Peg could dismiss the past months, the years, because there were no special ties, no plea to hold her. But I could not, not now, not without a sense of guilt at having left something pending, something I had thought—hoped—would drift off.

My book, open but unread on the cushion in my lap, slid off and struck Peg's thigh before I retrieved it. And she awakened, squinted over at the paperback *Guide to English Literature.* She groaned, "Gawd! You're into it already."

"Peg, I've work to do. You know I'm going for my master's."

"So go tomorrow."

"Oh, shut up." I turned back to the Pelican edition I had barely glanced at and ignored her.

I *had* work to do. And I had worked night and day to make it. Six concentrated weeks of it. English literature of the romantic period from 1780 to 1830. On scene.

The London scene at least. So many writers of that period had been born there. Blake, Byron, Coleridge, Lamb. More had lived there, died there.

I wanted to see their London, to feel it, to stand on the bridge where Wordsworth had looked back upon the river's ships, the city's towers; to walk in the halls of Westminster. . . .

"You've got the keys?" Peg dropped into the powerful silence of an air-borne jet.

Like a camera refocusing, my mind flipped to the present. The keys? Keys? Of course. The keys to her father's cousin's apartment. They had arrived two days ago via air mail express. I nodded, tapping my handbag.

Peg shifted again, slithering down in her seat. "Forgot to tell you. Cousin Nell was having the place done over last year." She sent me a crooked smile. "The pad may glitter a bit, but don't worry. All that gilt is not gold. Just a decorator's bonanza."

Weeks ago when the flat had been offered to me, I had protested that it would be an imposition. But Peg had cut me off. "No *way*," she had insisted. "Cousin Nell wouldn't set foot in London except in the season, whenever that is. In the meantime, if I know you, she'll get her pad aired and dusted daily in between her weekly char's possible appearances. Very mutual three-way deal."

"You don't seem too sure about the weekly appearance," I had murmured.

"If it's still Tilly, don't be surprised if she sneaks a few extra days in County Kerry."

Now, weeks after this warning she stared up at the overhead rack in the 747. "You know I'm sorry I didn't arrange for a London stopover for a day or two."

"So am I. My first trip. I am a bit——" I hesitated, and Peg leaned on the arm between our seats.

"Don't tell me you're actually hung up about London." When I did not answer immediately, she prodded me. "You aren't really afraid, are you?"

"That's not exactly the word. It's just a sense of isolation, somehow." I could not quite explain that a sense of loss was involved as well. "Everyone we know is back in the States. You'll be in Switzerland. And I'll be coping with someone's— a stranger's—apartment, new people, new curriculum, marketing."

"That part will be fun." Peg chuckled quietly. "Struggling with pounds and pence."

"Please."

"Picking up the language." Her lips twitched.

"Just a minute—it's English, at least."

"Sometimes you'll wonder, honey."

"Thanks a lot. That's all I need."

"Don't get uptight. You'll soon get used to the London scene." She leaned back, frowning. "Any questions about the flat, the neighborhood, nab the porter-doorman type. They know bus numbers. Nearest ironmonger, chemist, and all that." She giggled.

"Good."

"And Connie, I really would stop off with you if I weren't already a day late registering at the Zurich *Evangelische Hochschulgemeinde*. And don't ask me to say that again in my condition." She slumped back in her seat and closed her eyes.

Actually, Peg's German was better than mine. She had studied German and French formally; I had picked up mine from my Swiss grandmother.

Peg's courses started a day ahead of mine. She was continuing her religious studies, concentrating on the sociopolitical aspects. Convinced that the world's ills, from overpopulation to wars, were based on our outmoded religious beliefs, Peg's summers had been spent in European capitals absorbing what she irreverently called the angles.

Despite her protests, however, it was my secret belief that her interest in religious art was not incidental or paradoxical. I thought it was compensation, that she actually suffered in her own way, that what she had experienced and witnessed had battered her spirit, brought disillusionment.

Through the hours of that night I dozed and woke, my dreams ambivalent as my waking thoughts had been. Over the monotonous hum of the plane I heard Tony again, his strange last plea: *"Don't go . . ."* My mind warned: too soon for involvement; my heart: too soon for dismissal. . . .

Doubts rode with me into the brilliant dawn, which touched the cloud-blanket beneath us with rose and gold. Arrival jerked me from one world to another, from the past to the present.

The plane zoomed through the clouds, circled under a gray ceiling until the river was visible, the Thames, the clusters of the old city, the somehow familiar weather-washed monuments, green squares, and parks. We banked, streamed away toward the spread of the airport and the appointed runway, and finally cruised to a halt on English soil.

We had arrived. *We were in England.* I glanced around, wanting to share the rising excitement with Peg, but she was busy zipping her tote now—it was mine, actually; we had swapped at the last moment because mine was deeper, could hold more "extra junk," as she called it, in case she found anything of interest during the next six weeks alone. As she stuffed papers down beside her passport in her handbag, a crisp hundred dollar bill fell out.

12

She threw me a quick look, I suppose because she thought I would scold her for her careless habits with money, with any valuables. Then she mumbled, "Mom's parting gift. Found it last night, rolled into a hole in my bishop's head with a bon voyage note. There was a space behind the mitre . . ." her voice drifted off.

I was suddenly furious with that family of hers who blithely dispatched priceless objets d'art, dispensed crisp new currency, but did not appear to need her. If she had asked me even at this last moment, I might have abandoned my London plans and gone with her to Zurich.

I felt her pushing something into my hand, and I looked down. "Take this," she mumbled. It was the hundred dollar bill. "Pop down to King's Road and pick up a trendy outfit or two. Fun," she added. "You need . . ." She did not finish that sentence etiher, but I closed her fist around the bill and shook my head.

"Thanks, I'll manage." We had never quite agreed on clothes —or money.

She shrugged, and I thought she seemed embarrassed. I reached out a hand to touch her, but she edged into the aisle between two eager students who had sat across from us and uttered something under her breath which brought a burst of laughter. It was so like her.

Then she limped off toward the runway and the terminal passage where I joined her, walking by her side; I was speechless for reasons I could not entirely identify.

There had been a subtle change somehow. I wanted to comfort her now, to say, "It'll only be six weeks, Peg. In the meantime *do* take care. Don't be too careless." No. That was not the word. Generous. Peg was too generous. With her time, her money, her heart.

My face must have reflected my last-minute fears, for she nudged me with her elbow. "Come off it, Connie. You'll make out. I just hope you don't make out too well and get into trouble. Anyway, I'll be *agog* when you get to Zurich."

"Write to me," I said, with little hope. She preferred the telephone.

"You write. Practice your German. *Auf Wiedersehen.*"

Passport Control loomed before us. She swung left to join the in-transit passengers for her connecting flight to Zurich,

13

her long, dark-stockinged legs clearly visible against the summer pastels and white. At the door she turned and waved before she disappeared.

I was on my own. It was the end. Or the beginning. And although something inside me did not quite welcome the abrupt change, there was no time to gauge the effect, no time to think at all. Within a few minutes after I had waved good-bye to Peg, I was boarding the waiting coach for London.

The air, although damp, was cooler than in New York, the roads gleaming beneath a soft summer rain. And through intermittent showers the city emerged slowly: red brick and blackened chimneys blending with brown stone, flaking ivory paint, gray blocks. A Victorian mews whirled by, a Regency terrace; black, blue, yellow doorways, columned entrances, tiny shops, a few incongruous skyscrapers.

The coach swung off the London streets onto a ramp and braked to a stop in a vast terminal that buzzed with summer travelers. At first the taxi queue seemed endless, which somehow surprised me, but with curious self-discipline it moved.

Number 8 Crown Gardens, when the cab driver finally found it after a battle with awesome rush-hour traffic, was in a cul-de-sac south of Regent's Park, quite off any main road or street.

Looking up at the Georgian-influenced facade, I recalled Peg's words: "Not a large place. Four floors. Maybe twenty flats." She had neglected to mention the chic wrought iron balconies against rosy brick, the spanking white trim, the air of affluence.

Behind me I heard the taxi churn off and for a moment felt abandoned and a little chilled. Though the rain had ceased, the morning sky was November-dark; the leaves of the twin laurel trees flanking the entrance-steps dripped steadily. The sound was very clear, for the street was empty and singularly quiet. And no one, no "porter-doorman type" was there to greet me.

Discreet classic elegance was the keynote of the circular lobby, the only jarring accent a tiny box of a room adjoining the paneled door labeled "lift." The box was empty now. As I sidled into the small lift cage, I caught an angled view of a sagging bench, a ledge, a stained coffee mug, and an untidy straggle of papers.

Abruptly, on the top floor the elegance returned. Glistening enameled doors, gleaming brass, thick-piled carpet. Flat 19 was diagonally across. The key clicked properly. The door opened inward.

I stopped, uncertain. Had something, someone moved?

Propping the door open with my bag, I edged over the threshold and flicked the light switch.

The images that confronted me in the large square hall were so disconcerting that it was a moment before I realized they were all my own reflection. And the glitter of mirrors compounded by crystal sconces and chandeliers flowed through an open door into the room beyond. Its glowing beige and gold transcended the gloom of that dark morning. Daylight—such as it was—filtered through long rich brocade across inch-deep carpeting.

Last summer I had worked in a small antique shop in Rochester, and even at first glance I suspected that those must be fine porcelain and silver treasures on the escritoire, Baccarat or Lalique on that handsome pair of chests.

My first reaction was dismay that I had dared accept the responsibility for such a place, but as I stepped over the threshold of what could only be called a drawing room, indignation struck. The air that stirred around me was stale with flower rot, the dry smell of cigarette ash, and I suspected dust.

I had been prepared to air and dust "the pad" as Peg had indicated. But this place needed attention now. Long-dead white roses drooped in etched crystal vases. The philodendrons that spilled from golden cachepots were crisping for lack of water; a few yellowed leaves littered the floor beneath the mantel. Tilly had indeed overstayed her holiday in County Kerry.

I moved backward into the hall and closed the mirrored door on the room. I would straighten up later. "Living quarters" came first.

The Regency theme saved the bedroom. Over a broad window heavy black and white striped curtains were drawn, floor-length, against the gray day; the fabric repeated in cushions on the Empire sofa bed. Rose silk upholstery on lounge and desk chair, rose coverlet on the sofa, rose carpet fitted into every corner. Chest, desk, and small tables everywhere were cluttered with mementos of past and present.

At a touch the dressing room door slid back emitting a

15

jammed flurry of feminine clothing crackling in plastic. And an exotic scent.

I threw open the broad window on a jungle of gardens overspread with dripping sycamore and beech in full summerleaf, all motionless beneath a forbidding sky. The cool morning air was welcome . . . needed.

The kitchen, modern and streamlined though it was, reflected the same forgotten theme. Once I had flicked the light switch, a ventilator hummed, stirring only the dead air at first.

Cup, saucer, breakfast dishes, stood, half-rinsed, in the stained sink. The refrigerator revealed a number of unidentifiable objects plus milk reduced to translucent curds and whey. The flat had not been aired or cleaned for weeks.

There was no window in the room. Only a click-latch door that yielded to no clicking or tugging. I pushed it finally, and it flew open onto a landing, yanking me with it.

Clinging to the knob, I stared down into the gloom through the iron slats of a fire escape. Along the landing to my left three or four more service doors were blank and silent, marked by covered trash bins.

At least I knew where to cache the dead flowers and other items. . . .

That morning I scoured the neglected areas of the kitchen, down-graded the bedroom into a bed-sitter, increasingly aware as I worked of the silence that enclosed me within the walls of Flat 19. The peculiar quiet extended to the outdoors beyond the steel stairs, beyond the black and white striped curtains.

When I had safely tucked away the last delicate memento into a bottom drawer, carefully wrapped in my left-over tissue, I peered out the window once more.

Nothing moved except a branch where a starling perched and fled, nothing whispered. The short street and the wide road to which it led must be behind me, beyond the walls of streetfront flats, the elegant brick facade.

A bit late I began to wish I had listened to Tony's argument against the apartment and for the university's residence hall. "You'd be more convenient to libraries and lectures," he had insisted. "Probably safer, too." That had been almost a whisper, but I recalled it vividly now. "And the Hall is cheaper than rooms and meals in the States would be."

Peg's comment when I had broached the subject had been a characteristic, "Cheaper than free?"

By the morning's end I began to wonder whether I had made a bargain after all. I longed for a bath, hours of sleep, and eventually a hearty English tea. Which meant marketing.

Marketing. I swayed out of the flat to the lift. This time a figure leaned from the box of a room in the lobby. Square, solid, gray-uniformed, the man eyed me with something less than welcome.

"I'm Miss Farrar," I started, but he cut in.

"Who'd ye wish to see?"

"I'm—" I held up the set of keys "—staying in Miss Hobart's flat."

"She might've told me," he grumbled. "I must've been de-l.verin' the post when ye come. Too much to do around here as it is." He ducked back into the box, then out again, reading from a dog-eared note. "Month ago, right after Miss Hobart left, the maid rung up. On holiday, she said. S'pose ye'd guessed that by now, eh?"

His short laugh was not the friendliest I had ever heard, but when he started to slip back into his little nest, I clutched the door and asked him about the nearest shops.

"Left turning at the top o' the road," he muttered. "Five minutes walk to Marylebone High Street." As an afterthought, he added, "Name's Edwards, if madam wants me for anything." I hoped I would not need him.

Under other circumstances the next hour might have been fun, but I was so weary now that coping with strange weights, brands, prices to say nothing of strange money was almost too much. With little help from a harassed check-out clerk in a small self-service shop, I counted out the totaled pounds and pence although I had not the slightest idea whether my purchases represented my usual careful marketing or not.

Bread, cheese, eggs, milk, tea, coffee. I should have made a list. I should have stayed at the flat and cooked some of the Scotch oatmeal I had seen in a cupboard. I should have stayed home.

Home, wherever that was.

Yes, I was homesick that morning. I trudged back to Crown Gardens thoroughly disoriented. Too much had happened too quickly. And the excitement of departure and arrival had faded, leaving me with a queerly flattened feeling. I knew that jet-lag must be part of it, and lack of rest for a prolonged period. All I wanted was to sink down onto smooth sheets and drift into oblivion.

Yet even that was not so simple. Beneath the rose coverlet on the sofa-bed only a thin summer blanket lay over the mattress. It was an effort to recall where I had seen the linens, to drag out sheets, the case; to tug and turn and fold and shove. I sank down finally, lay back, and closed my eyes.

I have no idea what time it was when I awakened, but it was very dark and rather cold, and I was aware of the faintest lingering echo of a bell.

The ringing started again. Two short rings. I fumbled for a lamp, the familiar bedside lamp in the Long Island apartment. My fingers struck something solid. Wall? Another two short rings brought me upright. I swung my legs around to the other side, jarred into realization that I was in London, striving to recall the position of the china lamp and whether I had left the telephone in front of or behind my books.

By the time I located the central light switch, the pink instrument on the desk was silent again, the only sound in the room an almost imperceptible whir of the electric clock on the wide chest near the window. Its hands pointed to midnight.

I had slept almost the clock around, almost twelve hours. I leaned on the desk chair, gathering my wits together—what little appeared to be left of them. The bell pinged once more, the sound so close now that I had only to reach over and lift the receiver.

It was like Peg not to give me a chance to say "Hello," or "Yes?" or state my name. She cried, "Hi, honey! Have you been out?"

"Hardly." I had not meant to flatten her; I was ridiculously pleased to hear from her. I added quickly, "You called before."

"Yeah. Wanted to wish you the luck *I'm* having. Grooviest student body—wow! This country's changed since I was a girl." The giggle rippled over the hundreds of miles from Switzerland. I could almost see her. "How's London?"

"Quiet."

"That's a switch." There was a brief pause. Then, "You'll get into it, Connie. You've got six weeks. Or, maybe—" a burst of laughter "—maybe Zurich's where it's at, now."

I realized then that her words, her laugh, were a little too loud, a little blurred. I said, "You're smashed, Peg."

"Right on. The local wines are simply *organic.*"

I knew that if Peg were with me now she would complain that *I* was archaic, worse than her grandmother, but nevertheless I said it. "Go to bed." I started to cradle the receiver and stopped midway.

"A great idea." The laughter was muted now and distant, as though she had turned away. "But I just may need a little time to work on that."

She hung up first.

3

In a sense the past should have conditioned me for the next morning, but even then after four years away from home I still seemed unable to banish old memories: the days when I had been besieged by little fears and insecurities, easily wounded by a careless word from my elders or—worse—my contemporaries.

I should have been prepared for my first day at the university. Or, more important, as it turned out, I should have listened to Tony and bypassed the well-meant offer of a London flat.

The girls were polite enough at first. They said, "Hi!" and "Where are you from?" They mumbled a word about the weather. "Fab" was the word.

It was immediately apparent that while I had been coping with a stranger's flat, they had been settling in, forming friendships.

One girl asked, "You're not staying at the Hall, are you?"

"No. I . . . a friend loaned me a flat."

Glances flicked from my looped-back hair down the length of my navy sheath.

"An apartment. Groovy." The pretty blonde waved frantically to someone behind me.

I wished I could say, "I'd rather be with you," but these girls were so *together;* they did not encourage such confession. I said, "Do you like the Hall?"

"What's to like?" A girl from Nebraska shot back. "We're stuck with it."

A Carolina voice explained with soothing patience, "Rooms in a girls' hall are nothing like a *flat,* of course."

One of the Canadians murmured, "How *great,* living in digs." She flung up an arm suddenly and yelled, "Hi, Lynn! Here I am!" She was the first to drift off, to regroup with yesterday's friends.

From close behind me I heard a quiet, "snobs," obviously meant only for my ears. And turning, I caught the amused glint in a pair of the clearest blue eyes I had ever seen.

Fortunately at that moment someone yelled, "Everyone up to Room 4!" There was a general scramble for notebooks and ballpoints, and we were on our way to a day of briefings, instructions, assignments, the inevitable tour of scattered buildings.

My clear-eyed classmate moved along beside me, cocking her head, capped in short, ragged black hair, in my direction. I started an explanation of my position, "Well, I *am* late," I murmured. "And I suppose living off-campus——"

"Forget it," the girl said. "So do I. With an aunt in a suburb in the wrong direction. And if you think Victoria's ghost doesn't linger in this island, you don't know Auntie or that house off Putney Heath. Damned place is run like a base camp."

I laughed. "Better than living in a museum. I'm afraid to breathe in the drawing room for fear I'll blow over a Lalique vase."

Over mid-morning coffee in the refectory in Senate House, apparently the central building for the whole university, we exchanged names. Hers was Undine McCarthy, and of course by then I had already guessed that she was a New Englander. "Framingham, Mass.," she told me. "That's Framing*ham,* as in pork. Not *um* as in England."

By special permission, because Undine's aunt served dinner

promptly at 6:30 and "no nonsense about it," she left with a wry, "See you—if I don't fall down an escalator in the Underground staring at all the bosoms and navels on the posters that float by." Although she had said little during the day—we had been too busy with our notebooks—I was sorry to see her trot off.

By the time the rest of us completed our tour and rounded Russell Square behind our student guide, it was late afternoon. We stopped at the bottom of the Museum's steps.

Our guide's voice was husky now; she must have been as weary as we were. "Your identity cards will admit you to either of the libraries inside. Super, really. Dickens used the Main Room, and Thackeray." Her long braids swung as she smiled around at us. "You know, the whole bit. From Gray to Shaw, and the Bloomsbury Group."

They all moved off, but I stood below one of the stone lions and looked up at the dark mass of granite. I realized at that moment that I had at least one advantage over Undine McCarthy. I was close to sources. The flat was an easy walk from the University. I slipped out my identity card and started up the steps.

Except for a faint echo somewhere behind me, it was very quiet as I moved into the shadowed gloom. The echo followed me along the halls, ceased when I entered the long reading room, the North Library. With its tall pillars, its narrow green desks, its pools of lamplight at each place, the room was pleasantly inviting after the day's heat.

The librarian barely glanced at my card as I moved toward a reference counter, edging out my notebook again. It was then that I became aware of a prickly sensation that I was being watched, and I thought suddenly, perhaps that was not an echo behind me, perhaps someone had followed me.

I glanced around and met the man's eyes.

He was tall, seemed different. Dark eyes. Silver hair. When I turned back to the open reference book, I thought: silver? Was that possible? Or was it a trick of lighting? He did not look as old as his hair. A professor? But, whoever he was, why follow me? I had not met him, had not seen him before.

Then I heard movement, footsteps toward the librarian's desk, and I thought I had been mistaken. I risked a brief look to reassure myself and caught his glance again.

He was standing by the librarian and in that instant made a slight gesture toward me before he turned his back. Lamplight glinted on the librarian's spectacles as she shook her head. She was not smiling.

Nor was I amused. The day had been difficult enough. I swept my notebook into my open bag and quietly, while the man's back was turned, skimmed out the doorway. Via a circuitous route I left the Museum's south entrance, doubling back to the shops on Mortimer Street I had passed in the morning.

The flat, when I finally reached it, was cool and smelled pleasant enough after last night's airing. But there was no one to share the New Zealand lamb I had bought on the way, to appreciate hot rolls and crisp cold salad. The only voices in the flat were those of strangers, disconcertingly aloof, emanating from the BBC evening programs on Nell Hobart's smart TV set built into a bedroom wall panel.

The next afternoon was as still and sultry as New York in summer when I climbed the Museum's steps again and entered the long reading room. Loaded with books on the social setting of the nineteenth-century novel, I slipped into a chair and switched on the lamp. Today I was keenly aware of the scene, the priceless treasure of words surrounding me. It was a long time before I started scribbling.

I lost all track of minutes . . . hours. Until suddenly, next to me, a chair scraped and a lamp snapped off. Glancing up, I saw that the pool of light illuminating my books seemed brighter; the dark green desk and the shadows beyond almost black in contrast. Had I neglected time again? Had night come?

I looked at my watch.

"It *is* late, Miss Farrar." The voice was low, faintly accented, and came from a tall form across the table.

I stiffened, at the same time aware of movement outside the periphery of the lamp's light. My eyes were adjusting to the darkness. It was the man I had seen late yesterday. The man *had* followed me. I drew back.

"Permit me," he said.

Into the glow, a white card slid toward me across the table. It read, "Students' Travel Service (Overseas) Ltd.," with an address off Russell Square a few blocks away. And at the lower left the name: Guy Black. Tony's associate, I supposed.

The man persisted. "Haven't you done enough work for to-day?"

"*Sh-h-h-h*" someone hissed.

I left the card where it lay and stood up, gathering my books together. It was late, just on six, but I resented the interruption, the man's persistence, the peculiar approach.

Beyond the doorway after I had deposited my books and retrieved my identity card I faced him. "Did Tony Jenner ask you to look me up?" I was determined to learn the reason for his repeated appearance.

At first I thought the face, a half-head above me, was more than handsome; there was a classic beauty about the features. And yet when he smiled now, I saw that his mouth was a trifle wide for the chiseled jaw, his nose a fraction longer than perfection.

"You're annoyed, aren't you?" he said.

"You followed me." The statement sounded more like an accusation than I had meant, though now his obviously suppressed smile goaded me. "You have my name. Didn't Tony include my address?"

"That's just it." His eyes, almost as black as the triangular brows, sobered. "He didn't."

"And the Centre here?"

"Does not divulge addresses. Merely descriptions, which I found most helpful." He did not suppress the smile now, though when I muttered, "I'm sure," his eyes met mine in common understanding. "I also learned your possible whereabouts, which did not help yesterday, for the librarian had no record of your name."

I was moving along the hall toward the north entrance, fighting a peculiar resistance to this man, and then I stopped. "Is there anything special, any particular reason why you looked me up?"

"Yes. Checking over schedules I found your booking was incomplete." He was patient enough. "Jenner's office simply dropped you in London, where we lost you."

"I go to Zurich mid-September."

"I know. You see, we really should have a record of our clients' whereabouts in case of flight changes or cancellations."

"Of course." Now I found myself slightly irritated with Tony for having overlooked this for whatever reason.

We had reached the north doorway, and abruptly I knew

23

the reason for the early darkness. Lightning flashed. And I was startled briefly by the silver hair; he was too young, not past thirty I should think. I stopped just inside the door, uncertain of my next words, uncomfortable under the steady gaze of the dark brown eyes.

"I am forgiven?" he said.

"It is I, I'm afraid, who has been very rude."

"Please. You were right to be cautious." In the peculiar light of the storm his skin—in contrast to that hair—seemed rather dark; there was a tanned outdoors look about him that sharpened the white of his gray-striped shirt and dramatized the dark business suit. I watched him pluck a card from a leather folder, slip it into my open tote. "Now you will know where to find *me*," he said.

Beyond him I saw that the rain had slackened; I heard a few of those around us move off. I said finally, "Shall I give you the address now?"

"Not over a sherry?"

I stepped down onto the gleaming stone. Fortunately, the rain had ceased. There was no reason for me to remain here with him. "You're very kind," I said. "Not . . . today. I've a few chores to do. Marketing——"

"Marketing? You have a flat?"

"A friend loaned me one." I felt faintly defensive as I reeled this off again, but Guy Black seemed delighted.

"Jolly good," he said. "Is it convenient?"

"Off Devonshire. I can walk."

"Splendid. May I offer my services?" The bow was almost imperceptible, a mere fleeting gesture, distinctive and in character. But I wished we had not moved out to the landing.

The pretty blonde classmate and the one named Lynn were crossing Montague Street toward the pavement below us, not five yards away.

Their chatter ceased, their greeting to me a silent nod, a raised hand. I could guess at a topic of conversation in the Hall tonight. "Oh, *wow!*" One of them was sure to say. "A friend loaned her an apartment. . . ."

The marketing was more fun with a "friend" however. Guy Black knew the area—he said he lived not far away—and he knew foods. That day he introduced me to a pale Caerphilly

24

cheese and another called Kashkaval from a Greek shop; he steered me to small English tomatoes, fresh watercress, and Italian bread. He bought much more than I, confusing me, for I was not certain whether it was for his kitchen or mine.

As we left the shops in Charlotte Street and turned west toward Crown Gardens, he said, "Apparently you are able to cook."

The tension was building up again, and perhaps because I was not certain of the outcome of this innocent expedition, I could neither repress it nor quite understand it. Once more my words were sharper than I had meant them to be. "I cook because I like to eat."

I was relieved when he laughed. "*Bien dit!* Well said. And very practical."

Bien dit . . . was *that* the accent? I said, "Are you French?"

"My mother was Italian. My stepmother French. For a time I seemed destined to be volleyed between Paris and . . . Venice." The pause had been brief. The smile did not extend to his eyes.

"And London?" I added that city because his name was certainly neither French nor Italian. His father, I decided, must have been British.

"And London, yes."

Whether I had imagined the bitterness or not, his disclosure of this brief glimpse of his past brought a slight change in my attitude, a faint upsurge of sympathy. And, more relaxed, I said something about life between Paris, Venice, and London hardly being a miserable fate.

The smile remained rather more contemplative than wholehearted. "French schools merely added more language problems. Not a happy fate for a young lad shuttling about between families." He stopped and glanced away. "Fortunately, my father managed to untangle me from . . . various ties."

I was surprised at the subtle change in him; he seemed younger, more appealing, especially when he added, "You can see there are disadvantages in all this moving about."

"Yes," I said.

"Friendships become rather more difficult, you understand." He looked up at a street sign. "I am in Queen Anne Street today. Perhaps the Place Vendôme tomorrow. To seize the moment . . ."

I waited for an end to the sentence, but there was none, and I shuttled once more to uncertainty about the outcome of today's encounter, wondering how I was to dismiss Guy Black at the door to Number 8 Crown Gardens. Should I bid him "Good evening," add "Thank you so much," and "Now you know *my* address." No. *That* was wrong. Must I ask him to come up to Flat 19 simply because he was carrying the large bag of groceries? No excuse. I had carried larger bags than that.

My silence may have communicated something to him; he said, "You are preoccupied. I interrupt your thoughts, your plans, perhaps."

I stumbled over the words. "I was wondering how I should thank you."

"Not how you shall get rid of me?"

My lips parted to answer this astonishing surmise, but no sound came. I stared up at him and met the most understanding glance, not pitying, perhaps compassionate; in any case *different*— again the word that so well described Guy Black and his actions.

He said, "Why are you so afraid?"

"Afraid?" Wimpole Street seemed endless. I thought, Will I ever get back to the flat? I said, surprisingly, "Afraid of what?"

"Perhaps not of me, precisely. Of something more, something larger. Life?"

"I'm not sure I know what you mean."

He ignored that. "I speak from the wisdom of years. Observe my gray hairs."

I looked into his eyes instead and saw the laughter there. "You've been teasing me all along," I said, inexplicably relieved. "Haven't you?"

"Not exactly. While you have been plotting to evade me, I have been thinking of your work, believe it or not."

I frowned, casting him a suspicious glance.

"Once you have parked all this—" He tapped the brown bag "—in your flat, I propose to offer you a chance at further research this evening."

"Research?"

"Well, perhaps that is a bit overstating it. Will you accept

26

atmosphere? A chance to absorb atmosphere. How would you like to see a famous pub? It is said that Samuel Johnson——"

"Not the George?" The old George Inn was at the bottom of my list with a question mark beside the name because I had doubted I would venture there alone.

"The George," Guy Black said.

At the entrance to Number 8 Crown Gardens he remained ou'side in the short private street while I dropped off the groceries in the flat, zipped out of navy into mint green, switched from open tote bag to handbag, quickly whipped on earrings and bracelet, added lipstick. When I returned and stepped down to the drying pavement, Guy Black was leaning against the railing of one of the little Georgian houses at the dead end, looking as elegant as the backdrop. He strode toward me.

"*C'est si tranquille, ici.* So quiet here. You are most fortunate!"

"Yes." I made no further comment about the flat or neighborhood. "But it will be interesting to see a bit of London now."

"You've not seen anything of London?"

We had reached the wide street at the end of the cul-de-sac, and as he flagged a taxi, he looked over his shoulder at me.

"I'm here to work," I added quickly.

"We shall have to revise your curriculum." There was a hint of mischief in his smile. He looked ten years younger, a student; no older.

In the taxi with him beside me, the streets of London flowing by, I tried to pull my thoughts away from this complex man. One moment sophisticated, chic, a continental prototype. The next moment an appealing boy.

My first instinct had been right, I thought. The man was dangerous. I almost laughed aloud.

"That's better." I saw his hand move toward mine, and stop. "You are finally relaxing with me."

Somewhere in the midst of a traffic jam after we had passed the colorful closed shops in Regent Street, a sense of unreality overcame me. Trafalgar Square? I could not believe it. I leaned forward, all but pressing my nose against the glass of the door. When the cab swung away past a church I had seen in photographs ("St.-Martin's-in-the-Fields," Guy Black said, obviously watching me), I craned round for a last glimpse of it just as Nelson's Monument reared against a washed evening sky aflutter with starlings. Admiralty Arch. Down Whitehall, past the Horseguards Parade, Downing Street. Even those did not prepare me for the approach to the Thames.

It was as though all the elements had conspired to confound me. Against the last light of evening, a sky now yellow as a candle flame, the Houses of Parliament and the Big Ben tower loomed black as a poster as we moved toward the bridge. I turned to peer out the rear window of the cab. I wanted to hold the moment, never to forget the sight.

But it was soon blocked by a bright red bus that swerved in behind us, and I turned just as we sped over Westminster Bridge, the river rippling black and gold in a strong tide. I was wondering with a sense of loss whether it was the bridge of Wordsworth's meditations when Guy Black interrupted my thoughts.

"The Royal Festival Hall is down the river." He nodded to the left. "Your studies will take you there."

I floundered, adjusting from bridge to hall. And then he explained. "You'll be attending theatres, concerts, galleries, opera. They are all included."

"You know the course I'm taking?"

"It's part of my business. Students' Travel, remember. Besides, though you're the only one Jenner sent us for your particular session, we've thousands of others all over Europe."

"Did you book Peg Hobart in Zurich?"

"Swiss bookings would be handled by our offices in Geneva or St. Gallen."

The streets around us had changed abruptly past the bridge. No longer distracted by historic scenes, I had noticed the proprietary emphasis on his use of "my business" and "our offices." I wondered why I had not thought of it before. I asked, "Are you the owner . . . is the travel business yours?"

"Not quite. It's . . . a family operation. Someday——" He stopped, and turning, peered out the window. "We go around Waterloo Station now, toward London Bridge."

Since my teens I had dated boys, cycled with them in small American towns, munched frankfurters and hamburgers at counters, whirled along highways in rebuilt sports cars, in compact

28

sedans, had consumed my share of capuccinos in Greenwich Village coffee shops, had been dazzled and impressed by candlelight 'and starched linen in a few fine restaurants (until I had worked in one).

But nothing had ever touched that evening. During the minutes of that drive through a fading post-storm twilight the panorama had shifted so frequently that my sense of place became confused with time. In the cobbled courtyard of the George I was simply plunged back three centuries, and silenced by the shock.

Beyond the low doorway to the tavern I could see nothing but the glow of lantern light, the gleam of pewter, a multitude of dark forms against half-timbered stone.

Mesmerized, I followed one—a steward, I suppose—and still mesmerized, agreed to sherry while Guy Black ordered a Cinzano, which turned out to be merely Italian vermouth. I simply was not with him; I was far away and regressing down through the days of Dickens, Pepys, Johnson. I was with them. They moved like shadows across the pages I had read before I had come to London, since I had come here.

"You've left me again," Guy Black said, and I was spun back through time, space. I gazed at him and blinked a little at the speed of the transition. He touched his glass to mine, and I swallowed the mellow tawny stuff as though it were a glass of cool water, forgetting until it was down that it had been hours —nearly eight—since I had swallowed anything.

Whether or not my face reflected the glow that followed I cannot be sure, but my tongue was certainly affected. When Guy Black chided, "Where have you been?" I said, "From here to eternity and back to Russell Square." Then, leaning toward him, I went on, "You know it was a mistake living off campus."

"Off campus?"

"A mistake accepting the flat. Most of the girls haven't accepted me."

"Ah. So *that's* been on your mind, has it? But I should think you might have been warned about that."

"Tony did. And he was right, you see. I should have listened."

"So he was against it." He drank his aperitif and waved an order to duplicate our drinks which I was about to protest when he said, "You apparently don't always obey Tony." His eyes, dark and steady, held mine, and for the first time I felt gauche, unsure. Then he smiled and the panic fled and I thought: He's teasing me again.

But he persisted, using another approach. His glance had never left mine; I was still uncomfortable so that when he asked flatly, "How did Tony ever let you go?" I had to turn away to regain my equilibrium.

"Let me go?" I said, deliberating, examining every word this time; no longer trusting the sherry. "There really wasn't a question of permission. Tony Jenner is a friend."

"Good." His single word stopped me. I might have gone on, might have said too much, protested too much.

The kiss on my hand when he left me later at Crown Gardens was cool and light; it was . . . different.

But in that instant Tony's shadow rose between Guy Black and me. His words, uttered at the plane's steps, whispered across the silence of the London cul-de-sac. *"Don't let anyone . . . touch you. . . ."*

At that moment I would have given a great deal to be able to laugh at the continental gesture, at my reaction. But I could not. I could not even answer Guy Black's simple *"a bientôt,"* though I was perversely pleased that he had implied then, as he had all evening, that there would be another time.

4

Alone in the quiet flat, I wondered whether I had talked too much, responded too quickly to the man's magnetism, perhaps in overcompensation for my initial belligerence.

But after all, he *had* been delightful, had displayed considerable patience with me from the beginning. And he had marketed with me, *for* me as it turned out; conducted a private pocket-tour of a slice of Mayfair and Westminster; produced a logical literary setting for the sherry, which had finally loosened my tongue. It would have been a very strange female who would not have appreciated what Guy Black had done for her.

Admittedly, he was a man of charm, of striking good looks among other things. But this was a non sequitur. The manager of the Students' Travel Bureau (Overseas) Ltd. had given a client a very memorable evening. Certainly it could have been no more than that. To him.

In a sense, and of course in defense, I might well accuse Tony of neglect. Because *he* had not divulged my whereabouts to the London travel office, Guy Black had been forced to seek me out. For business reasons.

There was a point here which I was deliberately avoiding: I need not have enjoyed a business dinner quite so much, need not have relaxed so readily with a stranger. Or believed his *"à bientôt"* meant an actual promise.

To be pragmatic, this casual equivalent to an American "so long" could have been merely a kindness to keep wide-eyed foreigners and clients interested.

Accepting that sensible if flattening thought, I trailed into the rose room, zipping myself out of the shift I had picked up in the Long Island thrift shop at which we had all hunted for our date clothes. The dress was worth much more than I had paid for it, was basic enough to dress up or down. It was obvious that Guy Black liked it. Obvious too from little things: the cut of his hair, the width of lapels and tie, the glances he had cast at others this evening was the fact that he—like the girls at the University—might be inclined toward the mod touch, the trendy addition. Perhaps, after all, I should consider Peg's advice and prowl in Chelsea for a swinging scarf or chain, an over-the-shoulder bag.

The telephone bell trilled its double summons. I swung around to the desk.

"Where've you *been,* Connie? I've called every fifteen minutes." Peg did not wait for an answer. "You'll never believe it. *Here,* of all places! In *Zurich!"*

"What happened?" My voice bounced back, tinny and hollow over the wire.

"I got in around nine tonight. And my room had been turned upside down."

"What?"

"In Zurich!" Peg repeated. "Absolutely incredible."

31

But I was thinking: Zurich, London, New York. Anywhere. Peg could be careless. I had to squelch my instincts, which were to ask whether she had locked up and whether she had left valuables about; passport, keys, money.

I said, "Is anything important missing?"

"That's the oddest thing. Nothing. But you should see the mess!"

"Didn't anybody hear anything, see anyone?"

"Not a clue. Police did a routine check. That's all. But the baggage is a total loss. *Slashed,* would you believe it?"

Peg traveled with strong, heavy plasticized canvas bags, all expandable, because she continually needed extra room for her acquisitions. I liked her tote, the one she had exchanged for mine, very much. Though smaller, it was lined with pockets like her shoulder bag.

"You should see your tote." She groaned. "Peeled like a— like an onion. In layers."

I was attempting to visualize and understand the reason for such an outrageous tactic when she added, "Police think someone was looking for something specific. Detective warned about passports. Apparently there's traffic in them. So . . . be careful, Connie. It was wild, coming in here tonight."

I shuddered, thinking of the chaos, the responsibility if anything should happen to this flat.

"It's got me down," she said. "The first couple of days here were simply *cosmic.* . . ." her voice trailed off and picked up again. "There are the grooviest . . . but, you'll see. Possibly even before you get here. My absolute *favorite,* Dominic, says he may have to go to London on business. He's administrative or something. Not a student. In the meantime, darling, just remember: Take care! *Ciao!*"

The evening's mood was gone, replaced by a mounting uneasiness about Nell Hobart's flat. I crossed the golden sitting room to recheck the window fastening before I drew the heavy silk curtains together.

There was a moon somewhere, for the night was not entirely dark, the trees of the garden and few visible rooftops and chimney pots toward Regent's Park massed darker against the one-tone lighter sky. The windows, three in a row, almost a bay, were firmly latched as I had left them.

But I was uneasy about the bibelots and peered round at

32

all of them, mentally cataloging each one. The Neuchâtel pen-
dule stood slender and quiet on the mantel between the now
empty cachepots. No one had mentioned winding it. Now I
wished someone—the unseen Tilly—had covered it, covered
everything. Or stored these treasures.

The night dragged, of course. I lay on the Empire sofa in
the bedroom, staring for a long time at the tree shadows that
moved beyond the dark oblong open to the soft, still summer
night. I drifted off only when I had finally fixed upon a solu-
tion. I would leave my passport in the University's office safe,
ring Guy Black, and ask his advice about security, even short-
term insurance. The George Inn and a kiss on the hand be
damned. This was a practical matter.

But there was no opportunity to ring him the following day.
Checking my passport sent me in a rush from Tavistock Square
to Ridgemount Street. Then, from the first period we were
plunged into a series of intensive lectures by Cambridge and
Leeds professors, a hectic tea, a dash to the Sadler's Wells
Theatre for a seven-o'clock performance.

That evening, Benjamin Britten's atmospheric operatic version
of *Midsummer Night's Dream* banished—for the time—any lingering thoughts of a burglarized room in a Zurich flat, any fears
for the security of a London apartment.

Two hours later I edged toward the streaming pavement outside the theatre entrance listening to the shrieks and chatter of
my fellow students. "*Look* at that rain!"

"How will we get back?"

"This bus number or that?"

"Nineteen?"

"Thirty-eight?"

"One seventy-two?"

"What about the Underground from the Angel?"

Came a moan from one girl: "Change at King's Cross? All
those stairs?"

Someone settled it. "The bus is cheaper."

Then another said, "Oh, she doesn't go our way. She's got
a flat. Mayfair, I think." And I realized they were talking about
me. I heard a smattering of "good-nights" as the whole group
darted off, only two girls from Kansas bothering to ask whether
I would get home all right.

Undine McCarthy, of course, had not stayed in for the performance. Putney, I had learned, was an hour away from the University, and auntie was, to quote Undine, "prehistoric." *Any* theatre, even Shakespearean, was frivolous.

I waited alone in the shelter of the marquee while taxis edged up to the curb and moved off.

Then, the long snout of a silver Citroën glided to a stop. The driver's door snapped open. The street lamp gleamed on silver hair.

"*A votre service.*" The laughter in Guy Black's voice was exactly what I needed. I let him take my hand and lead me round the car.

"How did you know I'd be here?"

"Our modus operandi. I've got your schedule, remember." He slammed the car door, was around and into his seat in an instant.

"But, why?"

"*My* modus vivendi. I cannot permit a lovely creature to dissolve in London's treacherous atmosphere before I get to know her, can I?" We moved off smoothly, the way he did everything, said everything.

"The point is," he added, "are you pleased?"

"As a matter of fact I—" I stopped.

"Yes?"

"You haven't a telepathic pickup set in your pocket, have you?" I had no sooner uttered the words than I wished I could retrieve them. They were misleading.

And they misled him. He said slowly, "So . . . you've thought of me, too?" He was watching traffic, braked the car for a light. I caught the slight change in the tone and saw that his smile had broadened.

This was not precisely the trend of conversation I had intended. I said, looking straight ahead now at the dazzling lights of an intersection, "I've been wanting to ask your advice."

"Ah? Well, I suppose even that is encouraging." The gay mood had left him, and we drove for a minute or two in silence. An awkward silence for me; I was choosing my next words more carefully than I had earlier, not happy with the sudden change.

"I've lost you," he said abruptly.

I shook my head, drew a breath before I plunged into a not

entirely truthful opening. "I didn't know quite where to start. Zurich, I suppose."

"Zurich?"

Rather too fast, we rounded a corner in a faint whine of tires, a skid on wet tarmac before we throttled down. We were off a major street now, not far from Devonshire Place. I recognized the Georgian crescent we were passing.

"My friend Peg Hobart rang up last night. Her room had been burglarized."

Before I had finished, a low whistle escaped him. "In Zurich? *Really?*" Then, "Anything serious?"

"No. No. But that's not the point. I'm afraid that if it should happen here while I'm in her cousin's flat, I'd feel . . . responsible, don't you see?"

"Of course. But the block of flats seems safe enough. Your benefactor—hostess—whoever she is, would certainly carry insurance. You've a porter on duty. There must be a maid?"

"No maid has appeared yet. And I didn't see a porter last night," I said. "Although he might have been shut up in his cubicle."

"Well, we shall see about the porter, at least, right now."

The long car made the turn into Crown Gardens and drew to a stop. This time Guy followed me into the checkerboard lobby.

"Miss Farrar is staying in Flat Number—" Guy turned to me. "Nineteen," I said.

The porter nodded. "Edwards told me. I saw you last night, miss."

"Good." Guy was brisk. "Miss Farrar is a little anxious about security. She has had disturbing news from a friend whose room was vandalized."

"There's so much of that these days." The accent was elusive, of Slavic origin, I thought. "We do our best, sir."

"See that you do your best for Miss Farrar." Something small and folded passed from his hand to the sad-faced man, a pound note, I think. "What's your name?"

"Mikhail." Quickly, as though he felt he must explain, he added, "I am Polish. And thank you, sir. Thank you very much."

Guy turned to me, then. "I'd like to look over your flat if you don't mind."

35

Such is conditioning: Even in the less than a week in Miss Nell Hobart's elegant flat I had grown accustomed to her mirrors, had forgotten the first impact of that hall. Now when I clicked the light switch (and instead of two people crossing the threshold there seemed to be a dozen), it all came back.

I started to smile, but Guy Black stopped just inside the room as I had on my first day.

"*Sapristi!*" The sibilant whisper left him before he moved again. And then he smiled, gazing from the crystal chandelier and sconces to the inlaid chests to me. "I had not quite expected——"

"Nor I, believe me. After two rooms over a garage. Practically a Cinderella story." I had meant this to be amusing, but I had not anticipated a foreigner's reaction, especially a man who had been everywhere, seen a good deal more than I had.

"Believe me," he said, "this is a vast improvement over any residence hall." He was quite serious. He liked the decor, and I could soon see that he liked the apartment.

And what was strange, with him there, the rooms seemed different to me, lived in. Perhaps because they were the perfect background for Guy's own elegance, they seemd to enhance his presence; he gave life to the place. I could only think of the word "rapport." A mutual rapport had been established between him and Miss Hobart's flat.

He strolled into the sitting room, murmuring, "Exquisite," as he stroked a Sèvres vase, and "delightful" about a Dresden figurine. Before he reached the curtained windows, he said, "I quite understand your concern." At the window he turned, his hand on the curtain cord. "May I?"

He had not drawn the curtains more than a yard when he stopped, and nodding, reached out to the latch and raised the center window. For a moment he leaned, motionless on the sill, gazing out into the darkness, which though faintly luminous because of the rain, was veiled, too. Roofs and chimneys were blurred beyond the beech and sycamores. Guy, still as a painting, was framed in gold. . . .

And then he moved again, commenting matter-of-factly that the windows seemed secure enough, asking to see other windows, doors, fire escape.

"Now this," he said as he thrust open the kitchen door onto the black, steel-barred landing, "is a necessary evil." He slipped out and glanced up and down the stairwell. "Top floor." He shook his head. "Roofs are sometimes used as an intruder's means of entry. Or escape."

Back in the kitchen he added, "I don't mean to alarm you, but do keep this door latched at all times." Underlining this, he snapped the latch and slid the brass bar bolt across as he had found it.

"I check that every night," I said as we reentered the hall.

"If you did not, I would." He sighed and looked beyond me at his reflection. Or mine. I could not be sure. "But I shan't always be here. I *can't* be here. Damn."

"Are you going away?" The news was not entirely welcome at this time.

"Not really away, Constance. A few days at the Paris office. Problems." I caught a slight narrowing of his lids before he went on. "Perhaps someday all this shall not be necessary."

The kiss on my hand was feather-light, as it had been the previous evening; his murmured, " *'revoir,"* almost as impersonal as his *"à bientôt"* had been. I found myself wishing tonight that he had been a little more specific.

This time days went by before I heard from him again— days during which I reminded myself that I needed the quiet times for all the little feminine chores besides lecture notes, the special assignments. Besides the letters I must write. To Father. To Mother. To Tony.

The letter to Tony was the most difficult. I postponed it. In the varied and hectic days since I had arrived, the first impulse, which had been to pour out my loneliness to him, was no longer valid. Only now, as the hours ticked away—the night hours especially—only now was the loneliness, in addition to the apprehension, creeping back.

The days were different. The work at the university different enough from the curriculum at home, it never failed to hold our interest. Undine McCarthy and I were agreeing on that over pots of strong black tea in the Refectory one afternoon.

"Maybe it's because we're actually over here where so much *happened.*" She leaned across the table, half whispering. "I may seem flippant sometimes, Connie, but secretly I'm in constant awe of the whole city. Can't believe I'm walking through literary history. Do you feel that way?"

37

"Every day."

She sat back, her blue gaze fixed on some object beyond my left shoulder. Her brows drew together slowly. "Don't look now," she said, "but there's a female in the doorway, staring at you."

Of course, I turned. And the girl—woman—turned away as quickly, a dark fall of walnut hair swinging over the shoulders of her slim beige dress. She moved out into the corridor, one gloved hand curved round the handle of a chic brown handbag.

"Know her?" Undine asked.

"Not from what I saw. You're sure she's not one of our group?"

"No, and a bit older. Sort of foreign."

"Isn't everyone?"

She laughed. "Touché. But that one was Dior-type foreign. Did you notice?"

I had. However, by the time we had returned to the lecture hall, I had forgotten all about her.

Before Guy Black arrived the next time, there were roses. Edwards, who was still on duty in the lobby, rang me on the house telephone to announce a messenger.

Roses from a man in London . . . a fascinating foreigner in London. Certainly, I was to be forgiven if I felt that something that had been missing had returned. A touch of magic . . . I smiled at the thought but could not quite laugh. I took up the card. He had written in a strong hand:

> Unique one,
> I am not acting my age. Eager as a schoolboy to see you again. Shall it be Chelsea tonight?
> > Yours,
> > G.

I floated about the flat arranging the perfect blossoms in tall crystal on one of the hall chests. Selecting a white sheath and wide-banded sandals, pretending I had a difficult choice. Bemused? Yes. And yet I reminded myself sternly that I should have been a cold creature indeed if such attention did not slightly derange me.

38

For the time Long Island and the upstate New York town and Wisconsin dimmed. I forgot the summers of polite acceptance of my ping-pong existence between two families; forgot the kitchen clatter at the restaurant where I had worked for months. Bless the place. It had helped to bring me here. Bless Father. Bless everyone.

I whirled round and round to symphonic music from the radio; crossed the bedroom, into the dressing room, the bath, to the mirror. Lipstick, muted, with the dewy look. The new eyeshadow tonight, the smoky turquoise from the set Peg had given me. How right she had been. Gray eyes needed something. . . .

I was ready for Guy when the bell chimed, ready for his compliments, and I parried them with banter of my own. He seemed as light-hearted as I until after we had been bowed through the lobby by a servile Mikhail now on duty.

In the silver car Guy backed off far less smoothly than he had at the theatre a few nights ago. The car stopped at the exit of the cul-de-sac, and before we turned out, he glanced down at me.

"Just one promise. Don't retreat into your own world even for a moment tonight. I need you after the rough days I've gone through."

An enveloping chill . . . thrill. . . . I could not name the reaction, though it was physical and abrupt and silenced me.

And then he said just two words in explanation: "You're different, Constance."

I shook my head. "You're the different one."

He laughed. "That's what I mean! You have an *esprit neuf—*" His next words were new to me; I thought he had fallen back to his native Italian. "*Ch'el s-chusa!*" He snapped his fingers. "How do you translate this, '*esprit neuf?*' "

"I believe 'a fresh mind,' or better, 'a new approach.' And thank you, I think."

"Your French is not merely from school, eh?"

"My grandmother was from Biel, near Bern."

"French Swiss, then?"

"She spoke both German and French. She taught both in the States." I did not like to talk about my grandmother. I missed her too much since her death three years ago. In a sense she had been the anchor in my life.

"These clever Swiss." I felt his glance and turned away, watching as the car joined traffic. We sped down Bond Street this time, and after some detours rounded the two palaces— the somber Tudor St. James's and far grander Buckingham. Then, Grosvenor Gardens, Eaton Square, Sloane Square. The Kings Road.

Chelsea. An unfolding stage-set of boutiques and pubs, antique and coffee shops, bistros jammed with odd mod types in breathtaking gear. It was the swinging London Peg had told me of, that I had read about.

We window-shopped. At one, I stared past Lowestoft and Crown Derby jumbled together with Bristol and Waterford, at a carved wooden angel.

"How much do you suppose that figure would cost?" I asked Guy.

He stepped back for a look at the shop's facade. "Too much here. Do you want something of the sort?"

"For Peg, not me."

"Your friend collects such things?"

I nodded. "Even broken or imperfect pieces. She restores them."

"We shall do the outdoor markets, then. You'd like that, I think." He ticked them off. "Camden Passage. Portobello Road. Caledonian." A sense of well-being seemed to possess him. "We've lots to do, haven't we?"

We sipped vermouth cassis in the flagged courtyard of a mews pub, leaning against the low stone wall, watching others who were watching us; certainly watching Guy, whose magnetism was spun of commanding looks, exquisite manners, insouciance.

We ate a Tournedos Rossini in a most intimate hideaway, Italian with a French menu.

"Everything in London is foreign," Guy said. "Haven't you noticed? The British themselves fade away each night into their remote suburbs and leave the city to us—delightful."

That night I believed him.

There were gossamer saris; turbanned men, some sleek and black-haired in silk suits; small Orientals difficult to identify; shining Africans; West Indians. There were Greeks, Spaniards, Italians, Germans. And there was, I remembered, Mikhail, the

40

Polish porter; Edwards from Eire. Guy, who came from one continent; and I from another.

I was in London. And I was utterly enchanted.

At the end of the evening I tried to thank him.

"Don't say a word," he said. "Just be here when I return."

"You're going again?" I controlled the brief flicker of dismay, picked up the sentence quickly. "For a long time?"

He had turned so that the street light was behind him, and I could not see his eyes. But faintly, I caught the curve of his lips, and I stiffened, moving back toward the shallow steps.

"What is it?" His hands came toward me, clasped both of mine. "What troubles you?"

"You're laughing at me."

"Laughing? *Dieu!*" He said. "I was happy. I was hoping you would miss me."

Too much had happened too quickly. I had not really had time to live with loneliness in London; I had merely feared long periods of silence, of isolation. Perhaps Guy Black had pampered me too soon. The silent time that followed this departure was slightly different. And although I reminded myself that I needed the time, there was no particular comfort in the thought.

The second afternoon after the Chelsea sortie I discovered quite informally that I should not be needing extra time for *household* chores at least. Upon entering Flat 19 earlier than usual with more home assignments than usual, I heard a crackle of voices from the direction of the bedroom.

Tilly O'Ryan, whose presence I had just been prepared for by the porter, Edwards, was propped among the pillows on the Empire sofa bed, a mug in her hand, her rapt gaze fixed upon the TV screen. When I stepped into the room, she sprang up, a younger, spryer figure than I had somehow expected.

"Ye 'd be Miss Farrar. And ye're early, miss." While she straightened her coverall, flicked a wisp of fly-away black hair out of her pale eyes, I suppressed a smile. Tilly apparently adhered to the theory that the best defense was attack.

I dropped my books on the nearest chair, not entirely certain whether to act the mistress of the household, and briskly suggest some activity that would send her bustling. But she took instant command.

41

Flicking off the TV program, she announced, "Hours nine to five Thursdays. Ye was gone when I come. And all I can say is that some ladies sure do live different. Not much to do today. I was finished with me work—even yer washin'—in a wink." She nodded toward the open door to the dressing room. Piled in neat rows on the built-in chest were stacks of pressed linens and lingerie.

What could I possibly have said after her disarming compliment and this surprise? Even a stern mistress certainly would have withheld a rebuke. And I, not accustomed to such attention to begin with, accepted her offer of "a cuppa," repressing a smile now that was as much of gratitude as of amusement.

At the door to the hall she turned and waved a hand toward the desk. "Ye got a couple o' letters there, from the States."

That night there was no excuse to postpone a letter to Tony. But what could I write him? What could I tell him? London is beautiful? Work is . . . work? Guy Black—your associate —has been . . . what? Delightful? Attentive?

The problem was that I truly was not happy that in so comparatively short a time another man could even vaguely intrigue me. I dared once to consider the thought that if this were so, if another man *could* interest me, perhaps Peg was right, and Tony was not the man for me after all.

A week after the Chelsea evening I was still fighting this nagging worry, this weakness, hypervulnerability, whatever flaw in character I feared I saw unfolding, when Mikhail announced that a Mr. Regli, "a friend of Miss Hobart's from Switzerland," was calling upon me.

5

Certainly I had not anticipated a meeting quite like this, although I am not sure I had expected anything. I had simply forgotten that Peg had mentioned him. And without previous notice I was not inclined to welcome such interruptions. But Peg had obviously given the man the address, and she *had* told me of him. I should not want her to think I had been rude to a friend.

There was barely time to brush my hair back into its twist and fasten it, to snap the creases from my skirt, before the doorbell chimed.

I am not quite sure what set the tone of the next scene; I would have denied that I had braced myself to disapprove of him on sight. The fact was, now that I was ready to meet him, I was quite suddenly curious.

In the unflattering gloom of the corridor light above him and the dazzling reflections of the mirrored hall he faced, Peg's friend from Zurich was not the handsomest man I had ever seen. But rugged . . . yes. All male . . . yes.

"Tough" was the word that more accurately related, yet— strange paradox—from his posture I felt that he belonged to an older world than ours: the almost imperceptible drawing together of his heels, the stiff bow from the waist. Again, another paradox, the gestures did not seem native to the man.

"Dominic Regli." He rolled the *r*, pronounced his surname *Recklee*. "Miss Hobart was kind enough to give me your address."

A minute ago I was antagonistic to Peg's generous gesture. Now I simply stared at him.

He stood a head taller than I, tawny haired, the quiet hazel eyes combining oddly with the wary look of a mountain cougar, once he had relaxed his greeting posture. He belongs on fast ski slopes, I thought, on paths hewn through forests. I had to be wrong, of course. Peg had said he was involved with the school, administration, if I recalled correctly.

"Forgive me." His deep voice cut across my thoughts. "I think I have come at an inconvenient time for you." He did not move, however.

"No, no. Please." I held back the door while he stepped into the hall, and for just a second I caught a gleam of what could have been derision as his glance swept over the room.

What was he thinking? For some reason I wanted to know.

"Rather elaborate, isn't it?" I said.

"For you, perhaps. And me." The simple statement seemed right for him. I would have thought he would not waste words. Or dissimulate.

Indeed, he seemed already to have dismissed the surroundings. And the pause that followed, though brief, flustered me. I moved backwards toward the sitting room so abruptly that I might have struck the closed mirrored door had he not caught my arm.

With his hands circling my wrists, a current seemed to have traveled from him to me. I felt it. I could not move for a moment nor utter a sound. What was this strange reaction—so subtly different from any I had known at another's touch? Fear? No. . . .

If it had been fear, I should have drawn away quickly as I did with others, should never have stood quiet so long. Would I? *Would I?* What *was* the matter with me?

And was he aware of this odd sensation?

Perhaps not. He dropped his hands, reached past me, and grasped the elaborate handle of the door. "You wished to go in here?" he said.

I could release my breath only when he had released me. "Yes." Gathering the remnants of my shattered poise around me, I moved ahead of him into the beige elegance of Miss Hobart's living room.

"I . . . haven't used this room much." My voice was not quite steady.

The overhead light did not flatter the setting; it served rather to emphasize the museumlike impression. The effect was uninviting, cool, and aloof.

I hesitated, uncertain whether to lead him to a sofa or to one of the frail bergères, but he seemed to have been put off by the room as I had been. He had not moved from the threshold behind me.

"It's very beautiful," he said, "but not for living, I think."

"I agree. I use the other room."

He waited, though I recognized the same swift appraisal I had seen in the hall. "The other room is more modest?" he asked.

"Yes. Less formal. But it's a bedroom." Hastily, I added, "Rather a bed-sitter, as they call them here."

This time his lips betrayed him. I saw him press them together instantly, revealing an indentation, a scar, perhaps the result of some boyish prank, at the corner of his mouth. It somehow rendered him less formidable.

44

"If you don't mind," I said, and led the way toward the mirror that opened into the rose paradise.

"I am privileged," he murmured, but this time I did not glance at him, for I did not wish to be tempted to analyze any further nuance, to form any more impressions.

In the evening light the room's color theme, though excessively feminine, was muted. The scene looked very comfortable, and with the wide window open on the summer evening, the air was fresh and cool.

Lamplight shone on my books at the back of the desk, one open beside a pad and pen. I was about to offer Dominic Regli one of the two chairs when I felt rather than heard him move away. He moved as soundlessly as the creature I had first likened him to, and when he reached the window, he stood looking out on the garden and reflected glow of the city.

"This *is* pleasant," he said, then turned. "Would you have time to join me for coffee somewhere?"

"It's not the time, really. I don't know any coffee houses round here." I stopped, appalled that I had been so gauche, that I had not offered this small hospitality to Peg's new Zurich friend. "Would you join me for coffee here?" I offered.

If he had been an American, he probably would have said, "I thought you'd never ask." Instead, Dominic Regli straightened, gave a ghost of a bow, a ghost of a click of his heels. And although I had not invited him, he followed me to the kitchen.

I heard him stop at the door, and I turned to see his glance travel swiftly from the ventilator, which had automatically snapped into its low whir, down to the door below it. Then he moved into the room, watching over my shoulder, apparently intrigued by every detail including the touch-spring cupboards, table-top range, built-in oven, electric kettle.

When I switched on the kettle, he said, "Most efficient, all these electrical appliances, aren't they?" His glance had returned to the door again, and the ventilator above.

It was the opening I had wanted. "I should have thought Switzerland would be far ahead in such things."

"Not everywhere. Not where I come from, not even where I live now."

45

Perhaps because a peculiar thought had crossed my mind in that small instant—was he Peg's friend or a friend of her father's cousin, another Miss Hobart—I spoke abruptly in German.

"Dann sind Sie kein Zürcher?"

The silence in the room, except for the hum above us, was complete until the kettle commenced its first-phase simmering.

He shook his head finally and gave a short laugh. "No, I am not from Zurich." In a soft German, slightly different from the version I had heard around my mother's house as a child, he added, "And you do not speak a true school German, either. Where did you learn it?"

"My grandmother was from Biel." The kettle was spouting steam, but I ignored it. "Where do you come from?"

"A small village in the high mountains. You would not know it."

I had been right then, I thought, diverted for the moment, pleased with myself that I had guessed correctly. He was from the mountains, he did belong there.

But something still disturbed me. "I'm not sure I understand. Are you the Zurich friend Peg mentioned?"

"Peg?"

The kettle had overheated, snapped off automatically. I persisted, "Peg Hobart, my friend from the States. She's attending the *Evangelische*——"

"Of course. Margaret Hobart. *She* suggested I visit you." "Mar-gar-ett," he had said, separating each syllable, pronouncing the name precisely, and although I was relieved at the answer, I felt that something I could not quite identify was wrong. What was it?

His accent. I could not place it. It was not German, not French. In German, again, I asked, "What is your language?"

There was the faintest bow from the waist again, and suddenly I resented it. I felt he was mocking me. "Similar to your grandmother's." His German was swift and easy, and I was not expert enough to detect regional variations.

"You are German Swiss? Not Italian?" His name puzzled me too.

He gazed down at me from the doorway, a little quizzically, as though he were gauging an adversary. "I spoke only what the Italians and Austrians too often ignore, and what the Swiss

46

chose to call their fourth language—Rätoromanisch, Sursilvan idiom—until I was able to walk the many miles to school."

He stepped across, unplugged the kettle, and briskly poured the boiling water into the coffee filter. "I am from an area in the Engadine, the Val Sinestra."

"Toward Austria and the Italian Tirol?" My grandparents had talked of the rugged beauty of the Engadine in eastern Switzerland.

"You know it?" He glanced up quickly.

"Only from family stories. Lonely mountains in some parts, deep valleys?"

"Yes." He was watching me.

"Are some areas really isolated . . . cut off for months by the snows?"

"Not so much now, with better roads, powerful plows. But of course we who lived in such areas learned to live with the mountains."

Again I thought how much he looked the part. I glanced at him, but he was looking past me at the bolted door to the fire escape.

"The language you mentioned—you called it something a little different." I said. "I thought it was known as Romansch."

"In general use in Switzerland, yes. Italian scholars cling to Ladin or Ladino. Germans and other students call it Raetoladinisch, Rätoromanisch, even Romaunsch.

"Is the language found *outside* of Switzerland, too?"

"In 'pockets' all the way south and east through Austria to Venice and the Yugoslav border."

He picked up the tray on which I had been assembling cups, coffee pot, and biscuits. With a faint smile he added, "Shall we return to the rose room?"

I tried to relax after that, wanting more than ever to act the perfect deputy for Peg. But I had to be aware, too, that he was Peg's friend, her "favorite" she had said. So I sat stiffly in the more comfortable chair drawn up to the desk while Dominic Regli sat in the straight chair, smoking a Turmac from a flat white box, which he had offered me, absently tapping the firm ash into a silver cigarette tray.

I wanted to know all about him, why he had come to London, what he was doing in Zurich, how long he would be here. Or did I?

But he talked of the Zurich theology students, of Peg and how clever she was, how much the students liked her. He smiled as he talked of her, as though he saw her, heard her. . . .

When he paused, I asked, "What did you think of the burglary?"

The change in mood was subtle, but I watched the slight steadying, hardening of his eyes, the slight strain at the corners of his mouth, the whitening scar. "I think it was in error. Nothing was missing."

"Error?" I had not thought of that. "But, why at all? A student's flat could not be expected to yield much——" I could not think of the German word for loot, did not think he would understand the English.

"Loot?" he finished for me. And we both smiled.

"I was not certain you would know the word."

"Mar-gar-ett educates us, you understand." The light mood had returned. He went on, "But you can help me with another word, perhaps. When she suggested that I call on you here, she said, 'Call any time. Connie doesn't need any warning to pull herself or the pad together. She's a neat freak.' "

"That's so *like* her!" I laughed.

"Yes, I think. But 'freak'? In my dictionary I found so many variations. And none suits you."

An awkward silence filled the room prolonged by my inability suddenly to cope with language, idiom, slang; with men like this. I held my glance away from him while a veritable glossary filtered through my mind. Freak: abnormal . . . monstrosity . . . bizarre . . . unusual.

I said, "I would prefer 'unusual.' " I was thinking that Dominic Regli, like Guy Black, was unusual. They were different. That was their charm for us. And perhaps the danger.

Beyond us, beyond the wide window open to the summer night, leaves rustled lightly. A fragrant earthy breeze trailed in like a wraith, chilled my bare arms. I shivered.

He rose swiftly, his face as devoid of expression as I hoped mine was. "It is late," he said. "I have interrupted your work too long."

At the hall door he shook hands briskly and thanked me. "Perhaps before I return to Zurich," he added, "you will have time for lunch or dinner with me."

Later, in the bedroom, which was still pervaded by the not unpleasant aroma of a new—to me—blend of tobacco, I could not remember whether I had answered him or not.

The very next morning the doorbell rang before eight, and to my surprise I faced a slightly less than placid Tilly.

"Sorry to bother ye, miss. But me purse was snatched last evenin'!" She was clasping and unclasping a shabby brown bag in her hands, her eyes searching mine as though she were looking for an answer, as though I might help her.

I said, "Come in, please. Is there anything I can do?" I was thinking she might need money, but she quickly put in, "It's the keys. I'll need yer key for a copy."

"Of course." While I dug in my handbag, I commiserated with her.

"Gettin' as bad as the States, it is," she grumbled. "There I was mindin' me own business——"

"Where *was* it?"

"Round in Thayer Street. Ye'd better watch out, miss. It's happenin' even in the good neighborhoods," she muttered darkly. "Just carryin' Mr. Zeller's suits to the cleaners—he's the gentleman in Flat 4 downstairs—when I was fair jerked off me feet."

"Did you get a look at him?"

"That's just what the copper asked. But between the suits that were slippin' and fallin' from me arm and the late shoppers on the sidewalk I couldn't even be sure it *was* a man."

She tucked my key into a small purse inside the larger envelope. "I'll leave this with Edwards today after I get a copy, if that's all right with ye?"

"Yes . . . yes." I held back the door for her, puzzled and not too happy with this development. "What about money?" I said. "Do you need any?"

An almost impish grin disclosed several crooked teeth that somehow suited her. "*Somebody* was disappointed last night, I'll wager, miss." She tapped her spare bosom. "Keep me quids folded up into a safe place like me mum taught me. Ruddy thief couldn't 'a got thirty pence out o' that purse."

Before she reached the lift, I started after her. "About the key," I said. "Was there any identification on it? Any name or address?"

"Nothin', miss. Not even me own name in the bag."

49

Despite her reassurance and Edward's insistence a short time later when he returned Miss Hobart's key, the incident disturbed me. I found it difficult to concentrate on Shelley and Keats that morning, sorry I had chosen that day to work in the flat. I actually found myself listening for sounds that never came, a footstep, a key turning in a lock. . . .

By lunchtime with little accomplished, I tore myself away from books and doodled notepad, and double-locking the flat's door, departed for the Chelsea spree I had promised myself.

The day was deliciously cool for August, with London's gentle overtone of diluted pearl muting the summer sky. The King's Road, thronged with the youth of all nations, was diversion in itself. Chains, scarf, trendy bag, were all an excuse. I did not need any of them, though I did the King's Road thoroughly, down one side to the turning for Battersea Bridge, back the other to the flower stands in Sloane Square.

En route I did stop to yearn over a long silver chain, the Guatemalan wedding design, and I backtracked, mentally weighing pounds sterling and pence against a swinging addition to a square wardrobe.

I bought the chain finally, slung it over my navy dress, and found a not too bulky over-the-shoulder bag I could use for school and the Austrian walking trip.

Queuing up for a bus to Regent's Park, I suddenly remembered I had left a couple of books I needed at the Student Centre. It was growing late; it was after tea time. The underground would surely be faster than the bus.

It might have been faster, but it was a bit more complicated. I came up out of the depths of the earth at Russell Square and promptly walked in the wrong direction. Hurrying, I rounded a corner, looking for the Square, and stopped short.

Halfway down the block, not twenty yards away, Dominic Regli was walking toward me, looking over his shoulder at the broad, small-paned window of a shop. In gold on the white Georgian-influenced facade was lettered in Old English type, "Students' Travel Bureau (Overseas) Ltd."

It was the first time I had seen Guy's office, the first time I had realized it was quite so close to the University. But there was no time for me to equate the bureau with Peg's friend's presence, for, although I had stopped, Dominic Regli had not. And now he saw me.

I was puzzled by his reaction when he looked from the shop straight at me. Was it resentment? Suspicion? Certainly he was not pleased to see me. The smile seemed slow, forced, and I noticed that he did not shake hands, nor stop. Instead, when he reached me, he glanced at his watch and, murmuring something about coffee, eased me around to walk in his direction, the way I had come.

Something, and I am not at all sure what, forced me to blurt out, "Were you coming from the travel bureau? That's the London associate of the office Peg and I booked through."

He nodded. "I know."

"Oh." Slightly deflated, I added, "Do you know Guy Black?"

"Who?" He looked down at me, frowning.

"He's the manager."

"No. Actually, I was not coming from that bureau. I was going toward the University to look for you."

That's a lie, I thought, appalled at my suspicions. I had not smiled at all. And he may have noticed, for he went on quietly, "I saw the bureau and might have stopped there, but then I saw you."

Try again, I thought, cynically. I said, "Are you booking your return?"

His laugh was as sharp and short as my question. "I'm booked." He did not elaborate.

"Your business is finished, then?"

"My business is with travel agencies such as that." We were a full block away now, and he looked back. "You say the manager is a man named Black?"

"Yes. But he may not be there now. He's . . . been out of town."

"I see." He stopped and stood looking down at me, but he seemed not to see me, seemed to be contemplating something beyond me. "You know, I think I may go back, if you will excuse me."

And then he pressed his lips together again as he had last night when he had suppressed a smile. "I am frustrated, you see. I do not want to lose you, yet I *am* here on business. Will you wait for me somewhere? Perhaps a clerk at the bureau might suggest a little excursion for this evening."

We had nearly reached Tavistock Square now, having come the long and wrong way from the underground station. I could see the lovely terraced Adams buildings opposite, the doorway of the Student Centre where I had left my books. It would be simple enough to tell him to meet me there. We could walk. We could talk. We could compound the confusion that had plagued me last night.

I glanced away quickly from the hazel eyes that, now in the late afternoon sun, were cool, almost mocking, challenging me, daring me to say, "Yes."

"Thank you," I said, "but I really must work tonight."

As it happened, I had more than a simple assignment to tackle that night. When I had retrieved my key and opened the door to Flat 19, a white oblong envelope lay on the velvet carpet repeated a dozen times in the hall mirrors . . . a dozen reminders of my ambivalence. A letter from Tony.

"Why haven't you written?" he wrote. Why hadn't I? And: "Guess what good news I may have soon?" Good news? For whom? For him? For me? "Darling, if things go as I hope now, don't be surprised if I join you in Feldkirch in September."

I stood at the window for a long time while gold faded from the sky and a delicate green mist descended over the garden. I closed my eyes against London, tried desperately to retreat, tried to visualize a reunion in Austria in less than a month. The dark brooding eyes of those last two nights before I had left Long Island eluded me . . . the lips . . . the outline of the unsmiling face . . . I could not bring Tony into focus.

Sleep that night was fragmented by images that coursed like ghosts across the shadowed room, the black oblong of the window, the moonless sky. Endless night drifted into day again.

Dawn. A not very convincing one. The gray of thunder lay over the city.

I sat at my desk beside a lighted lamp and my half-finished breakfast, composing, scribbling, erasing until I had completed a final draft of a letter to Tony. No assignment, no essay had ever been as difficult.

And what had I written? Mere prosaic statements. I had been busy, as he might have expected. The flat and marketing and

laundry and schoolwork seemed to fill every hour. (*Seemed* to
. . . that was weak.) I quickly added:

By the way, you were right about the flat. I should have reserved a room at the Residence Hall. But never mind. In
a few more weeks school work will be over, and the holiday ahead.

Then cautiously, I ended:

Perhaps you ought to write to Peg about any possible
Austrian plans of yours. It was her idea, that trip. And you
know Peg.

At least and at last that letter was behind me. Preoccupied
as I had been, and not entirely organized, I left my plan to
condense the contents of my purse and tote into the new shoulder bag until it was too late that morning. It was almost nine
when I slid my tote up to my elbow, slipped the handbag straps
over my wrist.

Already aware of Edwards' duties with the delivery of the
morning mail, I was not surprised when I stepped from the lift
to see that the porter's booth was empty. But I did not expect
the light sound close behind me, though I can remember tensing before I tried to turn.

It was too late.

In one incredible instant pain seared my wrist, my throat
was caught by fingers that pressed . . . pressed. . . .

The black and white tiles loomed larger before darkness began to enfold me like a blanket, before I felt the savage push
that catapulted me onto a jumble of objects that whispered and
crumpled around me.

Somewhere near me, behind me, over me, a door clicked
shut.

53

6

I have no idea how many minutes went by before I became aware of the pair of frightened eyes peering down at me.

"In God's *name!*" Edwards was leaning over me, breathing the same words again and again. "In God's name, madam! What's happened?"

He seemed not to know whether to touch me or not, and even in my dazed state I could understand that. In the confined space of what I perceived to be the porter's booth, I found it difficult to move. And painful.

I was obviously jammed into the tiny place; my head must have struck the shelf as I had fallen. And I was half doubled up across a jumble of objects including a mound of something flat and hard that felt like books. I could not extricate my right arm, which was bent beneath me and numb.

I reached up my free left hand to Edwards. "My arm . . ."

My bruised throat ached when I uttered the two words. My head throbbed as Edwards edged me to a sitting position and freed my right arm from the cutting strap of the tote bag full of books that had spilled out beneath me. For a moment I leaned back against the booth's wall. Above me, surprisingly, the wall clock indicated that only a few minutes had passed since I had left the flat. It was just on nine.

"Are you all right, madam?" He seemed as unnerved as I had been, and when I put my hand up to my forehead and winced, he whispered, "Did someone *strike* you?"

"Pushed me." I was struggling to my feet now, feeling a little dizzy, trying to sort out the recollections. But it had happened too fast. Before those strong fingers had grasped my throat, there had been that light step behind me. And something else, something . . . elusive. . . .

A scent.

"I think it was a woman," I said.

54

Edwards stopped shuffling my books into the tote. He straightened. "A woman, ye say? But, madam, why? What did she want with ye?"

I gazed around me on the floor of the booth, at the lobby. I stared at the open tote in Edwards' hands.

"She wanted my handbag," I blurted out. "It's gone."

"Stay there!" Faster than I would have believed he could move, Edwards crossed the lobby, whipped past the entrance door.

I followed him, surprised that I could walk a straight line over the dizzying checkerboard. And at the open door I saw the porter crouched over the pavement near one laurel bush, scooping up the contents of my bag. He heard me and looked up. "It's here!" he called out. "Whoever took it dropped it!"

I was immensely relieved to see that he was tucking keys into the bag, incredulous to see that he had also collected the folded wallet that contained several pound notes and coins.

"I'll call the police," he said, handing me the bag.

"No, please. Please . . . I'd rather not. It's all right now." I was going through the pockets, checking the wallet. "You see, I've got everything. There's nothing they could do now. I'd rather keep it quiet, if you don't mind. And thank you very much, Edwards." I managed to extract a pound note, which seemed to render him speechless. At least, he added nothing but a whispered: "Thanks," as he held the lift door for me, and I returned to the flat for repairs.

Undine was waiting for me when I reached the study room at Tavistock Square two hours later. "What happened to you?" She said. "You missed Jane Austen—say! You look *ghastly!*"

Over a quick lunch in the Refectory, I related the bare outlines of the mysterious "snatch," as Undine called the experience.

"*And you say nothing's missing?*" She was as shocked as I had been. "I don't get it."

Neither did I.

All during the performance of *Hamlet* at the Aldwych that afternoon I found it difficult to concentrate on the Prince of Denmark and the ghost at Elsinore.

Tea and a couple of aspirins had eased the aches; my chat

with Undine had been a healthy release. But I had not been able to sort out a *reason* for the attack.

Although the performance was over early, the afternoon seemed dim as twilight when the matinee crowds emerged into the bustling Strand. But despite the threatening clouds there was no rain, and it was brisk and cool.

Undine glanced at me as we started toward the bus stop. "You going to be all right tonight? Alone?"

"Yes, I think so. It's safe enough *inside,* apparently. I'll just be careful, that's all."

"I could call my aunt if you'd like to come out to Putney." She giggled. "All you'd have to do is remember to salute. . . ."

I thanked her, echoing her laugh, pleased with her offer, but when she left me at her bus stop, I felt quite suddenly at loose ends. And I walked, aimlessly, following the rush hour pack, which seemed to be doggedly headed for the whirling Square, the confluence of pigeons, starlings, top-heavy buses, panting motor cars. Just past Charing Cross Station I stopped, wondering whether I could find a quiet riverside walk that would take me back toward the city to Shakespeare's London where I might wander in silence, conjuring up another world as it might have been those centuries ago.

After all, I had come to London to savor England's past. And in too short a time too many elements had intruded . . . Dominic Regli and Guy Black overlapping the pattern of my life; Tony interfering with Peg's plans. And today, a touch of violence I had never expected.

I hesitated at the corner, finally turned into Craven Street, away from traffic, and stumbled upon reminders of still another age. Narrow eighteenth-century houses leaned one upon another; surprisingly, a plaque read: "Benjamin Franklin Lived Here," and nearby, "Heinrich Heine." The names drifted by much as a stream of ectoplasm might evolve and dissolve, their importance vying with today's preoccupations.

At the street's end I glanced back, regretful, feeling somehow that I had passed old friends without greeting them. The wider avenue at the end entered the Embankment, and I passed under a railway bridge, startled to find a garden—an elongated "V," an oasis in the gloom—set quietly back, away from the thrust of traffic.

The colors drew me, blossoms jewel-bright and vivid against fine lawns, bright cannas and other summer survivors banked against England's hardy roses. August was moving toward September. September would inevitably end. And where would I be?

Back in the States, alone . . . but where? With which family?

My steps slowed. I had not meant my thoughts to take this theme; the day had been difficult enough. But before me now I saw that the garden's benches were filled with the aged, the lonely; with lovers. . . .

Lovers.

Two were drawn together, whispering, fingers intertwined. The boy's free hand reached out to touch the girl's fair hair . . . as Tony's had touched mine not many nights ago.

I felt an almost involuntary shrinking, a pulling away from the remembered touch . . . I had been wise, after all, to wait. Yet now there was a subtly different conflict, a forbidden interest I was striving to submerge. I moved slowly, reluctant to leave the peaceful little world behind me.

At the walk's end traffic edged solidly along the river road. And I stood waiting, listening to the suck and hum of tires on tarmac, seeing beyond the blur of westbound traffic shimmering in early city lights.

When I finally crossed the road, I leaned on the parapet, watching the river now at obviously low tide, black in the shadows, steely where the east wind rippled its waters. Below me a wide flat boat to Greenwich was gradually filling up with stragglers. Sightseers? I did not know, but I envied them despite the chill gray canopy of the sky, the ebb of the polluted water. Never mind that it smelled of mud and dank stone, it was London. . . .

Downstream, launches gathered at a neat dock. River police, I realized with a start.

Police. The thought remained while I watched a tanker with an odd squat chimney chug upstream against the tide. The thought of police brought a further sense of disquiet, perhaps because of this morning's odd experience which, added to Peg's intruder in Zurich, equaled anxiety. The thoughts combined with the reverberation of a not-too-distant *bong* to alert me to the time. Big Ben, it must be. I counted the strokes. It was six.

Perhaps three quarters of an hour later I emerged from the Underground at Regent's Park, having been properly initiated into the London rush hour, a counterpart of New York's, except for the permissive smoking. At the top of the steps I breathed deeply, grateful for the comparatively fresh air off Marylebone Road. The day's cooler temperature had not yet found its way into the tubes; summer heat permeated stations, trains, escalators, travelers.

In the lobby of Number 8 Crown Gardens Mikhail peered out at me, then stood up, seeming startled.

"Oh, miss—er—I permitted the gentlemen to go straight up. I thought, excuse me, that you were at home."

"But who—" I started, then thinking that the gentleman must surely be Guy, I stepped into the lift, pleased yet faintly disturbed.

The top floor corridor was empty, but next to Flat 19 the single unnumbered door marked "Service" stood ajar onto a slab of darkness, the strip of fire escape.

I hesitated until the lift door clicked firmly shut behind me, and I saw the service door move back. The man who slipped into the carpeted corridor was not Guy Black. It was Dominic Regli.

"What are you doing here?" My voice shook.

But he only smiled. "The door was open. I wondered where it led. Mind you, I don't think it is very safe."

I ignored his glib response. "How did you get up here?"

"Miss Hobart. I had only to mention Miss Hobart's name, you see." His tone was recalcitrant now. It was as though he were attempting an object lesson. He half turned then, to secure the service door, and I caught a glimpse of the ripple of pink carnations barely hidden in green tissue, and a brown-paper-wrapped packet dangling from the same hand.

In a flash I understood why Mikhail had accepted him, yet I struggled against the very fact of his presence, unasked, unannounced. I persisted: "Do you mean that Mikhail permitted you to come up here that easily?"

"Exactly," he said. The quiet eyes surveyed me. And as I started to turn away, his fingers encircled my arm. "You have been injured." He touched my forehead, and I tensed, aware of an uncontrollable reaction as I had been the first evening he had come to the flat. "Does it hurt?"

58

"Not now." I moved from him, inserted the key in the lock of Flat 19. "Come in." The "please" was added as an afterthought. I was not entirely sure I wanted Peg's friend here tonight. Or at any time.

"What happened to you?" He reached out again, but I backed away.

"I was . . . held up. At least, it was attempted———"

"Where?"

"Downstairs, in the lobby."

"And?" He was standing tall, rigid, oddly forbidding.

"Whoever it was pushed me into the porter's booth. I fell." I related the incident once more, but Dominic Regli probed more deeply than Undine had. When he learned that nothing had been taken, he said, "Not your passport?"

We were inside the mirrored hall by then, and I looked up, startled at my own reflection. All color seemed to have faded from my face.

Passport? A woman . . . of course, that was the likliest probability.

"But how would she, would *anyone,* have known I might have had a passport with me?"

"Gossip. Porters. Maid. Fellow students." He was watching me. "You did not have it with you?"

"It is deposited with the bursar at the university."

During the brief silence that followed that announcement I propped my shoulder bag beside the nearby chest. "It's rather late for coffee———"

"I had thought of that. It is really the time for an *apéro.*" The smile touched the corners of his lips, the scar, and fled. From his pocket he drew a bottle not much larger than a miniature. "Cynar," he said. He pronounced it "chinar." "Do you know it?"

I shook my head, still watching him, still not entirely at ease.

"An *apéritif.* French, but quite good." He laughed. "You see how nationalistic we are, how we . . . tolerate others?" Relieved at the change of subject, I laughed too.

He held the blossoms and the brown paper packet toward me. And when our hands touched, I noticed that he drew back, almost shyly. And he fumbled the next words, "I thought if you were free—if you would permit me—we might try the

59

Cynar here. Then, perhaps you would—might—join me for dinner."

As awkward as he, I looked away, undecided; then started toward the kitchen, stopped. I stared down at the packet in my hands.

"A little *Vorspeise*. Appetizer." He followed me as far as the kitchen doorway.

"How nice." I thought: *How disarming.*

"I met your agent yesterday, by the way."

"Guy?" I looked back at Dominic.

"He was leaving for France last night."

I wondered whether, in the not-too-complimentary light in the kitchen this perceptive man could detect the flush I felt rising in my cheeks.

So Guy had been back in London and had not called me. He must have been busy. I said, hoping that my voice was normal, that I sounded indifferent, "He's very busy, I believe."

"Very," Dominic said dryly.

"Did you manage to talk with him? About your business?"

"A moment or two. I left some material with him. Brochures, applications for students. That sort of thing." He stood watching me as I arranged the five carnations in a slender vase.

"They're so pretty . . . it's very kind." Why was it so difficult for me to thank him? Why did I suspect that these spicy blossoms were merely an afterthought, that he had picked them up at a corner stand off Oxford Circus? Or worse: that he had used these and his little brown paper packet as an excuse to waste an evening. Or to pry . . .

As I unwrapped the packet he had brought, a remembered aroma drifted up from the paper.

"*Schwarzbrot!*" I cried. "*Real* black bread! I haven't had it since . . . my grandmother . . ." I struggled again for the poise that seemed so elusive when this man was near.

He said, "I thought you might like it." It was a quiet statement, quieting me. "And the *Bündner Fleisch* You know it?"

Tucked away in layers of waxed paper was a sheaf of the thinnest cut dried beef I had ever seen. I edged out one slice with a fork. "We'd never had any as thin as this!" I said. "*Where* did you get it?"

"The Swiss Centre at Leicester Square."

I started to fold the slices onto a china platter, somewhat chastened to learn of the trouble he had taken. "It's really very kind. . . ." I was embarrassed, trying now to assume the role of hostess—gracious hostess. "Does this come from your canton, from the Graubünden?"

"Yes. Guaranteed fresh today. I hope."

"What is it called in your language? In Romansch?"

"*Puólpa.*" He spelled it out for me.

I searched my mind. "It doesn't relate to anything I know. What about the black bread? What's that called?"

"*Paun ner,* in my dialect. *Pan náir* in the *Ladin.*"

"That sounds like Latin."

"Yes."

I was disconcerted to find, when I picked up the tray I had prepared, that his eyes were on me; they met mine with such a searching gaze that I stood not two yards from him, for some strange reason unable to move. And although I could not have explained why I felt it, there seemed an implied question in the look.

He moved first, reached for the tray, and as he took it from me, he murmured, "You will join me tonight, won't you?"

In that instant I was suddenly determined to formalize his visit, to serve him in the drawing room where guests belonged. I passed him, opened the door to that room, so that there would be no question.

His voice was low, controlled, when he added, "You see, I don't know anyone in London." Even his smile was controlled. "And Mar-gar-ett thought you might have sympathy for me."

Mar-gar-ett, I thought as I pushed aside crystal and porcelain on the nearest chest for space for the tray, would have been better advised to withhold her generous gestures.

However, I murmured a polite word or two, explaining that I should like to change to something more suitable to the hour and cooler temperature, and excused myself.

Still uneasy, I hurried through the change. And when I left the bedroom not many minutes later, a draft was blowing through the partly open kitchen door and across the hall. At a glance I saw that the drawing room was empty.

Dominic had returned to the kitchen, and I wanted to know why.

From the doorway I said, "What did you want there?" and he swung around, away from the door to the landing.

"You are very quick." His glance was encompassing and approving, yet I ignored the attempted diversion.

"Yes. But what did you want outside, on the landing?"

"Merely to help you." Apparently quite at ease, he shut and bolted the landing door. "Since I have already seen where you keep the *Abfallkübel*—dustbin, you call it, or garbage can? —I have discarded the empty Cynar bottle and papers for you."

For some obscure reason I did not believe him, but I could not say this; my manners had been bad enough. Even now I did not thank him for his efforts, for anything.

It was he who led me back to the drawing room, a strange reversal of roles. We took up our glasses and wandered to the windows, where I looked out across the trees and chimney pots, aware that he was watching me.

"Do you like it? The *apéro?*"

"It's odd." I was relieved that he had broken the silence; I added, "It's less harsh than whisky. Or gin."

"And far more suitable before dinner. Especially before wine."

Peg had mentioned the wines in Zurich. Peg had mentioned the men. Him. I watched him finish his drink and put down his glass.

"I've found a pub not too far from the university where many continental drinks are served."

"Already? You *have* been busy." Why did I mock him, I wondered.

His glance met mine, flicked away. "You see, last night you left me—what word am I looking for?—*im Stich gelassen.*"

"Abandoned?"

"Yes." He removed my empty glass from my fingers. "You abandoned me last night." He shrugged. "Shall we go and find the little place once more?"

The little place, as Dominic Regli called it, was at the end of the narrowest alley I had ever seen. With both arms outstretched he could almost have touched each wall. The lane's length was illuminated by a single pair of ancient coach lamps, their gas flames already flickering in the deepening twilight.

The place was rather secluded; in New York I should never have ventured past the lane's entrance even with a man.

And yet there was something innocent and singularly aloof about St. Mark's Row, Covent Garden. A sense of elegance pervaded the lane, which was immaculate, unsullied by any sign of current pollution. I felt almost as though we had stumbled upon a stage set.

Even the name of the ancient scaled-down pub, which straddled the lane's end, providing a cul-de-sac, was evocative of the sinister royal past of Westminster. The King's Head, it was called. Crowned, weather-worn, and weary as the monarch it depicted must have been centuries ago, a regal face stared down at us from a gold-leafed plaque as we passed through the Tudor doorway.

The blackened door had no sooner creaked shut behind us than, at the far left of the dim, low-ceilinged room, a shadow moved from the bottom of a staircase that could have been no wider than three feet. Except for the gleam of tinted glasses it was as though some of the darkness had detached itself and floated off. I found myself peering after the foreshortened bulk until, as my eyes adjusted to the peripheral darkness, I realized the man must have rounded the simple balustrade and vanished into the cellars.

It must have been minutes before I was aware I had not spoken since we had entered the lane outside, aware that Dominic Regli was watching me, that neither of us had moved.

"You know this place?" he said.

"No . . . no." I wondered whether he had noticed the shadow pause, whether he had seen the man at all. I added, truthfully, "But I am not sure I like it."

"Ah, I am sorry. Mar-gar-ett liked one of our old guild houses in Zurich's Altstadt. Quite as old as this must be."

"How did you find this pub?" I asked.

"By accident. I was—" he hesitated, "—looking for a certain address. Near here."

We had almost reached the bar, which was empty except for a whispering couple at the far end. In the reflected light from the glasses and bottles and the underglow from the bar I could see the hazel eyes quietly scanning my face.

In a moment he glanced toward the sideburned, mustached

63

barman waiting across the polished oak. And I listened, surprised, as Dominic Regli ordered a repetition of our former Cynar. Just as surprised, I found myself countermanding his order. I said, "I should like to try Pernod this time."

I cannot think what antagonism had sparked that sudden switch to a drink I had only seen, never tasted, unless it was the sense that this man was maneuvering me; he was certainly taking over without first requesting my permission.

The look he sent my way was brief, but I avoided his eyes, preferring to watch the jewel-green of the Pernod change to a milky cloud as the liquid plopped over the ice.

The colors may have fascinated me, but the taste did not. I wrinkled my nose at the first sip and set down the glass.

"Please." Dominic held out his glass. "Would you prefer this?"

"Thank you." His tolerance of my inexplicable behavior was more than I deserved. I felt chastened again, less defiant as we exchanged drinks in silence. There was something intimate in the act; I withheld my glance as I drank from his glass. And when I finally looked up, I only hoped the penetrating eyes did not see as much as I feared they might.

I was especially relieved when he did not suggest that we settle at a table or, for that matter, stay more than a quarter of an hour. The first impression of this place had cast a gloom over my already ambivalent mood, and now I fought a compulsion to look over my shoulder toward that shadowed corner.

On our way out of the pub I managed a sidelong glance. The corner was in deep shadow and as empty as darkness can be.

Outside, in the moonlit and gaslit lane I noticed that the wavering light reflected in Dominic Regli's eyes, yet he did not blink. The gaze was steady and once more holding mine. "You were looking for someone?" He said. The inflection was wrong.

I stiffened, turned my head away. "No one. Like you, I know . . . very few people in London."

Perversely, I wished he had answered, had challenged me, whether or not he suspected that this might have been less than the whole truth.

We angled toward Cambridge Circus, crossed it, and were plunged into the vicissitudes of Soho, where the sordid exists cheek by jowl with a certain leftover elegance.

At Greek Street he stopped, and I was touched when he said gently, "Would you like to have one of England's fine fish? Or——"

"Would *you?*"

"Coming from an inland country, I must admit I hoped you would agree. Do you?"

I nodded, and as we moved on, he added, "Though I was quite prepared to offer you a *Berner Platte.*"

"Thank you. Your *Bündner* was simply delicious, but I don't think anyone in England could make a *Berner* like my grandmother's."

"Could she get the Berner sausage in your country?" He said slyly. "The pig's ears?"

I smiled. "Whatever was on that platter around the sauerkraut tasted heavenly to us."

Later over the Dover sole he touched his glass to mine. "*En guete!*" he said. I had not heard that Swiss German equivalent of "bon apéptit" for a long time. And now I wished I had not heard it again. Those simple words brought back so much . . . from the happy days too long ago: grandmother presiding at the Sunday table; grandfather, mother, Uncle Ernst, Uncle Rudy, father . . . all talking at once in a scramble of languages . . . German, French, English; the wonderful aroma of herbs and baking bread that pervaded that wonderful warm, cosy home. . . .

"*En guete*" had brought all that back. I blinked, found it difficult to swallow. He leaned over, brushed my hand with the tips of his fingers. "Did something disturb you, Constance?"

"No . . . I . . . ."

I could not go on. I could not say to Peg's friend, "I felt at home."

The telephone was ringing as I entered the flat. I raced through to the bedroom, breathless when I took up the receiver.

"Connie, you've been out *again!* You see," she went on, "I *told* you that you'd get into the London scene."

The "scene" I had floundered into was not the usual London

one, due in part to Peg herself. *She* had struck up the friendship with Tony Jenner who worked with Guy. *She* had sent Dominic Regli to Crown Gardens.

"Heard from Tony?" She said abruptly.

"Yes."

"And?"

I thought I had better warn her. "He mentioned joining us in Feldkirch in September."

"No." The word exploded. "I don't want him!" Then, "Damn it, we'll skip Feldkirch if we have to." Almost *sotto voce* she added, "Who the hell does he think he is?"

I said nothing. This was no time to mention her Swiss friend's appearance in London.

But her mood, as it could, seesawed. "We don't need that man." The short laugh sounded like a bark. "Believe me, I don't know about you, but *I* never want to see any man from home again. Zurich's the greatest. All I want is for that gorgeous man to come back here." Her voice actually trembled. "Connie, it's paradise. I'm in love, I'm in love, I'm in love, I'm in love. . . ." She drew a deep and audible breath. "Details when I see you. Soon! Only a couple of weeks."

The connection was broken.

Almost immediately, the double ring of the telephone jarred the silence in the flat, the first words as jarring as the bell.

"At last you're home!"

It was Guy. Guy who had left for France last night, according to Dominic Regli. I had to remember that Paris was almost as close to London as Boston was to New York.

"And you. At last you are—" I stopped. I must not be flip; these men were different.

He prodded, "You are happy that I am in London?"

"Yes." I meant it. He was a delightful . . . host.

"Yet you have not been idle, have you?"

My fingers tightened on the receiver. "A friend of Peg's was in town."

"Peg is your Zurich friend?"

"Yes."

"You said 'was' in town. He has left, I hope?"

"I hope."

The laugh that followed was infectious. I joined him, though it provided only a slight release from tension, nothing else.

66

"You will save tomorrow night and Saturday and Sunday for me, won't you? We have work to do."

"Work?"

"The hunt for your angel, remember. The angel for your Zurich friend." His laugh was low, almost sensual. "I have *mine,* you see. Now we must find a nice little wooden one for your friend."

7

The sky beyond the leafy damask of the sycamores was a streaked and faded opal when I awakened after less than a peaceful night. The subconscious had not wrought a soothing miracle. The events of yesterday were still with me: the odd attempt at robbery, the strangely nostalgic hours that did not belong to me, and last, the words that could not have been meant for me. Guy's words: *I have my angel.*

I wished that none of the twenty-four hours had ever happened, that I could erase them, that everything would remain as it had been before. The routine at school and at the flat. The pleasant dates with a fascinating foreigner. No more. No less. Suddenly, though it was barely seven, the telephone intruded.

Guy's voice was low, intimate. "Forgive me for ringing at this beastly hour. I *had* to catch you. Complications. A shift of time. *Today* is Caldeonian Market day, and the blasted place closes at three."

"Should we forget the expedition?"

"*No!* I'm looking forward to it. You will see that I am addicted to bargaining." He paused. "At nine, then. I'll have you back for your afternoon session."

Before he appeared, Edwards rang me from the lobby on the house phone, very correct, very formal. "A gentleman, a Mr. Black, Miss Farrar. Says he has an appointment."

Edwards was remembering yesterday. I said. "Yes, thank you. He may come up."

Guy stood just inside the mirrored doorway, closing the door slowly behind him. He reached out both his hands, then, and held mine.

"Constance, it has been too long. Too many days." He was gazing down at me, his dark eyes sober. "I wanted to surprise you, to come to you and hold you in my arms. And now something is different."

He tipped up my face to his. "Downstairs the porter stopped me, interrogated me as though I were an intruder. Tell me what this is all about."

Moving back, away from the touch, the intense gaze, I told him of yesterday's incident, briefly.

"I don't like it," he said. "I'm not sure I like you being here now. It makes no difference that nothing was taken. Perhaps we should make other——"

"But, don't you see, it will be more secure now. Edwards is being careful. It is *already* more secure."

"For how long? A few days? *Chérie,* I don't like knowing you are here alone." Abruptly, he moved closer, held me close to him. It was a comforting embrace; I was grateful, but I did not, dared not allow myself to relax. I did not want, in this mood, to involve emotions that already seemed in conflict.

I pulled back.

His hands slipped down to mine, he still gazed down at me. "I must learn to control my true feelings. For a time, at least. Yes?"

"Yes, please." My voice sounded to me singularly small. And he laughed, drew my hands to his lips. Looking over them, he added, "You are like a little girl. 'Yes, please,' " he echoed, " 'I'll have that later.' Is that what you mean?" he teased. "Tell me, Constance, is it a promise?"

His glance flicked away for an instant, and he nodded toward the chest nearby. I had forgotten that I had left Dominic's carnations there last night, in the crystal vase.

"Do I have competition?" Mischief glinted in Guy's dark eyes. "You know, I like that." He paused. "Your Zurich friend, perhaps?"

"Friend of a friend."

"Then I may relax a little? He belongs to someone else?"

"Yes."

"Good. Though this was not the greeting I had longed for, I am patient. Shall we go now, and battle for a saint?"

68

The market was below Tower Bridge, which we skirted but did not cross. And from the south, the bridge itself floated like a ghostly schooner through the mist and the smoke on the river. Beyond it the square fortress and half-onion domes of the tower recalled the violence and terror, the shades of Richard III, Sir Thomas More, Ann Boleyn—the queen who had given England the first Elizabeth and lost her head for her pains.

"Oldest surviving medieval fortress in Europe. Built by William the Conqueror," Guy intoned. "You see how I have learned my trade?"

I murmured something complimentary, then added, "It's Shakespeare's London, too, isn't it, down here?"

"*M-m-m,* and other colorful characters. Claude Duval, for instance."

"Should I know him?"

"Perhaps not." Guy jerked the car's wheel sharp right, and we swung away from the river, off Tooley Street. "Duval was a famous highwayman. French. Hanged." A faint grimace touched his lips. "The English, believe it or not, buried him in Covent Garden Church. Near my flat. This is his epitaph: 'Here lies Du Vall: Reader if male thou art, Look to thy purse; if female to thy heart.' Delightful, isn't it?"

He braked to a stop outside an open market that seemed already seething with humanity. But I was only half with the scene. Something nagged at me, something he had said.

"Here we are, Constance." He leaned across and opened the car's door. "Wander a bit, *chérie,* while I find a car park. And, mind you," he tapped the tip of my nose, "don't look interested in *anything,* even if you long for it."

Quite soon we both realized that his warning was purely academic. We found only one figure, a worn, much-chipped stone mourner, too cumbersome for me to carry to Peg, too difficult for her to restore to anything like its original beauty.

"French, I think," Guy said, examining it. He glared at the vendor when the price was mentioned. "I could do better than that by half, by twenty pounds, in France."

When we came away after the fruitless search, he mentioned casually, "By the way, how much did you want to pay for your gift?"

"I thought you'd never ask," I whispered. "About five pounds."

"I'm glad you warned me." He choked on the words when he finished laughing. "I don't suppose you'll let me share a possibly higher price?"

"No. Thank you very much, though."

"Then your friend in Zurich may have to *reconstruct* whatever we find, not *repair* it, as you had indicated."

"Perhaps we should really give up the whole idea." Forty pounds for that broken piece, I was thinking. It was incredible.

"No," he said. "I don't give up easily."

An hour later we stood outside the car in Thornbaugh Street, the main building of the university behind him, its arms spread toward us, toward the square behind me. "Today's lecture session will be a long one," he said. "Rest well tonight."

Our hands clasped, I felt the gentle pressure, and looked up at him, not for the first time feeling an oddly desolate sensation. Not disappointment exactly; perhaps loneliness was part of it, and the vague anxiety accented now because of the disquieting events of the past days. And I could already see in prospect the empty flat, already hear the silence. I doubt I could have described the feeling accurately; it was a multitude of emotions compounded by the past, complicated by the present.

Guy leaned forward, tucked back a strand of my hair that had blown free of the barrette. "Off on a cloud again, Constance? Did you hear me?"

I nodded, now aware of the activity around us, a clatter of footsteps passing us, a ripple of voices. A figure waving from the steps.

It was Undine.

"Tomorrow we have two markets to explore," Guy was saying just as I beckoned to Undine. He glanced over his shoulder, and I saw her pause, apparently uncertain until I called out to her.

"At ten tomorrow," Guy said. "*Ciao.*" With an almost imperceptible bow that acknowledged both of us, he slipped into his car.

"Oh, *wow!*" Undine stared after him. "He's something else! Where did you nab that coordinated dream?"

"At the library, believe it or not." I steered her toward our assigned lecture hall.

"Nobody told me *that* could slip out of all those dusty pages."
She groaned. "I could dig that man."

The market at Camden Passage was, the next morning, a
"bomb," as Peg would have said. But Guy seemed as cheerful as ever about our prospects. "One more to go before we
sink to the depths and struggle through Petticoat Lane tomorrow."

The "one more" market was Portobello Road, a cluttered
street in Notting Hill Gate north and west of Kensington Gardens. "Best and oldest for antiques in London," Guy explained to me as we made several tours of its periphery, past
renovated Victorian terraces and their earlier neighbors, until
we found a suitable place for his silver Citroën.

The road, due perhaps to summer tourists, was a madhouse,
unlike anything I had ever encountered. I literally clutched
Guy's jacket as he wove his expert way among stands, into the
dim caves of jammed shops, pausing, probing, poking stacks
of incredible junk.

It was not long before I was onto the game and thoroughly
intrigued. But I could be easily diverted by a Maltese cross,
even a twisted iron key. Guy pretended diversion, I soon discovered, and ignoring the suspicious looks of the dealers, he
sorted through candlesticks, missals, dazzling crowns that could
only have been stage properties, chain armor, rusted scabbards,
chastity belts; the last marked as such and very popular.

Finally, I watched him push a fold of torn brocade aside
and draw from beneath it a wooden figure unlike any in Peg's
collection; battered but possessing a peculiarly primitive charm.

Rembering Guy's warning, I resisted the impulse to lean past
him for a closer look at the fluted surface of the saint he had
unearthed.

"Spanish." The dealer woke from his half dream, which
might well have been a pose. "Eighteenth century. Collector's
piece, and that's a fact. San Jaime."

Guy turned it over, weighed it in his hand. I could see there
was a lot to be done. Peg would have to remove layers of paint
from the fluted surface, and she would no doubt sandpaper

71

the rough spots. But she would love it. A little nervously I watched Guy put it down, shove it beside the brocade.

"Philippine," he stated bluntly. "Maybe nineteenth century. Maybe twentieth. Look here, you know they painted over those santos. This fellow could be St. Anthony—and *they're* ten pence a dozen."

The bargaining commenced. I would have paid twice what Guy finally got it for, twice the six pounds, even if it meant budgeting tightly for the next month. And when we were barely out of sight of the bustling road and its wary inhabitants, I was jubilant.

"What a *terrific* bargain!" I was almost dancing beside him. "Philippines, Puerto Rico, I don't care where it came from! Peg hasn't one like it."

"*Sh-h-h*" Guy hurried me on toward Pembridge Crescent, toward the car. From the smile on his lips it was apparent that he was as pleased as I with the newspaper-wrapped figure beneath his arm. But he said nothing until we were seated in the Citroën. Then his hand covered mine on the seat between us.

For some minutes, although we sat in silence, I was aware that excitement had built up in him, too. He was as elated as I, his pulse only now was slowing as mine was.

I spoke first. "How did you do it? How did you . . . *know* those things?"

"I've done a little research on antiques. Last night I reviewed a few old notes, checked a reference book or two." He shrugged his shoulders. His fingers spread, linked over mine. "That *was* a bargain, I think. And wasn't it fun, *chérie*? Didn't I tell you it would be?" He did not wait for an answer. The words rushed on. "Shall we celebrate at lunch or dinner?"

"Either."

"Or both! I'll give you a plate of those so-English sandwiches at the Royal Garden, *if*—" he leaned toward me "—*if* you'll come to the flat for dinner."

It should not have been a surprise, should not have bothered me at all; I had visited men's apartments before. But Guy Black was another man altogether. When I did not answer immediately, he said, "I've wanted you to see it."

Of course I wanted to see where he lived, how he lived. . . . "I'd love to," I said.

"Good. We've settled the whole day. After lunch I shall give you time for all those homely chores girls fuss with. But I shall come for you at seven."

I was ready long before then, done up in my white and silver, but the telephone rang while I was nervously applying lipstick for the second time.

"One little change." Guy was profuse in his apologies. "The maid—they call them dailies here, an example of British optimism—the maid was late, of course. I've had to do much more than I had planned. I do hope you won't mind too much—I've rung for a taxi for you."

"You shouldn't have. There's time for a bus. Or the Underground."

He ignored the offer. "The driver knows exactly where to go. You might never find it."

As a matter of fact he was wrong about that. I would have found it quite easily.

When the cab drew up at the entrance to the lane and I stepped down onto the uneven flags, I was at first disoriented, set back two days in time. I had seen this place before, this narrow lane. St. Mark's Row, Covent Garden.

I stood in a stunned silence, staring from that sign to the ancient coach lamps—their flames already flickering in the summer twilight—to the walls that seemed almost to lean in toward me, to the ancient pub that straddled the lane's end.

I had barely time to disguise my bewilderment before Guy Black strode from the doorway of The King's Head.

"Welcome," he said when he reached me. "*Bienvenu chez moi.*"

I hoped that I could bury my secret, that I could summon a reserve of poise. Especially as we passed beneath the gold-leafed plaque of The King's Head and through the Tudor doorway. Especially when he glanced at me.

I am sure that what he hoped for was some sign of pleasure from me, the same delight I had shown at the George Inn, at the pubs and restaurant in Chelsea, at the market this afternoon. I was too slow. I had not controlled the wary glance toward that tiny staircase.

Guy turned his back to the dim tavern, murmured only for me, "What is it, Constance? Tell me. Something is wrong, isn't it?"

73

"No . . . no." I suppose the fact that the masked eyes were not lurking in the shadows, that the bar was noisy and smoke-filled and throbbing with life, that neither barman was the one I had seen two nights ago, gave me the necessary courage to hold my tongue; to lie to Guy.

I said, "For a moment I thought I had been here before."

8

"Here? At The King's Head?" Guy laughed as we moved toward the very staircase I had indeed seen on another evening. "I don't believe you've been here. Unless, perhaps, in an earlier incarnation."

Though my hand was in his as he led me up the dark stairs, the treads were so short and steep that I clung to the worn-smooth banister.

"Perhaps you were surprised—charmed—with your first sight of the place. Yes?" At the top he turned almost eagerly to me. "I hope so, at least. I want you to like it. You see, it's mine."

"Yours?" I slipped my hand from his, still not at ease. And I had not entirely absorbed his meaning. "Yours?" I repeated.

"The building. The flat. *This.*" He gestured toward a long, low-ceilinged corridor, toward an open door at the end.

Despite the continuation of the color and the period of the tavern below stairs, the lingering aroma of ale and beer had vanished. A faint scent of roses, a hint of herbs, hovered in the quiet hall, which, like the staircase, was narrow and dim. But when we reached the threshold of the lighted room, a glow emanated from the very furniture, from the mellow paintings on the paneled walls, from apricot silk that rippled across the hidden windows.

The doorway was so low that when Guy passed beneath it, the blackened oak lintel raised a strand of the silver hair, which he absently smoothed down. He appeared too interested in my reaction to be aware of himself, and I was still too fascinated to be articulate.

Dazzled at the brash mingling of periods, the intrusion of the

74

rich, grave glitter of old French furniture—satinwood, rosewood, and mellow walnut—into that Tudor fastness, I simply stared around me. Now I understood why Guy had admired Nell Hobart's flat, though most of her selections paled beside these perhaps more honest examples. And—another difference—all of these beautiful things looked "lived with."

Returning to the paintings, still dazed, my glance was diverted briefly by a movement beyond a carved screen. The lacy woodwork was so exquisite, so dramatic that for a moment I was held by its beauty; the figure that had paused behind it was only a shadow, although when it did not move again, I turned to Guy.

"Vanko!" His voice beside me was so sharp that I pulled a little away from him while he jerked out a command in Italian. And the shadow glided into an opening at the screen's end, pausing long enough to form into a woman before it drifted on toward some dim reaches . . . pantry . . . kitchen . . . and disappeared.

An odd combination, the creature was shapely yet dowdy, and from the mere glimpse I had had of her it was difficult to establish her position. Her attitude seemed not so much servile as surly.

During the moment while Guy had ripped off his sentence the woman had stared through thick-rimmed glasses that stained her eye sockets an unhealthy hue. The dull, uncomprehending look had to account for the haphazard pile of dark hair on top of her head, the sagging rusted black dress. Only the crisp white apron looked fresh, even new.

One corner of my mind had recognized this, had heard Guy's murmured, "You see, in London everyone is foreign, even the help. Especially the help, I should say." But the words slid away and disappeared as Signora Vanko had, for I was now completely captivated by the paintings that had been so carefully hung against panels covered with what looked like raw silk between the hewn beams.

Was that magnificent triptych a copy of one of the fine Florentine painters? I wondered. Could that Venus actually be an original Bellini? No, of course not. It would be priceless.

But this scene . . . I stopped in front of it, enthralled. *Piazza at Evening,* ivory and gold and rose . . .

"This can't possibly be a Turner, can it?" I saw that Guy was watching me.

"I wish I knew. In paintings, I buy what I like, you see, whenever such things are offered. Do you know much about art?"

"Not much." This was no time to explain a summer of my past to him, although my interest in art had actually been induced by those months in the Rochester antique shop. I added, "I studied art history," which was the truth.

"Of course. For your classes. They are linked, the arts and literature." He waved a hand toward the walls. "But *chérie,* for what I paid for these we won't waste time in fantasy. Any original would be an accident."

"Never mind! Such things *have* happened." The idea was exciting. "And if there were one or two, you might go into the business, and forget——" I stopped, appalled at my audacity.

He had anticipated the conclusion. "Ah, Constance." He shook his head. "Dealing in art, one must be an expert or prepared to employ one. Besides, it is the travel boom that has made it possible for me to indulge my whims. So you see, I am trapped." He was close to me; an arm came around my waist, and he leaned his head wearily against mine.

I did not move for a moment, for quite suddenly I was caught up in all the memories of the morning, his touch, his enthusiasm, his obvious delight in bargaining. And for that moment I wondered whether it were not possible that this unique man could have stumbled upon something more precious than he knew. I could not quite accept his casually dropped statement that he "bought what he liked," which was the cliché of the amateur collector.

He stirred beside me. "Someday, perhaps, when I have enough —no—when I have too much of these, we shall see what they will bring."

"But——" I looked up into the dark eyes that were so close.

He touched a finger to my lips. "In the meantime I shan't call in Sotheby's for an opinion. *Until* I have time for more research."

Research. The word brought back his comment after we had left the market at noontime, and I remembered the santo. I was about to admit I had left the figure in the car when I felt the silence and looked up to see that Guy was watching me again. I saw his glance shift to a nearby table where the santo stood behind an ormolu rail, half wrapped in its newspaper, sadly out

76

of place on the gleaming fruitwood chest, overshadowed by tall roses in fragile porcelain.

"After all your trouble yesterday and today," I avoided his steady gaze, "I forgot Peg's saint this afternoon."

"I *hoped* I should have to remind you, hoped that you would be preoccupied with tonight . . . perhaps."

Glass tinkled nearby, but when I turned toward the sound, the woman in black was vanishing again. A tray of crystal goblets stood before the bank of assorted bottles that all but filled the marble top of a chest.

A peculiar smile touched Guy's lips as he glanced from the tray to the opening between the carved screen and the wall. "She is well-trained, the—Italian, is she not?" His voice dropped perceptibly. "When she wants to be. But I must teach her not to hide behind the reredos. It is not polite."

I watched Guy mix the gin and French he offered as an aperitif, realizing only when I had seen the bottles that he was in reality mixing a martini—without ice. I resolved to merely sip mine, not finish it.

As we drank and sipped, surrounded by the soft glow of a sitting room that might almost have been plucked from two other centuries, I asked about some of the lovely pieces in the room.

"That bergère you sit in?"

"From a château in the Vendée."

"And that sofa?"

His glance went to the golden Récamier confection. "From the Loire. One of my . . . family knew the owners who sold out three hundred years of treasure so that they might live on the Costa del Sol."

I caught the fleeting cynicism in his tone, his smile. But then he said, "You know, you may be right, Constance. Perhaps I should investigate what I have here. Treasures may well be hidden within these walls. Sèvres. Some damned good marquetry." He stopped, looked over my shoulder, and excusing himself, spun off an incomprehensible sentence to the silent and invisible servant. Abruptly, he looked angry as he had sounded when he had rung me earlier.

Then he set down his glass a bit sharply on a nearby table. "That one," he muttered, and rising, came to me, drew me to my feet. "Come, Constance," he said. "We are victims of today's schedules, we must submit to the demands of the lowly."

I glanced quickly toward the screen, hoping again that the woman had not heard him, but no shadow stood or passed behind it.

Beyond the fretwork of the reredos we dined amid candlelight and lace and polished walnut, the accoutrements of another period, another century altogether. The woman apparently had been dismissed from the room and with her had gone the only disturbing note of the evening.

Alone with Guy and sipping a ruby wine, I said, "Your *signora*— I've forgotten her name—might have been late today, but you must forgive so noble a cook. This food is divine."

It was good to hear his laugh, he looked so much younger, less drawn and tired than he had, especially these last two days. "This casserole? It is not Vanko's." Once more I hoped the woman had not heard the derision in his voice. Perhaps as a foreigner, I thought, she was trapped in her lowly position at least for the time. As Guy was in his bureau, as most of us were.

"This casserole," he went on, "had to be ordered from a Greek in Charlotte Street who understands these melanges. Instead of the lamb of his country, I ask him to substitute veal and pork for me. To these he adds tomatoes, herbs, rice, a fine boullion. And the gift of time. That is the secret. The woman brought only the salad greens and the fresh bread with her. Little more."

Though the deprecating note persisted, he did not sound as angry as he had earlier. I think he was content now, as I was, and relaxed.

I wondered if he felt the warmth and security that had taken possession of me.

It was not to last, of course, and of course I should have realized it and not permitted myself to slip into such an unaccustomed state of euphoria.

We drifted back to Crown Gardens in a silver mist—more accurately in the silver car. At least, I drifted. I only awoke from the pleasant dream outside the steps of Number 8, in the secluded cul-de-sac, when Guy said, "It may be some time before I see you again."

The eyes that met mine were searching. And yet there was an oddly lost, almost young, almost vulnerable look in them again, as I had noticed earlier.

"Miss me," he whispered. "Say you'll miss me."

I could say this; it was true. I should miss the attention, the comfort, the security he brought me, the *knowing* he was there. And interested.

"Yes," I said.

His hand beneath my chin, he lifted my face to his, brought his lips to mine in a lingering kiss, soft as silk, evanescent as mist.

Then, abruptly and fortunately for my ambivalent senses, he released me. "*Dieu!*" He breathed. Then, again, "*Dieu!* And I must leave! France, again. Grenoble. Do you know what's been worrying me? Student trouble. In Italy, too. God knows I don't need *that* now."

He slipped from the car while I clutched at a pose that was proving difficult to retain in London. And I was glad for the smile he gave me, pleased with his words when we stood together on the pavement.

"You may be right, after all, Constance. Perhaps I should offer paintings, instead—"

He did not finish the sentence but lifted my hand, brushed it with his lips. Then, with a short laugh he scooped the santo from the back seat and placed it in my arms.

Without another word, without waiting for one from me, he whipped back into the car, reversing so swiftly that he neglected to switch on the headlights.

Except for the few entrance lights the street was in darkness, somehow more profound without the Citroën's silver gleam to hold and reflect the pale electric lamps.

Something stirred at the street's dead end. Someone moved from the iron railing as Guy had, not many weeks ago.

I stumbled up the steps, pushed open the door into the lobby, hurried to the lift, relieved when Mikhail stepped out of his booth and uttered a polite if somewhat sleepy "Good evening, miss."

The silence with which I lived for the next week, more than a week, should have been welcome. There was work to be done, the work that had brought me to London.

But though I found I could live with the comparative loneliness now, I was missing Guy's attention, perhaps the diversion. I found myself recalling the exciting evenings together, the gay adventures at the markets. I caught myself thinking of the beauty of his flat, the fascinating possibilities of his casual collection, the subtle meshing of our interests.

And I was grateful to him. Except for that one quite sudden kiss before his last departure, that poignant *"Miss me,"* there had been no demands, there had only been his declarations, his attentive concern for me, his kindnesses.

Toward the last of the long quiet days and nights Undine McCarthy greeted me with a sly smile when we met at the Student Centre before a lecture.

"Remind me never to stay with an aunt in the suburbs, again, luv."

"What else is new?" I said, and instantly aware that I sounded like Peg, I laughed.

"Nothing *happens* in Putney, see? No M-E-N wander into *my* life. Has that silver vision of yours been around lately?"

"Not . . . recently."

"So, forget it. There's another character lurking in the wings."

"Another—" I looked around, straight into her brilliant blue eyes. "Who?"

She shrugged. "You tell *me*. Tall, tawny. In a way, tough. But, I'll take him, I'll take him."

My laugh was not entirely genuine this time, and Undine was not entirely stupid. "Don't tell me you know him *too*." She moaned. "Must be that Mona Lisa smile, that feminine mystique." She ran her fingers through her short black hair, musing, "Maybe blondes *do* have all the——"

I interrupted. "Where did you see him?"

"At the Student Centre. He was asking one of our compatriots about you. The one whose voice could carry to Piccadilly."

After her first few words I had let the others flow on. What was Dominic Regli doing here at the University . . . he should be back in Zurich, with Peg.

"Know him?" Undine prodded.

"He sounds like a friend of a friend."

"Wrong friend. Damn," she mumbled. "This just isn't my summer."

"What did he want? Did you hear?"

"Asked where you were, when you generally came in. Then he asked when our course was over, what date was the last."

A peculiar resentment was building up inside me, and in a

way I welcomed it. Though then, and later, I wondered why he had not asked me those questions.

That night after a long session Undine and I went directly to the Cambridge Theatre in Earlham Street for a performance of *Lear*. It was Undine's only evening "on the town," as she said, and she had been instructed to take a taxi to Waterloo Station, as soon as the play was over.

She insisted that she could drop me off just past Oxford Circus and not miss her train. And I did not protest because a storm was brewing. After she left me, I hurried and had not passed Queen Anne Street when thunder roared down from the direction of the zoo. I started to run.

At Devonshire I swung into Crown Gardens, raced up the steps of Number 8 just as rain pinged on the iron fretwork above me. Outside, I could hear the deluge that had threatened the last few moments and another rumble of thunder from the west. That had been close.

Though the lift door slid back onto the top floor corridor, it slid back onto darkness illumined only by the dim light from the elevator box itself. Either the storm had caught up with me after all, or a fuse had blown. Fuses short-circuited rather frequently in London, I had learned.

Fumbling with the key at Flat 19, I realized a bit late that I should have descended in the lift and reported the problem to Mikhail. I should at least have descended in that lift.

The moment the keys engaged the tumblers and the door opened, I knew that something was wrong. Cool night air swept through the hall. I never left windows or doors open. And from the open door to the bedroom a faint glow from the city cast eerie shadows. . . .

I should have backed out, run for the stairs even then. Instead, and instinctively, I reached for the light-switch. The flick had a hollow, dead sound; the darkness moved with me. Yet somehow those mirrors and the multifaceted crystal picked up the gleam of eyes, the planes of a face.

And then, although I wrenched myself away from a hand, a descending arm, a black curve that repeated itself over and over in the near-black mirrors, it hooked round my throat, the hot hand crammed against my mouth, and I was crushed back against the man, still struggling, clutching my bag to my breast.

81

I twisted, pushed, grunted, heaved. I jammed down a broad heel upon the creature's foot. Hard.

For that I was jerked up, and in obvious fury, slammed back against the closed door.

The effort had cost him too much. His hand left my bruised lips, and in the same instant, while I gasped for breath, I tore the receiver of the house phone from the wall.

And I screamed.

This time he dragged me away from the door and flung me across the hall, and although I landed flat upon my bag, I managed to push myself away, enough to see that the form seemed almost to shrivel, to shrink from the octopus-like creature it had been due to its many reflections. Without sound, the shape dissolved into the utter blackness of the kitchen doorway.

In a moment, a blast of air swirled along the floor, and caught in the cross-current, the bedroom door slammed not inches from my head.

9

Across the hall behind me the doorknob rattled. I heard Mikhail call out, "Miss! *Miss! Are you all right?*" But I do not know how long it was before I crawled over the carpet and reached up to let him in.

The shaft of his flashlight's beam stabbed the darkness tangled with the distorted reflections in the mirrored hall and his slim form bending toward me. With his hands beneath my elbows I managed to rise and stagger toward the wide chest. I leaned against it, breathing hard from the effort.

"He went—" I clutched the porter's sleeve, pointed toward the kitchen. And he took off through the open doorway.

I edged along the chest, holding tight to the kitchen doorframe as I watched Mikhail sidle out the fire-door behind the glow of his torch and disappear.

How I reached the fire-door at all, considering my unreliable knees, I shall never know, but at the threshold I stared down at the gleaming slats of the iron landing, at the faint gray smudges that might have been footsteps fast vanishing in the backlash of rain.

The cold damp night air and the spray of rain that spattered off the fire-rail must have revived me. Or perhaps it was the grating noise, the *eeeek* from above, the hollow clang of metal against stone, or brick. Then, from somewhere nearby there was a scrape of metal on metal. And after that, except for the hiss of the rain, the night was still again.

The porter loomed back into sight, muttering, "He used ladder to roof. I have fastened it. You want me to go now, to get help?"

"No." I tugged at his jacket. "Just the lights, please." My throat ached, my voice was only a whisper. "And *hurry!* I've got to see about Miss Hobart's things."

As it happened, and most surprisingly, not one of Nell Hobart's precious possessions had been touched. Not one figurine.

Not one bit of bric-a-brac.

In the kitchen's gloom Mikhail fumbled with torch and step stool, quite soon establishing that the flat's main switch had been thrown. Minutes later we were able to snap on every fixture, every lamp in the flat. Light shone down on scenes that were orderly, untouched, deceptively serene. And baffling. Even the bedroom at first glance seemed undisturbed.

Until the ghost of a trace of what looked like powder on the rose carpet led to the dressing room, the wardrobe.

I rolled back the doors. And stared, open-mouthed. It was as though I had seen that tote bag before. At least I had heard about it not many weeks ago. From Peg. ". . . *Slashed, would you believe it? Peeled like an . . . onion.*"

It was not difficult to visualize this now. The tote's lining was completely stripped. And, cast out from where I had tucked it for the time being, lying among the disarrayed shoes on the wardrobe floor, the little santo stared up at Mikhail and me with dumb, beady, painted eyes.

"*Police think someone was looking for something specific,*" Peg had said. "*Apparently there's traffic in passports. Be careful, Connie.*"

Well, whoever the intruder was, he had not got my passport,

83

he could not have, since it was not here. He had got nothing from the flat, nothing from me. For the only thing in my tote bag had been that garish santo.

Mikhail had not uttered a word during our hasty search. Even now he merely stared dully at the scramble on the wardrobe floor. And except for a possibly compulsive movement of his foot as he backed away from the wardrobe toward the bedroom door, he had done nothing. He appeared to be smoothing out the pale tracing on the carpet, frowning slightly, as puzzled I suppose, as I was.

But when I murmured, "Miss Hobart told me there's a market for passports. Perhaps that's what the thief was looking for," he repeated, "Passport?" and glanced around the otherwise untouched room, seeming unsure as I was. He peered at me. "It is gone, your passport?"

I shook my head, "It is safe."

The long sad lines that framed his mouth seemed less defined. "You do not want police, then?"

A moment, two moments passed while I thought of all that the police implied. After all, I was living in a stranger's flat. Alone. And what *had* been stolen? Nothing. What real harm had been done to me? A rumpled dress, hair loose and flung across my face? Not unusual these days. Weak knees? Bruised, swollen lip? I could have had a struggle with anyone, even an escort.

"No," I said finally. "No police." (Certainly I did not only imagine the relief in the porter's eyes.) "I want to ring up Miss Hobart's cousin in Switzerland, first."

The man stood motionless in the doorway, watching me. "Perhaps that is best," he said.

"But wait. Please arrange for another lock on that kitchen door tomorrow morning. *Please* don't forget."

"Oh, yes, miss." He backed into the hall. "Thank you, miss. It is good not to frighten—other tenants. You understand how police might—might question?"

I thought I could guess. Endless questions. Endless forms. Especially for foreigners. Neighbors disturbed—those few who were not on a holiday. But those thoughts were no comfort after the porter had gone, after he had secured the kitchen door and the flat was quiet again, and doubly empty. My voice was

84

not quite steady when I put through the call to the Apartment House Aurora in Zurich.

"It's nearly midnight!" Peg cried when she finally came on. "What's wrong?" Despite her accurate statement and assumption, I almost resented her reaction to my voice.

"I need advice. It's happened here, too."

"Happened? What? Oh, *no* . . ."

The pause was so long that I thought the connection had been broken. And then I· heard her indrawn breath clearly over the hundreds of miles of hills and fields and water.

"Yes, it's happened," I repeated. "And I need advice about police."

"D'you mean someone really got into Nell's place? Oh, God, what a mess!" She sounded even more shaken than when she had told me about her ransacked room in Zurich. "Anything . . . taken?"

"Nothing of hers."

"Of *yours?*"

"Your tote's ruined, that's all."

For the second time the silence was prolonged, and then her voice sounded small and as far away as it really was. "You mean—you mean—like yours was, here?"

"I'm afraid so."

"And nothing's missing from the bag?"

"There was nothing much in it."

"You're sure?"

I thought that was a strange question, and I reacted sharply. "Just a little wooden figure we—I'd found for you."

"What happened to that?"

"Tossed aside. The tote's plastic lining was sliced top to bottom."

Again, the too-long silence, especially considering that this was an out-of-the-country call. "I don't like it," she said finally, her voice low and not much steadier than mine had been at the beginning.

"Nor I. But Peg, what about the police? Did they help at all in Zurich?"

"Not a damned bit. We're foreigners. And students. That doesn't rate us tops on the popularity poll."

"Then I won't notify them." I was counting on that extra lock

85

tomorrow, certain that there would be specific precautions taken by the housemen; hopeful, at least.

"Look," Peg said, "why not quit your lit course, Connie? Quit London. Fly down tomorrow and join me."

"No. I'll manage somehow. *You* did. And I need that London U. certificate, remember?" I am not sure why I did not mention Guy then, and that he should be back soon, though I did add, "The Swiss police may have been right, you know. The prowler here was waiting for me. Could have been my passport he wanted."

"D'you mean you actually *saw* him?"

"No. The lights were out." I explained about the switch.

"But how did he get *in?*"

"I . . . don't know. Extra locks tomorrow, chairs against the doors now."

It could not have been minutes after we had bid each other sober good-byes that the telephone rang. Peg called me back.

"Why not ask the new man for his advice?"

New man? She could not possibly know about Guy. I deliberately had not mentioned him; she had been so critical of Tony, of almost any man I had known within the last year or so. I asked, "Who?"

"Come off it," she said. "There's only one from Zurich. At least, *I* only sent one."

"But Peg, he's not been here."

"Since when?"

"A week. No, more than a week."

"Oh." The single syllable was flat. Then, cautiously, she added, "Didn't you adore him?"

"Not particularly." I hoped that was the answer she wanted, though for some perverse reason I went on, "He reminded me of my Uncle Rudy," which, except for the Swiss-German, certainly was not true.

She giggled at that. "I suppose it's the Swiss connection." Suddenly she seemed much more herself. "Well, I've news for you. I've discovered that I groove on older men."

I had not thought that Dominic was so much older than we were. Perhaps six or seven years. And when I did not comment, she said, a little querulous, "Are you with me?"

"Yes, I think I am." I was attempting to adjust my thoughts

86

of Peg and Dominic, Peg and . . . men. "You were talking about men. Older men."

"Right on! And, Connie, if you can't take care of Dominic, at least take care of yourself."

"Believe me, I'm trying." I was about to say good-bye again when Peg burst out, "Oh, it's so great to share the same hang-ups! And with such a *beautiful* man! This new one knows almost as much about santos and angels and mourners as I do."

"He does?"

"He ought to. He's from those eastern mountains where holy icons are still household equipment. We're going there. Together."

"When?"

"Soon, I hope. When he gets back. Don't worry, we'll be back before you get here."

Guy came back from France the next day. Before the afternoon was over, he came to find me at the North Library as he had that first evening weeks ago.

This time when I looked up from the circle of lamplight, I was pleased to see him.

"Finished?" He whispered.

"No." But I smiled and started to shuffle notes and books together.

"It is late." He beckoned toward the clock.

"*Sh-h-*" someone hissed just as someone had on that first day he had come to find me. My glance met Guy's. I saw that he, too, was controlling the laughter, that he, too, was remembering.

"Come," he said.

Of course, while we walked through the cool September dusk toward Crown Gardens, the events of the night before poured out. And now, for him to see, the bruises concealed by a jacket's collar, a scarf at the throat; graphic enough proof. He stopped at the edge of Bedford Square and gripped my shoulders.

"We shall take a taxi." His dark eyes were angry now. "I want to see that kitchen door and the fire-stairs. I want to talk with your porter."

In the taxi he held me close within the circle of his arm, his cheek against my hair. And when I did not move, he murmured, "Perhaps I should be grateful for your intruder. I have a feeling that you have needed me, that you missed me."

I stirred, and leaning away, pretended to search in my handbag for something. But he drew me back. "Perhaps if you would tell me not to go . . ."

A memory slammed between us. An evening on Long Island, five weeks ago. A mere five weeks.

Don't go, Tony had said. *I don't want you to go.*

I said to Guy, "I'm glad you're back," but the words sounded stilted, not really as I felt. Why? I wondered. *Why* was it so difficult for me? I *was* glad. I was grateful for his interest, his concern. I was relaxing in the ring of security that seemed part of his . . . mystique. That was the only word for his quite special aura, that word Undine had used just yesterday when she had teased me.

I stirred again, thinking of her words this morning, her reaction to the abortive attempt in the flat last night. "Y'know, Auntie's may be dull, but never dangerous." She had peered closely at me. "Sounds like someone's out to get you, Connie. Or," slowly, "to get something you've got."

Neither her laugh nor mine could have been described as genuine. And unfortunately the thought, which I had been denying, would not leave me.

When Guy closed his hand over mine now, I responded to the warm clasp. Swiftly, he raised my hand, held it against his face just as the cab stopped at Number 8 Crown Gardens.

We were up the steps, beyond the doorway, into the marble lobby, my hand still caught in Guy's—when Dominic Regli stepped out of the shadow of the circular staircase.

10

Once more, as I had on our first meeting, I had the impression of controlled force in the cold, deliberate poise of the man who stood by the wrought iron newel post. Again, I felt he could be a most formidable adversary.

I made a move to draw back, but Guy's hand was firm on

88

mine. He held me by his side, returning the Swiss man's level gaze with his own. Only a slightly raised eyebrow gave any indication of his mood before he said, "It's Regli, isn't it? From Zurich?"

Dominic nodded, managing to greet both of us in that one gesture, though his eyes looked straight at Guy. He said nothing and calmly tucked the flat white packet of Turkish cigarettes into his pocket without having removed one.

Guy watched him, following every movement with a critical, almost contemptuous eye. "You left more of your brochures at the bureau recently." His voice was sharp, his accent more pronounced than I had ever heard it. "I thought I had explained to you that all such material should be submitted to our St. Gallen office. Or Geneva."

"I am here to call upon Miss Farrar," Dominic Regli said.

Aware of Guy's fingers tensing, then releasing mine, I moved a little closer to him, angry at Peg's friend's attempt at humiliation, justified or not. I thought it especially courteous of Guy when he stepped back, murmuring, "Please," to Dominic, and bowed slightly.

If the man from Zurich had been aware of any mockery in the tone or gesture, he did not show it. He ignored Guy, spoke directly to me.

"I shall ring you before I leave." The fact that he should have telephoned before he had come here did not seem to have occurred to him, apparently had never occurred to him. "You might have a message for Margaret," he added.

Guy had moved away, toward the porter's booth. Glancing sideways at him, I caught the faint narrowing of his eyelids, the compressed line of his lips. I thought he was preparing to berate Mikhail because of the intruder last night, and my attention was divided.

"Something is wrong?" Dominic said, his voice too low to have been heard by the men some yards behind him.

"No. Nothing." I went on quickly, "I have no message for Peg."

"Nothing at all?"

When I repeated, "No. Nothing," he frowned, still watching me.

"Goodnight," I said. Then corrected myself, "Good-bye." I

held out my hand. It was the least I could do. Besides, it lent a touch of finality. He clasped it briefly, his eyes gazing down into mine as though they would see beyond, would ferret out whatever reservations might be lurking there.

"Wiedersehen." The word was murmured as he moved past me toward the door, and I turned, staring after him. He should have said, *"Adieu,"* I thought. *That* was "good-bye."

From across the lobby, now that Dominic Regli had left, the sounds of voices rising in accusation and in protest sent me hurrying toward the porter's booth.

I put a restraining hand on Guy's arm. "Mikhail did all he could last night. He came up right away."

"When it was too late," Guy said.

The porter was pale, even paler than he had been the night before. And he was seething, I thought, beneath Guy's onslaughts. "I cannot watch door," he muttered, "and roof, also."

"What has the roof to do with it?"

"Sometimes intruders come over rooftops, you understand?"

"No, I don't understand. And if that *is* the case, then we shall see the management. We shall arrange for iron bars if necessary, and extra locks. Even though it is Miss Farrar's last week here in London."

"Management has added new bolt this morning, sir. But," the porter shook his head, "roof-ladder cannot be changed. British fire laws." I wondered whether there was not a hint of defiance in the man's voice.

"Damned frustrating," Guy muttered to me as we left Mikhail and proceeded to Flat 19.

The encounter with the two men in the marble lobby had affected both of us. Guy was critical of the flat's vulnerability to the point of implying possible carelessness on someone's part, even mine, which I resented. Most of all, I resented his questions about Dominic Regli.

"Who *is* he, actually? You say a friend of your American friend, but do you know this?"

"Yes, I know."

"How?"

'I've talked with her." I did not add that I was not likely to forget her blissful remarks last night.

"When?"

"Nearly every week. She calls me."

"About him?" His question was so quick it was almost an interruption.

"Not always. But she mentions him."

"You mean she rings all the way from Zurich to talk of—a man?" Now there was a hint of the teasing smile that intrigued me. "She must be either rich or reckless, your friend."

"She's well-enough off. And she's in love."

"In love?" We were standing at the wide window of Nell Hobart's sitting room, and even though we were ignoring one of my last London twilights, the memory of those moments were to remain with me for a long time. His eyes were dark; his silver hair was dark against the pale on-coming glow of the city's lights behind him. "In love?" He repeated, "with that Swiss—that Swiss *montagnard?*"

I was sorting out his questions and his comment, translating the latter in my mind. Dominic Regli was not the sort of mountain man that Guy implied. He was as intelligent, as presentable as Guy himself.

In abrupt defense of Peg's friend, I said, "He is an educated man."

"Perhaps," Guy was murmuring almost to himself. "Odd . . . that brand of cigarettes. I should have thought he would prefer something rougher. Gauloises, perhaps."

When he stopped, I added, "He is from the mountains, originally. The Engadine. His background is Romansch."

Very briefly, a glitter lighted Guy's eyes. "You see? I was right. And, *chérie,* they can be a rough lot." Then he persisted, "Your friend had told you that she is really in love? You—she —do not hold secrets?"

"My friend has told me this," I said quietly, controlling an unreasonable irritation. "She made it quite clear last night."

"Last night?" He edged onto the wide window sill and drew me toward him. "It appears that many things happened last night. Tell me, is your friend so quick to love? Or is she slow and shy? As you?"

I did not yield to his touch this time, to the magnetism of his nearness. I stiffened and looked away toward the darkening gardens beyond him.

"You are angry with me." He dropped his hands, slipped from the ledge of the bay.

"No. No. I am—it's difficult to explain—"

91

"Don't then. I understand." He leaned over, kissed my forehead. "Let us try to recapture the mood we have lost. Let us go out into the world and drink, eat, and be gay. For, who knows what the gods have in store for us tomorrow?"

At the door to the corridor he added, "Wear something dark and mysterious tonight. Eight-thirty?" Abruptly, his attention flicked to the bronze doorknob. He examined the inner latch and looked back at me. "Your intruder must have had a key, you know. Didn't you tell me that the maid's handbag had been stolen? Didn't she have your key?"

Of course. She had come to borrow mine for a copy. And if her handbag had been singled out, that could mean that someone knew what she had, knew what he wanted.

"You definitely need a new lock now. I'll make this clear to your porter," he said. And I agreed.

I had just finished dressing in the only dark and mysterious "something" I owned—a classic navy nothing of a dress to which I added a filmy scarf I had not worn before—when I heard the *clack* of the metal mail slot in the hall.

An express letter lay on the carpet, an envelope I recognized at once. It was a special delivery letter from Tony Jenner.

The mingled feelings that built up in the first few seconds as I stared at the envelope left me quite shaken. Guilt, of course, was uppermost. More than a month had passed, but my life had already changed. I knew somehow that it was in a changing pattern, and I wanted Tony to remain where he was, at least one fixed element.

In a flash of insight I thought it might probably be best if everyone remained in his place for the time. I opened the letter with reluctance.

My darling,
   Your enthusiasm about my proposed Austrian trip is not exactly overwhelming. But secretly, I'm a bit fed up and need a break. I could do business over there at the same time, so I won't feel like a dog leaving the last straggle of holiday work with the kids in the office.
   I'm aiming for Feldkirch. Check your schedule and dates, and you'll know about when to look for me.
   Write me, darling. Say something. Say you're homesick.

Say you haven't met any foreign charmer.

Which reminds me, if you happen to run into the boss, a guy named Black (Oops! Bad slip; his name is Guy),— and being the selfish bastard that I am; I hope you don't meet up with him—I'd appreciate it if you didn't mention my plans. What he doesn't know won't bother him.

Guy Black . . . Tony's boss? I had thought they were associates. I was folding the letter, disturbed enough by Tony's persistence, now puzzled by this information, when the house telephone rang. Mikhail announced that Mr. Black could not park the car. He would wait downstairs for me.

He was pacing outside the double-parked car, but he must have heard me, for he swung around. His glance lingered on my hair, the sheer pale scarf, the silver chain, the fitted frock.

"You're my obedient girl, aren't you?" he said softly as he helped me into the low car. Propped against the backrest of the seat was a worn gray figure carved of wood, not stone as I had feared a mourner might be, and not much larger than the santo. But it was taller, perhaps twenty inches, and narrower. An utterly enchanting piece. Peg would love it.

I took it up, preoccupied until I heard the first of his words.

"Can you keep a secret, Constance?" He whispered. "Can you guess what I have been planning for you, for us, after you leave Zurich?"

A tightness started somewhere beneath my rib cage. He leaned on the car's door, gazing down at me. "Do you know what I have in my possessive mind?"

I did not utter a word.

"I have been rearranging my schedule so that we may meet in Feldkirch."

I rallied somehow after the first wave of disbelief. Disbelief? Not exactly. I did not want to believe this complication. Guy and Tony . . . both planning to converge upon the same Austrian town. And Tony's holiday without permission from his boss, this man beside me. What if they met?

There were answers to that question: Guy would not like it, Tony would not like it, Peg would not like it.

The idea panicked me.

"What do you think, *chérie?*" Guy was pulling at my scarf. "Tell me."

How could I tell him I was thinking that I must not fail to cable Tony tonight?

I cupped my hand over the satin-smooth head of the mourner. "I think I'm flattered," I said. The words sounded stiff again, and he laughed.

"Oh, *chérie*," he said. "*Ma bien aimée.*"

We drifted through the evening, through winding streets, through the seventeenth-century elegance of a divine inn. We sipped nectar and shared ambrosia. My spirits rose to meet his eventually; my fears diminished in the heady topaz of the wine, vanished after the rich amber of the brandy. It was a lovely night. We drove back to Crown Gordens after a wide detour along the Embankment, where a waxing moon stood pale beyond the lacy towers of Westminster. We heard the first strike of midnight as we passed.

He swung the car off Devonshire into the cul-de-sac, flaring on all the car's lights before he switched them off. "I'm going up with you," he said. "After last night, I must look over that flat."

After last night, I did not protest. And he was swift. He searched the rooms, checked the fire door, the windows. At the last, at the bedroom window he stood silently before it, looking out onto the pattern of the motionless leaves, the black chimney pots sharp against the muted glow of the new moon.

And then he turned.

"Constance?" He reached toward me.

A pale glow that was of the city, of the moon, touched his silver hair with an unearthly hue, a cold light, blue and unreal. The same light glinted on his dark eyes.

"I want you," he whispered. "I want you now. I have longed for you since . . . forever." Tenderly, he held my face between his hands, then the tip of one finger traced my eyebrows, my cheeks, my lips. "But I want to be alone with you. Truly alone. In the woods, perhaps. In the high mountains with the murmuring stream, the scent of pines; the sky far above us, the earth warm and yielding beneath us. And I shall want to know that you are mine."

He did not move. Nor did I.

The evening had led to this, all of the times I had been with Guy had led to this: I should have known. In the magic of the

94

moment, the poetic dream he had evoked, the promise of love, I wondered what it would be like to be loved by . . . I looked past him, shaken by the thought that had almost formed, by the desire that had almost risen.

The kiss was as light as the first had been those days long ago. Then abruptly he moved to the door, where he turned. His face was a dim oval in the shadows beyond the lamplight; I could not gauge his expression. "In case anything should prevent me from driving you to the airport next week, *à bientôt,* dearest," he said. "Until very soon . . ."

And he was gone.

11

The bell rang before I was ready to leave for the university the next morning; Tilly was outside.

"Working for me gentleman downstairs, today," she explained. "And knowin' you're leaving Wednesday, I come to tell ye good-bye."

"How nice." I was glad to see her cheerful face.

"It's been a pleasure comin' to ye," she beamed. "Not like some of my ladies. Nothing to do, most of them, but fuss with their hair and nails. And never so much as pick up a towel." She sighed. "Well it's me job."

My experience with pragmatic coworkers at the Long Island restaurant gave me more than a hint of the real reason behind this visit. I dug in my handbag for the couple of pounds that Peg and I had agreed upon as a "thank-you" plus the fee Nell Hobart had already paid.

"Maybe this will help you buy another handbag." I tucked the notes into a pocket of her coverall.

"Oh! The good Lord bless ye! Thank ye so much, miss. But didn't Edwards tell ye? I got me old one back. At the police station in Marylebone Lane. Nothin' missin' but the keys."

Later, I told Undine about this during the midmorning coffee break at the Refectory. She lifted her starred lashes and peered at me over her cup. "Okay, London's been great. Most of the time. But if I were you I'd be glad to split on Wednesday." I nodded, not overjoyed at this tacit confession.

That was the day we said good-bye; her excursion ticket time had run out. And I knew I should miss her as I had missed Peg.

That night, the third night after Guy had left London, I was wrapping the long gray mourner, a grieving figure with bent, cowl-draped head, in folds of tissue, preparing to pack it. I could not forget Guy's gallantry when I had protested, when I had asked to pay for the figure.

"Please," he had said. "We shall call it a gift from Students' Travel, Ltd. to a treasured client."

At the time I had wondered why he had not used some more intimate word than client; had rationalized later that, after all, he did not know Peg.

Thinking of him now, of this surprise that he had remembered to bring me despite his busy life, I felt an unaccustomed warmth, perhaps more than the warmth of a deepening friendship.

The telephone rang. I caught it up, expecting his voice, but it was another's altogether.

"Regli here."

There was a moment of adjustment as the man intruded into my thoughts as he had intruded into my life so often during these last weeks. For reasons that I obstinately rejected, I continued to resent this friend of Peg's and yet for some unexplained reason I could not answer sharply. My "Good evening," was neutral enough.

"You are leaving soon," he said, "if I remember correctly."

"Yes. In two days."

"So." The hesitation was prolonged, it seemed to me. But then he added, "So now I wish you another *Wiedersehen.* I hope we meet in Zurich."

"I—we shan't be there long."

"No? Not for a few days with Margaret?"

It was my turn to hesitate. Peg had mentioned having a brief fling—no, she had merely said they were going there—in the eastern mountains where holy icons were still household equipment.

I said, "Shouldn't *you* be there now, in Switzerland?"

He laughed. "Am I to assume that's a proper dismissal?"

96

"But Peg had said—" I stopped.

"Yes?" He prodded.

"Peg had said that you—I thought that she was going to the eastern mountains."

"When did she tell you that?"

I counted back. "Four days ago."

"I see." His laugh was shorter this time. "I see, too, that girls do not hold secrets."

"Good friends sometimes share them." I was defensive, protecting both of us.

After a pause he said, "And how do you know I am not in Zurich now? Or in the mountains?"

Of course I did not know. Connections had been so good to the Continent, some London connections had been so poor; I certainly could not detect the difference.

The short *blip* indicating the end of the three-minute period was followed by a tinkle of coins. "Please," he said, "Forgive me. I am en route to the London Airport now, for the nineteen-fifty-five to Zurich. You see, I shall be there in time after all."

"But you'll be there only two days before I get there." The moment I spoke I wished I had not, and during the brief silence that followed I wondered if he was embarrassed too.

Finally, he went on, "Quite enough for a trip. Distances are shorter in Europe than in your vast country. In two or three hours from Zurich's Central Station one can be in the high Alps."

I had said too much. I changed the subject. "I'd like to wish you good luck with your search."

"My search?"

His reaction had been quick, but mine was just as swift. What did he mean by such a question? Peg had distinctly told me that this man knew almost as much about santos and angels and mourners as she did. If he was merely using her interest, playing up to it so that he might *lure* her into a mountain hideaway of his, I could think of no lower trick.

I said quietly, and distinctly, "Her collection is very precious to my friend. I hope you understand that."

"I understand," he said surprisingly. "You still will not permit me to carry anything to her?"

I looked across the room at the tissue-covered head of the mourner protruding from the open tote. And I wavered.

Into the silence, he said, "You do not trust me, perhaps?"

97

There was just a hint of amusement in the inflection, though it did not amuse me. And I could not answer. For more reasons than one, I could not answer. He was, after all, Peg's friend. . . .

"Thank you for your offer," I managed finally. It was difficult to suppress the hurt and anger that were rising, and I wanted him to know. I said, "We've had enough trouble, Peg and I. I want to deliver these gifts myself."

He ignored the implication. "What trouble have you had?"

Now I was ashamed at what I had started. Peg's friend did not deserve this, to be involved in my affairs as well as hers. "I'm sorry. You couldn't have known. I—we've had intruders."

"Here, in London, also?"

"Yes."

"When?"

"Days ago."

"And what was taken?"

"Nothing. A bag was ruined, that's all."

"You *should* have told me."

"When, for instance? You . . . aren't always here."

"You could have told me in the lobby the evening I met you with Herr Black?"

"I was busy that night." I was reacting to him again, trying without success to control the feelings he always seemed to arouse.

"I noticed," he said dryly.

This time I uttered a distinct, *"Adieu."* Whether the word was German or not, whether he was Swiss or not, he would understand that.

"Auf wiedersehen." It was a pronouncement, sharp and clear, as though he were correcting me.

The next morning, just as I left for the university for the last time, Edwards, the day porter, brought me my first note from Peg. Brief but important. And, tissue-wrapped within the envelope was a flat and shiny key.

Peg had scribbled in her generous hand:

> Just in case, here's your duplicate to the little flat in the Dolder Weg. I think we'll be back before you get here— we plan to.

98

I thought: Dominic Regli *had* left a bit late after all, and I was disappointed though not surprised.

The note went on:

> If we don't, this key opens both the front door to Apartment Haus Aurora and the door to Flat G, second floor rear. Mailbox key in desk drawer. Don't expect too much especially after Cousin Nell's pad.
> You'll love Zurich. Prowl around. Have fun.
> P.S. He's so secretive! Apparently I shouldn't even have told you!"

Late that night as I was fastening my valise, Guy finally rang up. Distantly, I heard him rattle off a sentence that sounded like Italian.

I said sharply, out of my disappointment, "You're not in London."

"Ah, you're there! No, *chérie.*" He mumbled a word to someone again, then added, "En route to Geneva. I think we've over-educated these students." His laugh carried clearly over the wire and cheered me. "They want to go everywhere, see everything, do everything." His voice was abruptly lower, gentler. "Do *you?*"

"I . . . have been spoiled."

"Ah, Constance. I cannot wait, I cannot wait. And *je suis desolé*—bitterly disappointed—that I cannot be with you tomorrow at London Airport. But it will not be long. I may surprise you."

There was a series of fading yet clamorous sounds, and the wire was dead.

London was cold and gloomy on the day I left, presaging autumn. In little more than an hour after takeoff I was plunged into another world altogether at the Zurich Airport, a bustling hub crackling with loud-speakers sputtering one foreign language after another. I was bewildered at first.

To a customs question I answered a truthful, "Yes." I did have two gifts for a friend. The value? One was about five pounds sterling. The other, I told the busy officer, had been a gift to me, possibly worth a few pounds more. I actually did not know the cost.

99

I used my German, which he accepted without question, though I noticed he studied a pad beside him before he waved me on. Directly after I moved off, I heard him stop a pair of long-haired unisex types who had been drifting behind me and instruct each one to unroll his lumpy pack.

Curious, I looked over my shoulder, and for that brief second I thought I saw a man who looked like Dominic Regli standing near the passengers' entrance some distance away.

Since I was in the path of the laden travelers, I moved toward a corner before I turned again, craning to see whether it was Dominic and whether Peg might be with him. But, though I waited until all the passengers had filed through and the door was closed, I did not see the man again.

Neither Peg nor Dominic were at the airport. Nor did Guy appear, although I had wondered whether he might have planned to surprise me here. It was probably Feldkirch where I should find him after all. He had mentioned that town, as Tony had. And he knew my schedule.

Tony knew it too, but I did not look for him. He should have had my cable days ago. In it I had tactfully explained that other plans with Peg and a friend made a meeting in Austria quite impossible if not inadvisable.

I had pondered that last word for some time before I had dispatched the cable. But it was pertinent. He, himself, had written that he did not want Guy Black to know of his proposed plan to join Peg and me in Feldkirch.

The Apartment House Aurora was in a narrow winding street part way up a hill called the Dolder, according to the driver, and just off Dolderstrasse. A compact, modern little block, the building nestled between two handsome villas, half hidden by tall pines and graceful elms.

During the coach ride from the airport I had been diverted by my thoughts at first, vaguely aware of disappointment in the outlying districts; I had expected mountains, I suppose. But after my transfer to a taxi at the city's air terminal I sat forward in my seat watching the river, the long quay, the tiny stone houses of what must certainly be the old town.

Almost immediately after we left the river, we started a steady pull uphill, skimming alongside blue and white trams, around avenues named Graben—I searched my mind for the translation

—"moat?" And streets called Gasse. I knew that one. "Lane." I knew Strasse, too; that was the most common: "street." We turned left at an open Platz, the driver shifted, and we slanted up Dolderstrasse to the Dolder Weg.

The Dolder Way . . .

When I looked up at the building where Peg had lived for the last six weeks, I felt a strangely happy sense of home at first. Even in mid-September geraniums spilled in luxurious abandon from every balcony, a sight that delighted me, for it brought back happy memories of early childhood, memories of home and grandmother and baking bread and noisy family dinners with my mother's brothers and father's assorted friends.

I hoped one balcony was Peg's—ours—and hoped against a now somewhat dim hope that I would find her at home and un-packing.

But of course she was not there. The flat was as empty as the one I had left in London, and cold. The straight tall pines held darkness in their branches and screened out what little of the sun's last rays managed to flicker through the moving leaves of the elms.

I shivered, longing not only for a warm drink but for someone to share it with. Perhaps there was a note. . . .

There was a note.

Against the lamp on the square table that cornered between two sofa beds there was a sheet of lined paper. If the room alone had not given evidence of a hasty departure, that scribble did.

> Sneaking this to you. Car waiting. Hate to do this but men—damn! Off to the Verlassenes Tal, the valley for carvings, so he says. If we don't get back to Zurich, see you in Feldkirch. Plenty of driving to do.
> Hundreds of miles apparently

There was no period. No signature.

The note disturbed me.

Again, I asked myself why Dominic Regli had left his re-turn to Zurich so late. This was Wednesday evening. And Peg and I were to have left for Feldkirch, the Austrian border town, on Friday. Instead, Peg was probably hundreds of miles away by now.

I read the note again. Hundreds of miles to the east would put them in Austria, well into Austria—I had been studying my map. If this had been the plan, why couldn't they have waited another day or two and set off from Feldkirch?

I seesawed between annoyance with Peg and with that Swiss —that Swiss *montagnard,* as Guy had called him. Damn, I thought, reflecting Peg's own comment. Damn all these complications. What had happened to our original plans for an Austrian holiday together?

The answer was simple: men.

The flat, I discovered was in reality a room with built-in bath, kitchenette, and the balcony I had hoped for. And I soon found that there were places for everything. No more, no less. I found, too, that Peg had taken all of her clothes with her, though she had left her books and school notes to be studied after our return from the planned ten-day trip.

In the kitchen I found the usual staples: milk that seemed fresh, several cheeses, eggs, and a loaf of bread that looked delicious, plastic-banded with the name Tessiner. After all, they probably were all fresh if Peg had left only two days ago.

Coffee or tea would do for now, however. The Swiss "collation" on the plane had been suffiicient to serve as supper. Besides, I was restless, uneasy, without quite knowing why.

Even the window-box gardening in the deepening twilight, the thin slice of the view of the lake below and beyond the screen of pines, the winking, shimmering lights of a city in motion as darkness fell, did not alleviate the depression that dogged me. I gathered the small dead blossoms of the geraniums, nipped off the few yellowed leaves with chilled fingers, and I am afraid, a chilled heart.

I was upset because Peg had left, had changed our plans because of a man. And I was ashamed of myself, deeply, heartily ashamed. Peg deserved this romance. I only hoped, prayed, that the man she loved was worthy of her.

It was not until the next morning, after a miserable mountain-cold, dream-filled night, that I found the second note. Looking for what Dominic had called the *Abfallkübel* to dispose of the usual small clutter involved with breakfast, I saw the folded sheet taped to the bin enclosed beneath the sink.

Friday next garbage day. Before you leave, tie up plastic liner with string. Carry out to entrance gate. Sorry— left a

few last-minute items in it. Taking last-minute qualms with
me. Only hope this isn't another mistake like Tony. Remind
me to tell you about that sometime. For God's sake keep
him out of our hair, whatever you do.

Another mistake like Tony? What had he to do with Peg,
except as a travel agent? I could not quite understand this reference.

I was holding open the cover of the garbage bin, staring down
into the black liner. At least that Swiss is neat, I thought. He
hasn't cluttered up Peg's flat with ashes and ends and boxes.

On top of a folded newspaper lay the bronze-banded and lettered box of Turmac, the brand I had seen him smoke. Unless
Peg had been wooed away from her American cigarettes, I
knew no one else who smoked them. I had never heard of these
cigarettes before I had seen the box in Dominic Regli's hands
in London. Wondering about them now, I reached into the liner
and took out the packet.

"New European Blend. Super Oval." As I turned the box to
read "Made in Switzerland," something slid across inside. There
were at least ten cigarettes left. I should not have thought this
was quite like a smoker, not quite like Dominic Regli, not like
the Swiss who never wasted anything. But apparently I was not
a very good judge of men. I would not have believed that Dominic Regli would have been quite as precipitate as he had been
about this search for saints and angels. He could have waited
two days. He could have dropped me off in Feldkirch and gone
on to his valley with Peg.

But, no. He was selfish. He had taken Peg away with him.

I caught myself up again. I was wrong. I had to remind myself again. Peg had wanted to go. Peg was enchanted by this
man. Peg was in love.

I dropped the Turmac packet onto the newspaper, was about
to close the container's lid, when the headlines stopped me.

It was yesterday's *Herald Tribune*.

Had they left only yesterday? The day I had arrived?

Dismay that amounted almost to shock was not relieved by
the hot tea or the heavenly bread or the dark mountain honey;
there were elements about Peg's departure, her notes, her haste,
her references including the comment on Tony, that cast a per-
manent gloom over my spirits. In my mind I began to defend

Tony. After all, he had packaged a good trip for her last year, which was why—she had told me—she had gone along with his plan for us this year. It was not his fault if Peg, if *we* were disrupting the holiday with our own individual excursions.

And exactly why didn't Peg like Tony? Why, if she was so against him, had she left it so long to explain?

The low ring of the telephone brought me back to the flat in Zurich.

"Fräulein Farrar?" A woman's voice inquired. *"Hier ist Students' Travel in St. Gallen."*

Students' Travel—was Guy in Switzerland?

But, no. The woman was merely instructing me to pick up my seat reservation on the Transalpin Express leaving tomorrow at 11:24 A.M.

"It is a reserved seat train," she said. "You must go to the Central Station immediately to secure your place."

In some ways Zurich surprised me. I had thought of it as a financial center, busy, impersonal, certainly not colorful. Yet that morning in mid-September all the parks and gardens that I had so loved in London were no more beautiful than the greens of Zurich's hills, the vivid reds and golds and violets of its sturdy blossoms. Color wove its way into the very heart of the city, into the public squares, the window boxes, the blue and white trams, red-tiled roofs, glittering shop windows. Flags of all nations flapped against a cloud-swept sky, bright sails angled on the rippled waters of the lake.

The station was an absolute madhouse of clamoring tourists, worse than any I had seen, and I was relieved to get away, after I had picked up my *Sitzplatz.* By accident, I left via a rear exit, finding myself directly across from the Landesmuseum, the national museum. I went in.

Captivated by the old wood carvings, the gilded and jeweled bishops and kings, madonnas, and saints, I lingered in one gallery, comparing these exquisite pieces with Peg's, wondering whether any remaining mountain hideaways might disgorge such treasures today. The four-hundred-year-old *Heilige Katharina,* the fourteenth-century crucifix, the magnificent *Armoire de Sacristie,* all from the eastern mountains where Dominic Regli had "walked the many miles to school," held me for the longest time.

If he could lead her to anything even one quarter as fine as these in the Canton Graubünden, I certainly was wrong about the man. I had been refusing to believe in his knowledge of such artifac;s, had questioned the fact that they existed. I had been so sure that he was misleading Peg, that somehow he was misrepresenting the possibilities of discovery in those alps of his.

I trailed back toward the Dolder Weg, wandering almost blindly along the route the tram had taken when I had come down to the station. Past the busy Central, I was aware of a change in the pattern of traffic and architecture, and consulting my small map, turned into Niederdorfstrasse, an ancient lane where the buildings seemed to lean toward each other over the granite paving. Students, tourists, the city's shoppers, jostled one another; cars and trucks rode the sidewalks, mudguards all but scraping the bordering windows of boutiques, cafes, prosaic stationers, bleating record shops. At Rindermarkt I checked my map again and swung left.

The madonna stood alone in a window at the corner of the narrowest lane I had seen since St. Mark's Row, Covent Garden. A figure almost as handsome as any at the museum, a *Maria,* a madonna with child. Thinking of Peg, I stood for some time on the tiny ledge of pavement, wondering whether she had seen this piece, whether she had priced it, whether I dare. I fingered my wallet in my shoulder bag, wondering whether I could afford a deposit to secure it for Peg.

While I thought of these contingencies, I saw beyond the window a tall, ascetic young man approach the shop's door. He opened it, cast me an appraising look before he slipped a small sign behind the glass: "GESCHLOSSEN 12.30–14.00." He was obviously closing for lunch.

I said, "How much is the madonna?"

In warning he offered the information, first, that it was from the sixteenth century, then added, "Eighteen thousand francs."

My brief contact with Swiss currency made it impossible for me to work out the specific sum, but I knew it was far more money than even Peg would spend; it was thousands of dollars.

I am not sure how I managed to murmur, "Where does it come from?"

"Austria. *Bitte.*" He bowed slightly, and his heels clacked off down Neumarkt behind me.

Austria, I was thinking. Perhaps that was their destination

after all. Hundreds of miles east of Zurich would certainly take them well into Austria.

I walked on, following the route of Tram 3, and it was well after lunchtime when I finally reached the flat. I doubt I would have noticed any difference in the room at that time if I had not decided to change into another pair of shoes.

All my shoes were in the new tote bag, which I had slid into the wardrobe. And I had left the bag open earlier. I remembered it particularly because the zipper was stiff.

The zipper was almost completely shut now.

I do not know how many minutes passed before I finally opened the bag; uneasiness was mounting to something close to fear. And before I touched the metal fastening I paused, listened, actually looked over my shoulder.

Someone had been in this flat. But how had he gotten in? The door had been locked, double-locked, for I had already learned that the key turned twice.

The tote's zipper moved stiffly, revealing first the smooth gray head of the mourner still covered in tissue, though the paper did not seem as fresh, somehow. Beside it the brash painted head of the little santo was tucked tightly between two shoe bags, too tightly.

I had removed one of the three bags from beside the figure which had left it tilted at a sharp angle. Now the santo stood upright.

It was not minutes later when I decided to telephone the St. Gallen office to learn whether Guy was in Switzerland. Even though nothing was missing from the flat, as far as I could tell after a frantic search followed by a more thorough piece-by-piece examination, I wanted to talk with someone. Perhaps his office would know where he was, whether he was in Geneva, which I hoped, or somewhere en route to Feldkirch.

The woman's voice in St. Gallen was not the same as the one who had called me this morning. "You wish to speak to Herr *Black?*" She sounded incredulous, and there was a prolonged silence before she continued still in German. "Who is this?"

"Miss Farrar, in Zurich."

"Who?"

I repeated my name. "Your office rang me this morning."

"A moment."

There was a hurried conversation, too low for me to hear.

106

And then a man's voice came over the wire, speaking correct, accented English.

"Miss Farrar, Herr Black never comes to this office. He supervises London, Paris, and Genoa operations."

Genoa? I thought. *He must mean Geneva.* But I did not interrupt the man, and he had gone on.

"And seat reservations were posted to you and Miss Hobart two days ago." He was obviously reading. "To Dolder Weg 12, 8032 Zurich."

"But, your office instructed me just this morning——"

"I beg your pardon," the man cut in. "No one from this office could have called you at any time."

12

My mind was spinning with the implications of what I had just heard over the wire from St. Gallen. Someone had obviously wanted to get me out of this apartment, someone who knew enough about Peg and me to know our schedule.

The itinerary might be on file in one of the other branches of the travel office, listing almost hour-by-hour plans. And what about Peg's school? Peg was sometimes overfriendly. She might have confided in a classmate.

After all, now there had been two intrusions. Someone must still believe that Peg or I had something important in our possessions.

Downstairs in the letterbox I found the envelope from the St. Gallen office, enclosing the two reservations. It could have been there since yesterday.

And there was a card from Peg! Stamped in Feldkirch, Austria, posted late yesterday.

> Super inn, food, wine. But, guess what? No man. He sent
> me on ahead. Business, he said. So here I am, guzzling *Alte*

Knabe St. Anton Spezial and eating something called *Schnitzel Donatal.*

Super valley, by the way, but no santo or madonna in sight. Superman no saint, either. Beginning to wonder who he really is, and what I'm doing here. 'Bye, now. Post-bus driver mailing this for me.

I read the message on the card over and over, a card picturing a street in Zurich's Old Town which gave me no hint of her whereabouts. Three sentences disturbed me. "No man. And "Superman no saint." Actually, I was more distressed by these two than I should have been, and I had to remind myself that I had already suspected that about the man, hadn't I?

But, most of all, her words, "Beginning to wonder who he really is" repeated themselves over and over in my whirling mind.

Why would Peg have raised such a question?

She had told me weeks ago that Dominic Regli was connected with the Evangelische Hochschulgemeinde in an administrative capacity, hadn't she? Recruiting. Yes, yes. In London he had been distributing brochures, calling on travel agencies. But . . . we had only his word for this.

I paused just long enough to consult my map again before I tore out of the lobby and down the Dolderstrasse to the tram stop.

I had to find the office of that school. And, since Peg was getting regular college credits for the course, the University was the only place where I might get directions.

One could not miss the tower. Its green copper dome rose beyond terraces and conifers to dominate the old villas and the old town that glistened like quartz and muted garnet in the sun. The main building spread up Rämistrasse, imposing and confusing with its many entrances, and it was too long before I found the correct bureau and a busy clerk.

"The EHG?" He thrust a folder at me. "Hirschengraben Number Seven." He must have felt the urgency, for he glanced at a wall clock. Then added, "They close at four-thirty, Fräulein." He gave me explicit directions.

I flew down the flagged steps, past gardens, villas, walls, sauntering students; across a traffic-mad road, an open cobbled *Platz;* raced through a low stone doorway, up a stone staircase.

The serious young man behind the desk in the bureau of the Evangelische Hochschulgemeinde replied at once, very quietly and distinctly, that there was no such person as Dominic Regli connected with the school.

I descended the steps in that handsome hallway slowly. And I do not know how long I stood outside the cream-washed building in the cobbled square, vaguely aware of artists sketching or painting, of a fountain splashing, of the spray carried by a sudden gust of cold wind, a change in the air, a dimming of the light.

I stood there while my shadow grew longer and darker, blending with the slate gray cobbles and the basin of the pool.

I stood there because at the time I could not think where to go next, and because I had no one to turn to.

A storm was brewing as I finally reached the curved roadway that led up to the Dolder Weg; the atmosphere added to the apprehension that had grown with almost every hour of my day and night here. I wanted the answers to the questions that had now become very important. I wanted to know who the man was that Peg was meeting and what his plans really were. I wanted to know who had gotten into Peg's flat, and how.

Someone could have another key. Peg might have given someone another key. A landlord or landlady might know. What *was* the word in German? I started to check the names on the bank of mailboxes. This could be it: Frau Knipfer, *Hauswart.*

Haus meant house, of course, and *wart* could mean tend, among other things. I rang the bell.

Despite a prompt buzz, which admitted me to the lobby, and a prompt appearance in the doorway directly opposite the entrance, the buxom and aproned character I presumed to be Frau Knipfer was obviously not pleased to see me. From the aroma that drifted through the open doorway I suspected I had interrupted dinner preparations.

"What do you wish?" The look she gave me was practiced, sharp, enveloping.

"I'm Miss Hobart's friend."

"She has several."

That stopped me briefly, but it was information, and that was what I wanted.

I said, "I'm the one from the States, the one booked here by Students' Travel."

She relaxed slightly. "Ah, now I remember. She said she was expecting you."

I did not mention, nor did she, that Peg had left. I said, "Do you know whether she, whether *we* had any visitors today?"

"They would not ring my bell," she said defensively.

"They never do?"

"Never. Except for deliveries from shops, that sort of thing."

I did not want to ask, but I felt I must. "It's possible, of course, that other people, friends of the tenants, could have keys, couldn't they?"

Now she was openly hostile. "If you are going to ask about that robbery shortly after your friend first came here, I want you to know that I am sure she left her door unlocked. Your friend is—how shall I say—*leichtsinnig?*"

I knew that word. My somewhat stodgy uncles thought that all young women were giddy and light-headed these days.

The landlady added quickly, "Perhaps Miss Hobart is a little too easily friendly. You understand?"

"Yes," I said.

"The Students' Travel Bureau has sent tenants for the past two years. I have never had any trouble with them."

"Yes. Yes, thank you." I was careful to repeat the almost too profuse Swiss, *"Ich danke Ihnen vielmals,"* as I backed toward the stairs. An idea had come to me; I wanted to examine it. I wanted to pull my thoughts about Peg and Tony together. Why hadn't I realized it before?

Peg must have gotten the house keys from Tony.

It was not much later that I decided I would have to leave Zurich earlier than the agency had planned. I would have to get to Feldkirch as soon as possible, even if I had to wait that much longer there for Guy. I had to do something. I had to move. I would take the very first train in the morning.

While waiting on line for the seat reservation earlier in the day, I had picked up a condensed timetable for Feldkirch and Vaduz, the capital of the principality of Liechtenstein, which was one of our planned stops. There were several trains each day.

If I arrived at the Gasthof Goldene Krone too early for the room the agency had booked for Peg and me, and if she were not there, at least I could hope that Guy would be. I decided I would tell him everything about Peg, about Tony, and this last evidence of an intruder. But specifically my anxiety about Peg.

In the meantime I had problems to solve, decisions to make. What to pack, what to leave. And why.

Having found the flat empty of everything except Peg's books had puzzled me. We had already planned to leave all our "city" clothes in Zurich and, of course, any gifts or figurines Peg might have acquired by now. If she had taken everything except her books, perhaps I should too.

But I wished I knew why she had, I wished I knew what these last few days had meant to her, had done to her.

In my indecision I removed both santo and mourner from the tote bag twice. The second time, I found myself weighing the santo in the palm of my hand. Wasn't it lighter than when we had bought it? Or was that my imagination?

The telephone rang while I still held the figure in my hand. It was Peg!

"Darling, it's me. Together at last in that valley of his! Paradise, or whatever."

The dismay that swept over me was more intense since I had learned of her man's deception. And because Peg sounded so giddy, so like the first time she had rung me in London, for a moment I could not speak.

"Connie, honey," Peg shouted, "are you there?"

"You're smashed, Peg," I said as I had those weeks ago. "Now, listen to me." It was all I could do to add the next words. "You were right. That man's not what he says he is."

Peg's laughter faded and returned.

It angered me. This was no time for laughter. I cried, "Listen to me!"

"Oh, I know all about him. He's a *business* man. Big business. And what a *pad!* Fantastic! We're going to do business together. Swaps, trades, that sort of thing. He's found a source for one of my figures already."

I thought of the madonna in the shop window off Neumarkt, and I wavered. Perhaps this was big business after all. . . .

"Connie," Peg cried, "didn't you say you'd found me a saint in London?"

"Yes, but——"

111

"Now, you listen to *me.*" There was a belligerent note in her voice. "Bring it with you. Bring everything but the books. Big deals going on here."

"Peg," I said in desperation, "that man is a liar. He is *not* with the school. I've ——"

Her laughter was thin and far away. "Whatever made you think that?"

"Peg, wait. Where are you?"

"We've *been,* dear. Fabulous valleys. The Montafon, the Silvretta, a place called . . . the Verlassenes Tal. I told you. But we're going back."

"Back to where?"

"Quo Vaduz?" Was that really what she had said; her giggle obscured the words, rippling over the wire, drifting before she added, "They're all mixed up, these crazy towns. Don't forget my santo." I heard a man's voice in the background, though not the words. "Oh, yes, that's right. Bring everything. *Bientôt* . . . Feldkirch . . . Vaduz . . . *qui sait? Ciao.*"

The receiver clicked, and a faint bell like an echo pinged in the room

Until quite soon . . . Feldkirch . . . Vaduz? What did she mean by "Who knows?"

Who was he, the character who had tossed stars into Peg's eyes? That tough, stiff paradox of a man? That curiously withdrawn, curiously curious man? Curiously European . . . but then, so was Guy.

Was that man exploiting Peg? Had she possibly discovered something quite valuable, and was he giving her the romantic fling I had feared—and I had feared it all along, hadn't I?—before he absconded with the loot?

That was a bit melodramatic, that thought. I repressed a wry smile, thinking that I should like to be around when that big business "expert" viewed the santo. If he thought that, at five pounds sterling, it would bring a fortune in one of those crazy towns, he did not know London dealers. They were known to be very canny. I had read this, and Guy had confirmed it. I was certain that Peg would have weeks of work to clean up the santo before it had any value at all.

I sobered quickly, thinking again of other possibilities, something more involved.

Passports . . . yes. The man knew we had them, of course.

Or he might be working on a mistaken premise; he might *think* we had something. The search of Peg's flat here in Zurich weeks ago, the London flat. The prowler today. All interested in our baggage.

What had all this to do with the man from the mountains?

13

Through the morning mist the train slid silently across the invisible frontier into the Austrian town. Until that day Feldkirch had been merely a name on my schedule, a meeting place.

Now I had come from Switzerland across the northern tip of the little principality of Liechtenstein and into the medieval town hours ahead of the scheduled Transalpin Express. At a little past dawn this morning after a sleepless night I had left Zurich on the Arlberg Express, instead.

As the train slowed, a customs official drew back the compartment door, requested the passports of a Hungarian woman and an Austrian couple, instructed them to open their valises. He merely glanced at my passport, referred to a pad in his pocket, and dismissed me.

I left the compartment to stand at the passage window, watching the approach to Feldkirch but I could not shake off the feeling that I was being watched. There was a silence in the corridor despite the half-dozen passengers who were standing along the window rail. I wondered, too, why I had been so readily dismissed until a voice spoke almost at my shoulder.

"And how long will you be staying in this country?" the same official said quietly.

He had startled me. I turned, not sure that he had addressed me, but his eyes, inscrutable, neutral, met mine.

"A day. A few days, perhaps," I said quickly, too quickly, for he looked from me to my baggage with what I thought was a contemplative eye.

"So. And nothing to declare?" The statement was as much a

question; he had already zipped open the tote bag just far enough so that the mourner's cowl-draped head emerged. As he looked up at me, his fingers smoothed the surface of the narrow figure just as mine had in London not many days ago.

"A gift," I explained, "for a friend who collects."

The officer lifted the figure, turned it, examined it. "Nice copy," he muttered, pressing it back between a shoe bag and a book that barely concealed the little santo. "Now, if that figure was an original," he added, "it would be in stone, of course, and its value could be considerable."

I said nothing, for I was aware of conflicting thoughts now, of a slight disappointment in Guy's perception, a slight amusement at the picture of Dominic Regli's attempts to negotiate a sale of this copy.

The official tapped my suitcase, smiling. "Any more like that figure in here?"

I shook my head.

"Be welcome in Austria." The man touched his cap and moved into the next car that clicked along the rails behind us.

The incident had disturbed me enough so that I was relieved when the train drew to a stop at the border town.

I stepped down onto the platform, not quite prepared for the enclosing fog, the darkness that shrouded the town, muting sound and color. And, although it was nine in the morning, the alpine cold had not yet left the valley. Shivering, I pulled the collar of my raincoat around my ears, tucked in my scarf.

By the time I arrived at the station square, the few passengers who had left the train had disappeared into the cobbled and granite-paved passageways and lanes as if the mist had swallowed them. A bus stood empty some yards away, two cars parked behind it. Inside or outside the station there seemed no one of whom to ask directions; the *Auskunft* window had been closed.

I turned back to the news kiosk, where I had noticed a broad female attendant. An instant before I reached the stand, a pair of youths barged between the newsrack and a slim woman in a sleek, shining black raincoat.

Whipping a journal from the outer rack, one of the boys slung a few coins into the attendant's hand.

The woman muttered something about *"Ausländer,"* under

114

her breath, adding in German to her chic customer, "Foreigners—we have too many here." And as I approached the stand, the slender woman stood aside for me, busying herself with the selection of a magazine at the far end of the counter.

I used my German when I asked the direction to the Gasthof Goldene Krone which brought a tolerant smile from the attendant and a kind suggestion that I use the shortcut to the town's center. The woman pointed to a back way out of the station.

The route proved to be little more than a lane, alternately flagged and packed earth between random strips of tarmac, a lane deserted and singularly quiet except for the occasional rapid sound of a woman's heels some distance behind me. When I turned to look, I caught a glimpse of a shining coat before the slim form vanished into a hedge-bound lane I had not even seen.

At the same time I saw a small boy wobbling along on a scooter and, some yards behind him, a tall man in the gray-beige trenchcoat I had come to think of as the European uniform; that was all.

At first in my weary and nervous mood I was disturbed by the interrupted sound of the footsteps until I realized that like me, the man was walking sometimes on, sometimes off the same irregular paving and that my footsteps too were muted when on the softer earth.

Nevertheless, this damp and lonely lane was my introduction to the town, and I did not like it. I wanted to run though that would certainly have been impossible with my two bags. Only the hope that I would find Peg here sustained me; and if not, that Guy could share my worries. Guy would know what to do, how to cope with the situation.

But there was no time to think about either meeting at the moment. Quite suddenly a main road was before me, and I was faced with trafffic as astonishing as Zurich's, on a much smaller scale but just as hazardous.

At the pedestrian crossing I set down my bags and waited for a letup in the steady stream of cars that swished past in both directions.

London traffic had been bad enough. Surprisingly, Zurich's had been worse. This road in this little city was the worst. I waited endlessly for a brief break in the flow of cars. Then, catching sight of an opening, I swooped up my bags and stepped from the curb. Instantly, I staggered back out of the path of a dark car that had rocketed from a lane somewhere at my right. Tires squealing, the car slowed for a fraction of a moment, skidded slightly on the wet tarmac, then spurted on, braking for the curve below a towering stone wall.

I stared after it. In the moment of the driver's adjusting speeds I had seen a face. A girl's face. The girl in the rear seat, her head leaning on the backrest, dark hair spreading over the shoulders of a green coat.

Peg had long mahogany-brown hair. Peg had a green coat. Could it have been Peg? Or was it merely that she was so much in my mind that I would see her everywhere?

I continued to stare, trying to convince myself that Peg would not likely be in a car with two men and a woman here in Feldkirch, and if she were, I would surely find her at the Gasthof Goldene Krone sometime today. I had to remind myself that I was early, hours ahead of our planned schedule.

With considerable difficulty I finally negotiated the zebra crossing of what must have been Feldkirch's main artery. And immediately was plunged into a medieval maze of cobbles and arcades and painted houses and ancient gates and arches; a town huddled beneath a brooding castle that seemed perilously close to collapsing upon what must once have been its feudal dependencies.

The faded and bracketed sign of the Goldene Krone—bearing the golden crown of its name—was more inviting than its entrance. At first I thought I had come to the rear of the place: The stone arch was like the opening of a cavern, dank and smelling of wet wood and stone that had never dried and of many unnameable odors, the most pleasant of which might have been stale beer or wine. I hesitated before I stumbled beneath the Gasthof's wide arch and into the forbidding darkness of the flagged court. When my eyes became accustomed to the gloom, I saw to the right above a wide stone step a door of ancient oak, black and rough with age. There seemed no means of opening that door until my probing fingers found the iron latch.

Beyond, the stairway was ill-lighted. And the small square hall at the top seemed empty. Empty, yet oddly rich with mellow wood paneling—linden I should think, from what I had seen in Zurich's Landesmuseum. In too small a space were crammed several ancestral paintings, too many fruitwood chests and chairs. On the uneven polished floor oriental rugs overlapped.

I was still staring when a voice spoke briskly in German. "What do you wish, fräulein?"

I swung around toward a figure who was straightening up behind a porter's lectern.

The man was foreign—no, *I* was the foreigner—thickly built, of indeterminate age, and swarthy, not the blue-eyed, pink-cheeked type I had somehow expected of an Austrian.

"You have a reservation for my friend, Miss Hobart, and me." Before I could give my name, he turned to a board beside the reception desk, then glanced up.

"Yes. Double room. But not ready. Not until thirteen hours, you understand."

I understood; indeed, I had been prepared for this. However, I asked, "Has Miss Hobart arrived?"

"Not yet. You are early," he added almost accusingly.

I had been prepared for this too. But not quite prepared for the answer to my query about Herr Black.

"Herr Black?" Did I imagine the faintly cynical lift of the porter's lips as he consulted the board once more. "No reservations in that name."

"For tomorrow, perhaps?" I wondered whether I could wait another twenty-four hours for Guy's help.

"None for this week." He tapped the board. "Only twenty beds we have. It is simple enough."

My disappointment mingled with a degree of respect for Guy's discretion. Connected with Students' Travel as he was, he probably preferred lodgings elsewhere.

My disappointment mingled, too, with a sense of loss. I had so looked forward to Guy's help, to his protection, had so needed a confidant.

Preoccupied with this unwelcome development, I watched absently as the porter moved my two bags into a shadowed corner behind the lectern. I was thinking of my next move, of what I might accomplish in the next four hours. I was thinking of a possible bus to the valley Peg had mentioned, the Verlassenes Tal. She had written on the card she had posted from Feldkirch, "post-bus driver mailing this for me. . . ."

"One moment, please," I said in German. "Are there buses available in Feldkirch?"

"Ja, ja." His black-button eyes scanned me swiftly. "Where did you want to go?"

"To the Verlassenes Tal."

"The Ver—" He stopped and stared at me, shaking his head slowly. "There is no such valley that I know of in the Vorarlberg."

"But there must be. My friend wrote me just a few days ago especially mentioning the Verlassenes Tal."

The porter's brows contracted into a puzzled frown, his eyes narrowed. Slowly, almost as though he did not wish to offer the possibility, he said, "The fräulein could mean the Verlorenen Tal, perhaps." He was watching me now.

"The Verlorenen Tal?" Peg could have made that error. "Is there a bus?"

I had a faint feeling that he was about to perform the sign of the cross as he added, "No bus. No one goes there." Then, stubbornly, emphatically, "No bus goes to the valley of the lost souls." He was still watching me.

It was not the Verlassenes Tal—the forgotten valley—but the valley of the forlorn, of the lost souls. I did not like it. I said, "isn't there an inn near there, at least?"

"No inn," he said in something like annoyance. "I have just told you, fräulein, that no bus goes there. The road . . ." his voice trailed off "is little more than a *Wanderweg,* only a *Pfad.*"

Little more than a wander-way? A footpath? I could not believe it. "Doesn't anyone live there?"

It was a moment or two before he answered, and then he seemed hesitant, unsure for the first time. "Fräulein," he muttered finally, "no one deliberately goes there."

He stopped, although he could not have heard the man behind him, for the door that had seemed part of the wall paneling had opened without a sound; the man had moved without a sound. And the man, obviously a member of the staff, did not move further; he merely watched from a distance of about four yards.

The porter leaned a little toward me as though to emphasize his point. "No one goes to the Verlorenen Tal, fräulein, because the place is said to be evil . . . haunted."

I was aware of a slight movement behind the porter's sturdy form, but still no sound.

"Haunted?" I hoped my inflection hinted at amusement rather than dismay.

The porter's black eyes looked beyond me as though he were seeing something I could not see. "Although recently," he appeared to be recounting something from memory, "recently it has been reported that some stranger is believed to return there from time to time. Some foreigner. Some have heard that he speaks a language that has almost disappeared from this continent—the old Ladin." His voice dropped. "There are Swiss who speak something similar," he muttered under his breath.

"Romansch?" It was Dominic Regli's boyhood tongue. I was no longer amused.

He nodded. "Those few who have heard it insist that evil will come to any who go near enough——"

"Then, one *can* reach there?" I cut in. "Perhaps I could find a car."

"No." The word was sharp. "Those who—those who have been close will not speak of the place. They are afraid."

"But," I persisted, "someone does live there."

"Live there, fräulein? That is difficult to know. There are lights at night sometimes. However," his voice grew firm again, "there is no roadway to the end, you see. No route. You understand?"

My nod was mere convention. I understood less and less. Except that Dominic Regli must have been going there for some time. . . .

As I started to turn, the tall fair man in brass-buttoned jacket and waistcoat advanced to the porter's stand. In an instant the expression of calculated interest in the man's blue eyes was gone, replaced by the calculated blankness of one attempting to ignore what he has heard, or to pretend he has heard nothing.

Behind me, as I reached the dim staircase, I heard the porter's gruff voice asking in his stilted German, "Karl, your name is? You want to be called that? Or you wish Ochsner?"

"Karl is good enough. And you? It's Luigi, isn't it?"

"*Ja, ja.* You speak Italian, perhaps? It would be easier for me, for us, especially in the beginning. Always new people to train . . . you understand."

I paused on the last step, blatantly listening for Karl's answer. Even I could detect the difference in the accents and in the men's backgrounds. The new voice was educated, incisive. His

Italian when he answered Luigi sounded clearer, more precise to me. But then, I had to remember that foreigners often spoke a language they had studied more precisely than a country's native. Although—the thought was fleeting—few hotel employees spoke so well.

14

Out in the damp arcaded street I turned past empty sidewalk tables into the café I had passed on my way to the court of the Goldene Krone, a restaurant obviously connected with the inn, for a golden crown was etched on its facade. I had just been given directions to the bus station by a pleasant waitress when I saw the tall brass-buttoned and jacketed figure of the new employee Karl descend a staircase beyond a row of booths.

He stopped when he saw me, then quite correctly came toward me. "The fräulein wishes a table?" he asked.

I shook my head, and thanking him, slipped off to pursue further inquiries at the bus station.

In my perhaps too sensitive and questioning mood I was unhappy with what I had heard from the Italian porter at the Gasthof. He had insisted that the valley Peg had mentioned must be the Verlorenen Tal, and the name, the legend—if that's what it was—worried me.

I wanted to reject his preposterous story as nothing more than country superstition, an oft-told tale that had burgeoned in the telling. But the Italian's reaction had stirred more doubts in my mind, his disclosures had brought some confirmation of my own more than vague fears.

Perhaps, I thought ruefully as I hurried over the wet cobbles, I was annoyed with the man because he had actually added to my apprehensions. What I wanted was assurance that all was well, all was normal. I did not want to believe that Peg had gone off to a strange spot with a strange man who spoke a strange and dying language.

This, of course, is what really haunted me. The porter's reference to the old Ladin, a dialect of the same root as the fourth

Swiss tongue, Romansch. Dominic Regli spoke that ancient language.

How long would it take me to find that valley if Peg . . . if Guy did not arrive in Feldkirch by one o'clock, the time my originally scheduled train, the Transalpin, was due?

Rounding the corner into the open square, I spied several yellow buses, one revving up its motor, its sign reading: "Montafon-Silvretta."

The Montafon was one of the valleys Peg had mentioned.

I started to run, waving at the driver, but he was too busy backing away from the curb. And within seconds the bus with barely a half-dozen faces peering through the rain-spotted panes churned into the arcade-lined roadway and joined the stream of cars and lorries that pounded through the little town.

I touched the arm of another driver who was lolling against his bus, smoking. "Is that—would that bus have gone to, or near the Verlorenen Tal?"

The remnant of a thin cigar came slowly from between the man's lips. "The Verlorenen Tal?" His eyes, the blue I had expected of an Austrian's, were cold and still; the eyes of a nerveless driver. And then he added, "No bus goes to the Verlorenen Tal, fräulein."

"But there *is* a valley by that name." I was determined to get another opinion.

"No bus goes there." He dismissed me with a glance similar to Frau Knipfer's appraisal just yesterday, dropped the last inch of cigar onto the damp cobbles, and squashed it with his heel.

Behind me another driver muttered, "You've missed the only bus today for the *Hochalpenstrasse,* the high alps road." He shook his head when I looked back. "And it's not a day for a walk in the mountains. Now, is it?"

"I just want to know how one gets there."

"Ask in the post office," he gestured over his shoulder, "about the post bus from Vaduz in Liechtenstein as far as Malbun."

Liechtenstein . . . post-bus . . . why hadn't I thought of that before? Peg had given her post card to a *post-bus* driver.

The driver was still talking, saying something about one bus daily from Vaduz. "From there, also a *Wanderweg* . . .*" his voice drifted off, and I saw his glance slide toward his colleague. "Though there's . . . nothing at the end, fräulein."

How could there be nothing? Peg was somewhere in one of

those lost valleys with that—that *montagnard*. At least, she *had* been.

"Nothing?" I persisted. "No inn, no cottage, nothing at all?"

"*Nur Zigeuner,* it is said. Only gypsies, strangers who do not belong. And deep ravines. Old, worn-out alpine huts, that is all. You understand?"

The words of the two drivers had registered slowly. *Hochalpenstrasse . . .* the high alps road. Post-bus. Liechtenstein. *Only gypsies, strangers who do not belong . . .* That is what Luigi had said about the Verlorenen Tal. . . .

I looked up at the man before me. Perhaps either driver would have seen something or someone, or heard something that might help me. Perhaps if I appealed to these men, explained that I wanted to find a friend . . .

I said simply, "I am looking for a friend." I lied slightly, "She could be lost in the mountains."

The urgency in my voice might have moved the man, and it was obvious that his colleague had heard my words; he had certainly been listening. He joined us, then. "A friend?" he said. "*Ausländer,* also? Young, like you? English?"

"American." I restrained myself from grasping the man's arm and shaking him.

"That bus to the Silvretta, the one that just left here." The man's cool eyes narrowed in concentration. "A couple of days ago the driver told me of a fräulein. On one of the mountain passes near the Swiss border. She ran out of a driveway. Gave him a card to post here. And five Swiss francs." He shook his head. "That's too much, you know."

It had to be Peg. She would give too much. "Where was that?" I said. "Is it——"

"Wait," he cut in. "You are sure it is your friend? She did not seem—" he appeared to be embarrassed now "—she did not seem quite right. Too much wine, perhaps. You see, when the driver mentioned that it was only a couple of schillings for the postage, the fräulein said something odd. 'Schillings'? She looked surprised, too. '*Austrian schillings?* I thought we were in Liechtenstein.' "

"She thought she was in *Liechtenstein?*" I stared at him.

"*Ja, ja.* She said they had business to conduct there, in Vaduz." The driver was shaking his head again. "My colleague said either it was too much wine, or she—she may have been hurt. An accident, he thought. You see, she limped."

It was Peg. She was somewhere not too far from here, or she had been somewhere not too far away. But I did not like the drinking. There had been a little too much of that in her calls these past weeks. And the confusion was not like Peg at all. She knew Europe almost as well as she knew Long Island.

At this point the other driver offered his advice. "If you knew where your friend might be doing business, fräulein, you might take a post-bus to Vaduz this afternoon."

"Yes . . . yes." I thanked the men and automatically started into the post-office building although I was not really clear why. It was only mid-morning. I had arrived ahead of schedule. Peg *could* be on her way here. Guy could be on his way.

I turned even before I reached an inquiry window and wove my way between wet raincoats back to the door, dimly aware of the unaired smell, a phenomenon that pervaded most public buildings. (Where did all the beautiful people go to post a letter or package?)

One passed me, surprising me. Though I caught only a glimpse of her, the impression was chic, the scent subtle.

I looked around, but she had slipped into a telephone box. Her hair, long and shining, the color of walnut, fell over her face as her gloved hands dug into her copious bag. She was different; it was the only reason I turned to look at her. She was elegant. And she was alone.

She did not belong there any more than I did, I thought wryly. But not for the same reason. Peg should be here with me. Guy should be here.

Neither of them had arrived, Luigi informed me when I returned to the Goldene Krone. No one had rung up.

I peered beyond him to the dark corner beneath the porter's stand. My bags were no longer there.

"My valise," I said. "My baggage? What have you done with it?"

"Don't worry about your lugguage, fräulein." He tapped a panel behind his lectern, his smile patronizing, almost cynical as if to say, "Don't fuss about your little bags."

"Wait." I was thinking of Peg, of her request for the santo. Despite my doubts of its value, and now of the mourner's, at least I wanted to deliver them to her. "One bag," I said. "The small one. I'd like that one locked up. I'd like a receipt."

"A receipt? That's not . . ." his voice slowed. ". . . necessary. Feldkirch is not Paris. Or Chicago. The bags will be here when you return."

"I'd like a receipt."

"Very well." He reached behind him and touched a panel in what looked like a solid wall. A narrow door swung out revealing both my bags among others. He slid out the tote bag and selecting a key from his pocket ring, moved to an adjacent panel. The lock into which he inserted his key was so unobtrusive that it might well have been a flattened burl in the wood.

In the darkness beyond I could see only the outline of what looked like a small safe; that was all. My bag was dropped beside it.

Once the formalities were over and the receipt tucked away in my handbag, the porter urged me to go down to the café next door and have a coffee while I waited for the room to be free.

"Will you send Miss Hobart or Mr. Black to me if either one should come?"

"If either one should come, of course."

I wondered whether I was sensitive to this negative repetition, and then he added, "Better still, you may take a seat at a sidewalk table and watch the Gasthof's entrance. *Ja?*"

The few sidewalk tables that were being set up were protected from a now relentless downpour by the medieval arcade that arched over the slabbed pavement along both sides of the street. And I suppose it would have been pleasant enough despite the cold and dampness if I had not been distracted by mounting worries.

I was so busy watching the Gasthof's entrance court that at first I did not hear the individual voices around me. They blended with the hiss of tires on the wet tarmac into what Peg might have called background music. And then gradually a few voices rose and fell above the others. I heard German, Italian, a Slavic tongue, then something rather different. I listened intently; I had to, for the man's voice was pitched very low. I found myself straining to identify the language.

"*Bun di.*" The voice was coarse, almost harsh. And a coarse German followed. "You've noticed the visitor has come."

124

The answer, a rush of German was barely audible. I could not separate the words.

Apparently the man's companion was having the same difficulty. "*Ch'el discuorra plü plan,*" the hoarse voice complained.

"Speak German. That jargon is rough, you know that."

"You manage well enough for the boss, I notice."

"Shut up." Continuing in German, the lower voice ordered coffee and bread, his tone more normal then. "*Und schnell,*" he added to the waitress. "Be quick."

"So you're in a hurry," his companion muttered. "Leaving me to hang around———"

"Be quiet. We do as we're told. It's your shift, anyway. And I've got to get back to *Il Cumün.*"

There was silence behind me after that, but the few unfamiliar words had somehow carried me back to my earlier conversation with the Goldene Krone's porter. And I caught myself wondering what they spoke in the Verlorenen Tal— if there was a strange tongue spoken there. If indeed there was a Verlorenen Tal.

Would it be Ladin?

What did I know about Ladin except Dominic Regli's mere mention of it? Derived from Latin, obviously. For that matter, what did I know about the Romansch of my mother's country, the language Dominic Regli had told me he had spoken until he was old enough to walk to school?

Something was eluding me. I wished there were not so many distractions now: the aroma of coffee as the café's door opened and closed upon the espresso machine; the smells of sausage and the omnipresent onion that managed to insinuate itself into so much foreign cooking; the pungent sour smell of cheese; the richness of chocolate.

A large family whose buttons and zippers had already reached the bursting point was happily indulging in enormous portions of Sachertorte gobbed with *Schlagrahm,* an iced sweet chocolate cake literally emblazoned with whipped cream.

I realized suddenly that it was lunchtime, one o'clock, the hour of my scheduled arrival at the Goldene Krone.

Neither Peg nor Guy had entered the cavernous arch of the Gasthof. I had seen only a few tourists and a postman.

By this time, although I had consumed a late morning collation of croissants and honey followed by innumerable glasses of hot tea, I was cold and thoroughly dispirited. Unhappily, I trudged back through the arch and up the dim stair way to the lobby.

To my surprise Karl Ochsner, the tall, fair porter-waiter-maître d'hôtel was now busy at the porter's lectern, scanning an open notebook on the stand. When he glanced up, he closed the book, and announcing that my room was ready, reached behind the stand and slid out my valise.

I questioned him about a message, a telephone call, but without even a glance over his shoulder at the mail pigeon-holes he shook his head, then murmured something quite irrelevant about the weather.

"The afternoon will be fine," he said, making his way up the narrow staircase to the second floor corridor.

Although I did not answer, he persisted. "Perhaps the fräulein will enjoy a little sightseeing in this ancient town?"

"I think not," I said. "I am waiting for a friend."

At the door to Room 5 he offered, "The fräulein could leave a message for her friend. There is always someone on duty at the desk."

It occurred to me that the man might be about to suggest an arrangement with a specific local travel bureau, and I abruptly diverted him.

"Perhaps you know of some shops in town or close to town that are well-known for wood carvings? *Not* souvenirs," I added hastily. "Older pieces, religious objects."

The man set down my bag outside Room 5. He seemed preoccupied with the key. "I should not recommend this town," he murmured as the tumblers clicked. "Not for finer things, you understand. This is . . . a tourist stop. In Austria I would suggest the Tirol for art objects, wood carvings especially."

The door opened into a low-ceilinged room so dim that I could barely see the outlines of the two puff-covered beds lined along the left wall. Opposite the door at the room's end dark curtains were drawn across the faint outline of a tall window.

The porter dropped the valise onto the luggage rack, moved to the window, and pulled back the heavy fabric. The onion domes that rose above tiled roofs and random skylights and capped chimney pots thrust me back momentarily to London, the Tower . . . I shook off the memory.

Karl was right. The rain had ceased, and the sky behind the almost fairytale silhouette was a misted pearl.

"You see? The fräulein should take advantage. . . ." The man slipped past me, and doors creaked as he added, "Here is your bathroom, the wardrobe." I heard lights click on and off, but I did not turn from the old town view.

The man was probably right about taking advantage of the afternoon, the clearing weather. It was already past the time of arrival of the scheduled Transalpin Express on which I was to have traveled, a time that Guy knew as well as Peg. Perhaps now I should follow the bus-driver's advice and go to Vaduz. There was the chance that, on the spot, I might find that "Total" business that had so excited Peg. I turned from the window and almost absently said, "There is no place here to sell old objects, art objects?"

"Sell, fräulein?" His voice seemed different, somehow wary. "Excuse me, you wish to *sell?*"

"No." I gave a deliberate short laugh. "Not I. My friend had mentioned something, some firm—rather large, I believe. It's possible she meant in another town near here."

"Not Feldkirch." The man's face was impassive again. "A large business, you say?" He was at the room's door now, still apparently contemplating the aspects of my question. "Perhaps in Liechtenstein," he said finally. "The capital, Vaduz." There was a very slight lift to the corners of his mouth. "For such a small place, much business is conducted there."

Liechtenstein. There it was again. "Big business' had been Peg's words just yesterday.

Total. The name was something of the sort. *Totall?*

I did not stop to open the window, not even to open my valise. I followed Karl out the door and locked it behind me.

When we reached the lobby, I said, "Would you mind taking a message for Miss Hobart? Or . . . Mr. Black?"

Without a word he pulled a pad toward him.

"Just say that I've gone to Vaduz for the afternoon."

"You—" he looked up quickly. "Excuse me, you mentioned it was your friend who wants to sell. Should you not wait for her? For them?"

"No." One did not tell a stranger that one was worried about the friend as well as annoyed with her behavior. Or that one

127

was slightly hurt because the man one needed had not appeared. "No," I repeated.

I had not reached the bottom of the stairs to the court when I heard the whir of a telephone dial from somewhere in the area of the reception desk.

15

As it hummed over the smooth highway toward Vaduz, the post-bus skirted the border mountains between the Austrian Voralberg and the little principality of Liechtenstein.

In the valley where the two countries blended we rolled through meadowland of loden green, gold, and emerald spangled with campanula and dandelion. Farmhouses, grazing cattle, cream-washed cottages . . . an innocent landscape . . . alternately shimmered beneath a brilliant sun and brooded under clouds November-dark and mercifully transient.

It was only during the pause at the Austrian-Liechtenstein frontier that I became aware of my fellow passengers, a dozen or so, apparently local, most carrying market bags. The checkpoint seemed a mere formality, a pause to examine passports, little else.

While the official passed along the bus aisle, I was alerted by a half-familiar sound diagonally behind me. The same voice timber, the same low rush of German I had heard a few hours ago in the Feldkirch café.

I turned. Beyond the official who was questioning the man I caught a glimpse of amber-tinted spectacles spanning a boney nose and high-boned cheek. The glimpse was in profile and hidden by dark hair that swept over the collar of a soiled raincoat and curved down the man's cheek in a bold sideburn.

Foreigner, I thought, as I had so often during the past few days. I restrained a smile, reminding myself once more that I, too, was a foreigner, and dismissing the odd coincidence of the man from the café, I glanced down at my map.

I saw that I had traversed a few miles of this same valley earlier today en route to Feldkirch in the fast train from Zurich. Now, in the sturdy bus, I was retracing those miles as far south as Schaan where the road forked south, away from the route back to Switzerland.

The hills seemed to rise higher and higher as the valley narrowed and we approached the capital of the principality, Vaduz. Its castle, though perched on the edge of a cliff, seemed somehow immensely secure beyond the pines that clung to the stone walls and terraces beneath it.

An early autumn sun was angling over the jagged mountain peaks, and colors shifted . . . cerulean to viridian . . . the palest rose to the lavender of heather. By contrast with the snow mountains to the south the effect was staggering. I was so entranced that I was not prepared for the ugly square at Vaduz, cluttered with buses of all colors and apparently of all nations. And I was disappointed with the seething mass of tourists, the noise, the commercial look of the place.

In the post office above the open square I discovered that the telephone directory for Liechtenstein was incorporated within the Swiss Number 10 book, which covered Appenzell, St. Gallen town, Thurgau, and Graubünden.

Graubünden . . . I paused before I opened the directory. Dominic Regli came from the Swiss Canton Graubünden, from the eastern finger of that canton. I could still hear his words on that first night in London. *"I am from an area in the Engadine, the Val Sinestra."*

The Engadine, the long valley of the Inn River, bordered the frontiers of Liechtenstein as well as Austria.

I turned the pages to the Vaduz section, scanned the T's for *Totall,* found what I was sure must be the correct name: Totallia, S.A. It was listed simply at Malina 10.

Malinastrasse, the busy postal clerk informed me, lay a half kilometer away. "Along the main road past the cathedral. Left at the second lane. After a few hundred yards, look carefully, for number 10. There are many trees. One could miss the driveway."

"Look carefully" was good advice for Vaduz in general. I learned that, even as I crossed the busy road at the zebra marking, passed the geranium-banded Engel Hotel. Its terrace restaurant was deserted now, for a chill wind was whining across the

129

valley carrying a scent of pine with a more subtle air of fresh-fallen snow from the high alps.

And oddly, as it had upon my arrival in Feldkirch earlier to-day, the mist was swirling down, enveloping the little town. Tourists surging outside cluttered souvenir shops were buttoning their coats, pulling up their collars as I was.

The town, the principality's capital, was little more than a village. On first impression it was merely a main street lined with souvenir shops to catch the unwary with its almost frantic signs: "Quick Tourist Office," "Quick Change Office, Best Rates!" "Our Clocks 'Cuck' and 'Coo' Oftener, Louder, and More Melodically!". The show windows crammed with charms, glassware, silver, cloth, cameras, scarfs, and diamonds all gave the impression that somehow Vaduz was the last place on earth to buy *anything*.

Traffic on the main artery was spasmodic; at times the cars crawled only to be assailed by soiled hitch-hikers complete with bed-rolls and lettered signs realing, "Zurich or Bregenz or St. Gallen." Once more, as I had in the café in Feldkirch, I heard a half-dozen languages all around as I passed the tourists' shops, local food and wine markets, and a small though elegant hotel-restaurant called Real.

Under other circumstances I might have been lured into the Postal Museum, the Historical Museum, the famous Art Galerie, but this afternoon I was hurrying toward a destination that might lead me eventually to Peg, which might help to prevent—what?

A foolish action? A *more* foolish action than her already impulsive dash from Zurich to—where? A mountain hideaway where business schemes were blended with romance?

My footsteps slowed, almost faltered. The first faint questioning of my own motives insinuated itself into my mind; I rejected it. The man was treacherous. He had to be. He had lied to us. Peg had to be warned, at least.

Warned. Why did the mere thought of that word chill me? Or was it an external sense, a feeling, a sound that had sent out a beacon, a warning signal to *me*?

Sound . . . that was it. Somewhere behind me, as my foot-steps had slowed, another's had slowed. I glanced over my shoulder and caught a glimpse of tinted glasses, bold black side-burns . . . and profile again, as the man's head moved sharply right.

The gray stone walls of the cathedral rose at my left beyond its steps and gardens. I almost turned off the walk and climbed those steps—I might have if I had not suspected closed doors at this hour in the afternoon, closed doors leading to a dead end and retreat.

I moved on, listening now. At the first lane beyond the gray mass of the church I hesitated long enough to permit any stragglers behind me to pass by.

No one passed me.

It was then that I heard a car stop, so briefly that the flow of traffic was barely interrupted.

I turned. No one was behind me. The sidewalk was empty as far as a city block. Only cars, bicycles, motorbikes, purred by in both directions going toward the mountains to the south and to the town behind me.

Here the village started to straggle off into what seemed rolling countryside again, innocent country. Vineyards beyond the churchyard were misted in lambs wool pulled thin over their laden vines. And now as I moved on, watching for the second lane, apple orchards spread toward the hills in the east, toward a clean neat little farmhouse nestled in its clean neat little garden.

Innocent country? That was a hasty judgment. What was it the new porter-waiter-factotum at the Goldene Krone had said about Vaduz? "For such a small place, much business is conducted there. . . ."

Directly behind the farmer's wall I was astonished to see a parking lot fringed with low concrete business blocks bearing such varied names as Dr. Siegried Mannheim and St. Martin's *Bürohaus.* Their flat facades, one bedecked with hanging geraniums, one bordered with a formal moat, displayed signposts indicating that a dozen or more professions and businesses were housed within each cool impersonal exterior.

There was something familiar about this sort of complex. I had seen similar conglomerates on Long Island and in the upstate community where my father lived. Though here, dropped at random as they were in a valley not far from the Rhine's source, the word "phony" occurred to me. I smiled, bolder now, relieved that I was alone, that no one was following me.

I had reached the second lane, Malinastrasse, when I felt the icy blast blow in along the valley floor, and as though a light had been dimmed, a blue veil of fog muted the mountains. From somewhere down the road, and not far away, I heard an abrupt beat, an oddly muffled sound of what I thought might be a helicopter. But I could not see a machine, for the rain-heavy clouds were even then rolling toward me.

The irregular sidewalk ended where the second lane cut off, a lane that seemed to lead only to a dense wood.

Or so I thought.

I thought the barrier was a pine wood surrounded by the blue of spruce, and I was prepared for a long walk on the Malinastrasse. I had almost forgotten the directions I had been given. "Look carefully for Number 10," the postal clerk had said. "Many trees, you understand."

Indeed Malina 10, I soon discovered, stood well off the road, well beyond the grove of pines. At first I saw no building, only the turnoff—a strip of tarmac wide enough for a car—and at its entrance a small discreetly lettered sign that read simply, in German: *"Bürohaus, Malina 10."*

Until I had traversed half of the one hundred yards of smooth-enough drive, I saw nothing but the silent woods, heard nothing but the distant hum of the town.

In the dying afternoon light the structure that finally emerged before me seemed remote from business operations. A turn-of-the-century villa, it was completely incongruous in this setting. Even its faded old brick exterior, its strange half-onion dome atop a squat tower, offended me. Its color blended almost too perfectly with the ridged bark of the pines, and standing as it did against a hillside, the camouflage was rather too effective.

I slowed, half reluctant to proceed. The place was dark, there were no cars parked in the outer court. Why did the thought occur, from something I had read: *Holding darkness . . . whoever walks there walks alone . . .*

My footsteps on the narrow roadway made only a faint sound in the stillness, yet I half-expected a face to peer out of one of those long dark windows, a pale hand to pull back a curtain and beckon me on. I hesitated, an almost hysterical giggle rising in my throat when I thought of what Peg might say. "Let's split, Con." I could hear her. "We're in the wrong pew."

Then, laughing inwardly at my own gothic imaginings, I reminded myself that this was *Bürohaus 10* in the capital of Liechtenstein, that the principality was under the aegis of law-abiding, law-ridden Switzerland. What could happen here?

I crossed the court briskly if not boldly and climbed the three shallow steps to the imposing door. By this time I was thoroughly prepared to find only a single name engraved over the bell-pull, *Totallia, S.A.* It had already occurred to me that "big business" in antiques would not be easily contained nor in fact well-displayed within the limited and perhaps too functional walls of any of the concrete blocks I had passed.

In response to my touch on the bell, a long *bong* echoed beyond the tall oak door; it was the only sound. I waited long enough to warrant one more attempt to rouse the company's receptionist, official greeter, anyone connected with the enterprise. When no answer came to my second ring, I glanced at my watch.

Just on five o'clock, and now the clouds had masked the sun completely; it was darker than twilight.

Perhaps offices such as these, I thought, adhered to rigid hours; opened early as European firms were rumored to and closed precisely at this time. And yet I had seen no person, no car leaving the long drive through the woods, nor in fact anyone leaving the house at all.

If the place had been neglected, I should have been less surprised at the quiet. The villa bore rather the same turn-of-the-century air of affluence that it must originally have presented to the community. The borders of chrome-gold and vermilion dahlias were neatly tended, the stone pots of boxwood flanking the entrance were clipped tall and narrow, resembling tight-grown cypress.

I had not moved more than a few yards from the last step when I heard the low *br-r-r* of a motor on the Malinastrasse, the lane at the drives' end. And I started forward, thinking that an employee or employer might be returning from some business negotiation, perhaps. I was in the drive when I heard the motor accelerate disproportionately for the confined length of drive and court.

In a flash I thought: *He'd better have good brakes!*

But it was too late—it was almost too late for me. The dark hood of the car came straight at me, seemed almost to rise like a jungle animal pouncing on its prey, the gleam of the metal bumper a stretched mouth, the grill of the radiator its teeth.

I leaped sideways and fell, the entire right side of my body striking the drive's soft shoulder with a thud. The fall had not been voluntary; the car's fender had caught my left hip as I flung away from it. But I did not lie even for an instant on the resilient blend of pine needles and black earth that had cushioned the fall for me. I had heard the sharp squeal of brakes as the driver brought the car to a very short stop in the court, not many yards behind me.

16

The shock had dazed me . . . it was sheer reflex that took over in that instant. It was no accident. That driver had seen me moving toward him on the smooth tarmac of the drive and had deliberately aimed his car at me.

I scrambled up from the soft verge and tore through the woods with no thought but to get away from the madman behind me. It was not until I stumbled onto the road that was called Malina that I became aware of an aching leg, a bruised hip. But pain or no, I plunged on, relieved to see cars ahead even though they were yards off, toward the main road, and driving away from me.

Never mind. There were the modern office buildings, the parking areas now comfortingly astir with the home-going activity of Vaduz. I dared a quick glance over my shoulder.

The lane behind me was empty all the way to the tall pines, which formed a screen between the more normal movement of the town and the silent villa where I had rung the bell.

Who had driven that car? And why had he deliberately driven at me? The thought repeated itself over and over. I did not know anyone in Vaduz. And no one knew I had planned this half day here. In fact, I had upset the Students' Travel schedule completely for this day, had arrived hours ahead of time at Feld-

kirch. And no one could possibly have known that I had abruptly decided to call upon Totallia, S.A.

Despite the smooth tarmac I staggered, panting now, aching,
breathing painfully until I finally reached the highway beyond
the cathedral, the road that was the capital's main street.

My mind still seethed with questions. What about that man
with the black sideburns, the man who had mumbled German
in the café in Feldkirch, the one who had complained about that
other language, had said that it was "rough?" His presence in
the bus, in Vaduz, might not have been coincidence after all.
But who was he? I was afraid to look back now, afraid I might
see him again.

In the gathering darkness the lights of the cars swept by as
I limped on toward the huddled mass of the town. One car
slowed behind me, its light spreading a wide fan across the
road and bordering walk.

A voice called out in German, "Can I help you? Do you
want a lift?"

Without daring a glance, without pausing, I drew on all my
strength and started to run again, keeping close to the lighted
buildings, the Art Galerie, the Stamp Museum, the little shops.

Beyond the Café Real I stopped, attempting to control my
shattered nerves now that the lighted town was closing around
me and I could begin to feel comparatively safe. I was bracing
myself against the stone wall of a building, shifting my handbag
to my other arm when I heard a woman's voice almost at my
elbow. I jerked around.

"Did you want anything before we close?" Her voice was
kindly enough.

Only then did I realize I was beside a doorway, and even as
I turned, lights were dimmed inside the shop behind the rotund
figure. The woman's arm was extended, her hand grasping a
metal newspaper rack. She did not move; only her glance traveled from my face, my hair, down the length of my light raincoat
to my stockings.

"Are you all right, fräulein?" she asked.

I had managed to control the labored breathing by then but
had not yet taken stock of the damages. Now I realized that
because my hair had loosened, tumbled over my shoulder, and
blown across my eyes and I had been brushing it back with mud-
dy fingers, my face and my hair must be streaked and caked

with dirt. My coat was damp, stained by a combination of the earlier rain and the pine-cushioned earth of the verge. One stocking was simply shredded.

I shook my head. "Thank you. I . . . fell." The explanation was weak but to a degree accurate.

"I see," she said a little primly, and it was not until she had yanked the newspaper rack back over the threshold of the shop that I wondered whether she had classed me with some of the bedraggled hitchhikers. I had seen several in town before I had turned off the main road on my way to that singularly secluded "office building" in Malinastrasse.

Very shortly I might almost have settled for a hitchhiker's sign reading: "Feldkirch." I learned at the terminal that the next bus returning to that Austrian town just over the border did not leave the post office until seven twenty-five that night.

It was then five forty. And rumpled and grubby as I felt, I did not want to sit conspicuously bedraggled for all that time in the bare little waiting room provided by the government. Already, I was looking over my shoulder at the sound of every male footstep behind me, listening for the particularly hushed timber of that German male voice.

Vaduz had been worse than a dead end. It could have been a fatal mistake. And I longed to tell someone about the strange near-accident at the villa that housed Totallia. But there was no one, certainly no one in this town.

And certainly not the police. I would have no answers for the questions they could hurl at me. A dark car had almost run me down. There are many dark cars, fräulein. The license? I had not seen a license. Not even the initials that European cars are required to use if they are driven across borders. And surely by now that car would not be lingering in the courtyard of that turn-of-the-century villa at Malina 10.

Besides, if I went to the police, I would be delayed, could be delayed long enough to miss the last bus, the seven twenty-five back to Feldkirch. And Peg could be there right now. Guy could be there. Tony might have ignored my cable and might be on his way.

I decided to clean up and have something warm and cheering to drink. Coffee. Soup. Sherry preferably. The weakness that had been stealing over me was altogether forgivable; I had eaten nothing since early morning in Zurich but the forenoon croissant at the Café Goldene Krone.

Turning from the posted bus schedules toward the steps that led up to the road, I stopped and stared at the sight above me. Dominating the street lights, the shops' lights, the gleam from hotel windows, a cool reflection lay over the town, an almost eerie glow from the floodlit castle that rose so sharply from its pine-clad cliff.

There it is again, I thought, suppressing an unbidden sense of derision: that aura of picture-postcard innocence. In daylight or in twilight the valley with its noble hills rising toward the country's towering frontiers with Austria and Switzerland gave that impression.

I wanted to get back to Feldkirch, to find out whether Guy had come at last and if Peg had turned up. I would have been willing to endure any amount of Peg's saucy chatter and Guy's abject excuses. In the meantime, all my conjectures were shuffling about in my befuddled brain, and none of them were pleasant. If Peg *had* said Totallia, if Dominic *had* taken her there for any reason, why was *I* so unwelcome?

I crossed the road to the lobby of the Engel, and while the reception clerk was rolling a letterhead into her Hermes typewriter, I asked to be directed to the powder room.

"One flight up." Her last word fell to a whisper when she looked at me. This woman was half the age of the shopkeeper; she recovered quickly when I gave her the same excuse. "Walkways are so wet today," she commiserated. "You'll find towels up there, I'm sure."

Cheered by her kind words, I paused at the first step and turned back to her. "Could I have dinner here?" The place did not look cheap, but it looked comfortable.

"Yes, certainly." She indicated a door to her left, and dismissing me, settled to her machine again.

Brushed hair, clean hands and face, and a decision to discard my ruined stockings lifted my spirits somewhat. Ten minutes later I edged into the first seat at the first table inside the restaurant's door, grateful for the warmly lighted tavern room and the respectable number of diners even at this early hour. My table was a vantage point. I could see everyone who came in through either doorway. And I could hear everything.

Tourists were complaining in English and German about their feet, the prices of souvenirs, the weather, their tour guides.

In a booth some yards away a confident American came to the loud conclusion that "Europeans are afraid of the English language."

"Yeah," her companion answered sarcastically, "Y'know, next year we oughta take a tour of the United States—no language problems, like here."

In the doorway next to my table an Englishman murmured, "I'm ready to get out of here any time."

"Yes, Henry." This, meekly from a little woman. "I think we've seen it all."

"Had it, y'mean. If I ever see another cuckoo clock again . . . Where's the loo in this place?"

"*Sh-h-h*"

A harried waitress bustled toward me; I recognized the weary, almost grim gleam in her dark eyes from my own experience in waiting on tired and irritable customers at the end of a long day.

"Something to drink?" She pushed a menu across the table.

"Dry sherry, please."

While I was looking over the French and German menu, four young women sank into chairs at the table directly in front of mine, littering floor and chairbacks with large limp bags.

One raised four fingers and called out, "*Vier Sausers,* Anna!" To the others she mumbled in British-accented English, "And do I need that drink. God! His lordship was a bastard today!"

"You can say that again," a North American voice said.

"You'll become accustomed to it." The third voice was German-accented and sounded amused.

"Not *me,*" the first and loudest stated emphatically. "I'm cutting out. Going to Italy."

"Me too." The last was a new voice, quieter. After a time I had her pegged as Australian, one of the others as probably Canadian; the other two were certainly British and Austrian.

They all worked in a tourist shop operated by a character they referred to as his lordship, and all of them obviously felt they could show his lordship how to run his business.

All four agreed that the boss was right about the lawlessness that seemed to have struck even this "sequestered paradise"—a

138

phrase used by the Canadian that brought chortles from the other three.

A robbery at the Galerie, for instance—that "bugged" the Canadian. "The papers and radio didn't give it enough publicity," she said. "His lordship claims that sort of thing is getting to be big business. Too big to cope with."

When Anna brought my sherry along with four tumblers of a light-colored drink for my talkative neighbors, I asked her whether the *Alte Knabe* Peg had raved about was available.

"That's Austrian." She tapped the wine list as though to remind me of the restaurant's limitations.

"What about that?" I nodded toward the *Sausers* the girls had already started to consume.

"Young green wine." The waitress shook her head. In a low voice she added, "Try two deciliters of *Vaduzer.*"

I thanked her, ordered a veal ragout in a rice ring, and settled back, sipping the sherry, feeling the warmth instantly, and grateful for it. A few moments passed before the chatter came through again.

"What I can't understand is: Who *buys* the stolen stuff?" The Canadian muttered.

"I read a report in *Time,*" the Australian said. "Claimed that some of the rich collectors with more money than conscience don't care *how* they get what they want."

"Too many greedy people." A British dismissal. "God! How I needed this drink!"

The Australian shrugged. "Perhaps some people buy without knowing."

"Especially if there's been no publicity," the Canadian repeated. "His lordship's right about that. Police here made an awful mistake not to raise a big stink about the Rubens."

The Rubens? I stared over my wineglass at the long pale face of the girl who had said that. A Rubens *was* big business.

"Don't worry, luv," her British co-worker put in. "Interpol is probably into it. They'll get their man."

"It'd be more practical if the Prince would insist on real guards at the Galerie in the first place. Everything's so damned *open* here."

Open? My experience had been slightly different. "Deceptive" would have been my choice of a single-word description.

Though the girls grew more garrulous as they finished their wine, their conversation remained local, mostly gossip about their boss and his unjust treatment of his employees. It was a break for me. I let my mind drift with theirs, remembering some of my experiences when I had worked in the antique shop.

When I had paid and finally rose stiffly from my chair to return to the bus terminal, I felt as though I had been back in a familiar world. I was pleasantly drowsy from the light red wine, the delicious food. If it were not for the dull ache of the bruise on my hip, I could almost have been convinced that I had imagined that incident at Malina 10.

The bus plowed on along unlighted roads to the Austrian checkpoint where we encountered not only passport and customs controls but a curtain of rain. I roused briefly to produce my passport, aware again that the examination was as cursory as it had been when I had entered Liechtenstein not many hours ago.

No hushed German voice disturbed me, however, no black sideburns or tinted glasses. When we started off again, I sank back in my seat, almost mesmerized by the rhythm of the giant windshield wipers that swept the panes with synchronized precision. Surely, I thought, Peg would appear at the Goldene Krone eventually. Certainly by now Guy would have rung up, would have left a message. . . .

I might have dozed, for the next thing I recall was the jerk resulting from the swerve of the bus as it angled between the stone buildings and entered the terminal square at Feldkirch.

The square was asleep even at this early hour. Our lights glittered on the post office facade, on the hulks of empty buses, on wet cobbles. Outside our arc of light the depot was dark, apparently deserted, although the time was only eight fifteen in the evening.

The six or seven passengers descended, and before we reached the post office corner, the bus lights were snapped off. The town's street lights seemed suddenly inadequate; footsteps behind me seemed too close.

Despite the stiffness that now persisted all through my body, I started to run, already apprehensive about the courtyard of the Goldene Krone. The arcaded street cast its own shadows, but I was relieved to find that the café lights glowed out onto the walk, flowed onto the flagstones in the court. And very faintly

140

in the court an old coach lamp glimmered above the heavy oak door.

The stairs were as dim as they had been earlier, but the lobby was singularly empty and poorly lighted. From my several entrances and exits through this rather attractive room I had noticed a bell on the reception counter; I rang it now.

The silence that followed was so complete that I could hear the muted sounds of dishes in the restaurant next door, the rise and fall of voices. There must be a door nearby; I knew there was a stairway leading down to the café. If I could hear the clatter from there, someone should be able to hear the clang of the metal bell I had rung.

By this time I was impatient with hotel formality; there was a limit to old-world charm. I decided to slip behind the registration desk, lift off my key, and check my pigeon-hole for messages.

I stepped out firmly and stumbled over something bulky though soft, and apparently immovable. I grasped the wooden stand at my right and pulled back.

That was cloth down there on the floor. That was a jacket. *That was an arm. . . .*

I gasped. That was Luigi, the Italian porter. I leaned over, beginning to tremble.

Behind him, the door of the cupboard that had been locked this past noontime was standing open. And even from where I stood, I could see that my tote bag was gone.

17

In a panic I struck the desk bell until the small lobby echoed with the metallic clang. I was about to plunge down the stairs to summon aid from the café when a strong broad hand came down on mine. I jerked around.

"You wanted something, fräulein?" It was Karl, porter-waiter-maître d'hôtel.

In that stunned moment I could only point.

Before his gaze could take in all of my own disheveled condition, he followed my outstretched arm. Swiftly, he was down on his knees beside the man on the floor. In a moment he muttered, with merely a glance at me, "Good. Have no fear. His pulse is strong."

His fingers probed the porter's head and his neck while I watched, somehow not surprised at the man's efficiency. Karl Ochsner had the look of an athlete, moved like an athlete, a skiier, a man who might have seen many accidents in his thirty or more years.

He opened Luigi's collar, unbuttoned his waistcoat, was massaging his wrists when he added without looking up, "Tell one of the girls in the café to bring brandy. For you, also."

I did not question the peremptory order; in fact, I was relieved for the chance of action. And by the time I had returned with a waitress, Luigi was lying flat on a bench Karl must hastily have drawn up behind the registration desk. In this position no guest could have seen the man.

Karl dismissed the curious girl with a brisk nod and the curt words, "A fall. I'll take care of it." Then, as the girl backed through the panel door, he raised his glance to mine over the limp form. "In such a place," he said, "it is best to say little, you understand?"

I shook my head. It was he, Karl, who did not understand the full significance of what had happened there . . . and elsewhere . . . today. Any more than I did. But I waited as he lifted Luigi's head, touched the brandy to the pale lips. Though I was nervous enough about the missing tote bag, a man *had* been injured. . . .

The Italian coughed, grunted, lifted his lids with an obvious effort. His eyes blinked up at us, small black coals in the white face. He started to talk, rambling in Italian at first, then German. The last thing he recalled, he told us, was a movement behind him. That was all.

He attempted to sit up but slumped back, stifling a groan. "My head," he repeated. "*Per Dio,* my head." Then, feebly, "What has happened?"

I looked up at Karl at the very instant his gaze had slid toward the open cupboard door, toward the key dangling in the lock. *He knows,* I thought. *He has already seen it.* His glance came back to me. "It is best to keep everything quiet, I think," he said again.

I shook my head once more, but this time I said, "No. It's more complicated. Something of mine—a bag—was in that closet."

Luigi struggled to rise now, but Karl eased him down, adjusted a chair cushion behind the man's head.

"A bag?" Karl said.

"*Si.* The fräulein had left a bag. My key—" Luigi fumbled in his vest pocket. "My key—" he rose on one elbow. "*Per Dio!* It is gone!"

"Take it easy," Karl murmured to the frightened Italian.

"But you must tell the *signor,* the director," Luigi mumbled over and over. "Tell the Herr Direktor. There will be trouble."

Room 5 was cold when Karl, sent by the manager to accompany me, opened the door. At the flick of the wall switch a low-watt glow shone down on the empty room; a too-dim reading lamp lighted the pillow of the single bed that had been prepared for me.

The room was cold because the French window was open. In the draft from the hall door the long curtains had billowed toward us, were sucked back against the shallow balcony's rail when the door shut behind us.

"Stupid maid," Karl strode across the room. He closed the windows firmly, drew the heavy latch. He looked around then, eyed the valise still resting on its rack. "You had not unpacked?" he asked.

"No." For a moment I wondered why the questioning, then realized he was double-checking, had probably been instructed to report anything unusual.

He opened the empty wardrobe and peered into the bathroom. At the door to the hall he asked solicitously, "The fräulein would like a little tea, perhaps. *Pfefferminz Tee?*"

"No. No, thank you." Though the offer of a tisane touched me, I was impatient now despite all the assurances. The manager had insisted that I would be compensated for any loss. He had requested that I estimate for him the value of what I had lost, but this had been no comfort at all.

The trouble was that I did not know the value. And even more, the trouble was that I was afraid, more afraid now than I had been a few hours ago on the driveway to Malina 10. More afraid than I had been that night in London when I had stepped into the mirrored hall and had been frozen by the sight of the octopus-reflections, choked by the encircling arm.

I looked into the cool blue eyes of the superefficient ubiquitous Karl who had slipped quietly over the threshold into the hall, was now pulling the door toward him. "The fräulein must not worry," he said. "Everything will be taken care of."

No, it won't, I protested, silently as the door clicked shut, as I quickly turned the gigantic key in the lock and shoved a little side chair under it. *It can't be all right. It isn't that easy.*

If only Guy were here . . . or Peg. Or Tony. Now, this evening, I would have welcomed all three—even all three at once. All those plans. All those promises. What good had they been?

With irony I recalled my original misgiving about a confrontation between those three. Now I would have been overwhelmingly relieved at the sight of all of them. Coping with so simple a matter as temper or temperament might be the perfect foil for these past days. For today.

The memory of the tree-shrouded drive at Malina 10, the empty, echoing villa in which Totallia supposedly operated a big business, now superimposed itself upon the yawning cupboard downstairs, the injured Luigi who had heard only a light footstep before he had blacked out.

I was shivering, literally shaking now, but not just from the stone-damp chill of the room. I simply could not control the trembling, which was no doubt a reaction to the total unexplained events of the day. The flood of fatigue, the gnawing pain, the mounting apprehension . . .

And something else here in the room was wrong. That window had been closed and firmly fastened when I had left here. No maid would open it in this uncertain weather. No maid was *that* stupid.

The cold inward creeping persisted. My teeth started to chatter. I suspected even before I touched the locks on my valise

144

that they had been tampered with. They sprang back before I used my key.

My clothing in the tightly packed valise had been turned upside down, then jammed back with no semblance of order.

One of the clocks of Feldkirch struck midnight before I had unpacked everything, repacked everything, before I had determined that not a thing was missing.

Not a thing was missing, I was sure, because no one wanted what was in the valise. It was the contents of the tote bag that someone had wanted; perhaps the santo, perhaps the mourner. But why? I had to know why. If Peg did not come, if Guy or Tony did not come by morning, I would board that bus to the high alps road and try to find Peg. And . . . that man.

Through the night my mind seethed with unwelcome images that conspired to keep me on the edge of sleep, conspired successfully to keep me fearful of sleep. I was afraid to close my eyes.

Could a man move so silently, I wondered, that I would not hear him? Could the darkness conceal all motion, the swish of traffic through the medieval town—spasmodic though it was—and muffle all sound?

There were stretches of time that seemed like some unformed dream, and I fell . . . fell into a bottomless cave, a cavern like the courtyard of the Goldene Krone, only to grasp at nothing in the darkness. And finding nothing, to grope wildly for the light switch, to convince myself that the dream had not crossed the boundaries of sleep.

I was afraid for Peg, afraid for myself. But I did not know of what I was afraid, or why I should be afraid. Only Dominic Regli knew the answer. And where was he? Dear God, where were he and Peg?

There were stretches of time during those long miserable hours that were lost to me . . . dreamless lapses when I drifted through a valley, a lost valley; no *a valley of lost souls* . . . so dark, so dark. . . .

The oblong of window beyond the curtains was a tone lighter than the wall when the brisk knock aroused me.

I sat up, stared unbelievingly at my travel clock. *It was ten o'clock!* Ten o'clock in the morning. The bus! I had missed the high alps bus. I bounded from the bed.

145

"What is it?" I swung my soiled raincoat from the wall hook and drew it around me.

"A telegram, fräulein." I had the door open before Karl added, "And the manager sends you your breakfast."

I snatched the telegram that was propped against the coffee-pot as the man edged past me into the room. Even as he slid the tray upon a round table near the window, I noticed that his glance did not miss the tossed bedclothes, the closed valise, the absence of normal clutter.

"The fräulein is leaving today?"

"I hope." I was tearing open the envelope, willing the man to leave. He seemed deliberately slow, had not reached the door while I was reading:

YOUR LONDON CABLE RECEIVED AND NOTED BUT ANY FRIEND OF YOURS A FRIEND OF MINE ARRIVING FELDKIRCH SATURDAY EVE PLAN-NING MEMORABLE REUNION WITH OR WITHOUT ENCUMBRANCES ALL MY LOVE

TONY

So he was coming after all. Coming today . . .

I looked up to find the eyes of the new factotum of the Gasthof Goldene Krone watching me. The man was standing in the doorway, obviously waiting.

"There may be a change in plans," I started, then fumbled. "I—wait! Is there a Mr. Jenner booked here for tonight, do you know?"

"Jenner. Yes. I have seen the name. Room number 6." Bowing, he stepped back, and just as he pulled the door closed behind him I could see the brass numeral six clearly on the door opposite mine.

The mingled reactions were difficult to assess. At the moment I could not think beyond a deep sense of relief that at last I could share my problems, that perhaps Tony and I could solve them if Guy did not appear, if Peg did not.

Still clutching the telegram, I moved slowly across the room, past the table and tray to the French window, and drew back the curtains.

The fairytale aspect of the view no longer held me. A certain disenchantment with view and color and composition had

146

begun on a main road yesterday and had ended in a lane in Liechtenstein, the driveway to Malina 10. Beyond my window now, beyond the iron rail of the balcony, the steep roofs and gables and onion domes were stained and streaked with dampness; dormers and casements blank, dark-curtained as mine had been, or shuttered.

And—something I had not seen yesterday—broken shingles hung over a ledge just to the left of my room.

I yanked open the window and leaned out. The shingles covered a narrow ancient staircase leading from the back alley to the rooftop of the old stone building adjoining the Goldene Krone.

Anyone could easily have managed the distance from the wooden balustrade to my balcony ledge.

I wondered whether I should alert the management or wait for Guy, or Tony. And tell either one of them the whole story, of my fears that involved Peg, and that man . . .

Had a henchman of his slipped in and searched my room, and not finding what he wanted, had he slipped down to the lobby, attacked Luigi when his back was turned? He would not even have had to know about the cupboard. Most inns and hotels recommended checking one's valuable with them, most porters and concierges carried keys.

I felt helpless while the hours slipped away; guilty because I had not been aboard that high alps bus this morning. I should have found that driveway Peg had dashed from. Now I could only wait.

During that endless September afternoon I did not see much of Feldkirch—jewel of the Austrian Vorarlberg—beyond the gloomy scene from my fastened window in the Goldene Krone. But I could describe all the furnishings of the lobby, all the tourists who trailed in and out, every item on the menu of the café downstairs, practically every flagstone in the court. I must have been up and down that dim staircase a dozen times or more, must have made life miserable for Karl and the pale Luigi and a shy relief porter.

I could have described every diner in the café, even the dark little round-faced man who had sidled into the restaurant while I was inspecting the menu. I had wondered about the name *Schnitzel Donatal* that Peg had mentioned and the specific *Alte Knabe* wine, the *St. Anton Spezial*.

147

Neither was listed, which did not surprise me. I doubted that Peg's man would have initiated a romance or carried on a romance in such a mediocre village *Wirtshaus,* a mere tavern.

But I had certainly expected Guy to come, to ring me, to leave a message. All he had said, all he had promised, could not have been forgotten in this short time, could it? Little more than a week had passed since the night he had said he would be with me in the mountains.

Those words, "*à bientôt,*" had lingered because I had wanted them to. I had wanted to believe that I was cherished, that he had meant, "until very soon." But perhaps the words were as empty as our own "so long."

Or *Auf Wiedersehen.*

There were moments of that afternoon that were like the distant dreams of the night just past. I do not know when it was that I realized the day was over. Unless it was when the sound of the wind and the rain ceased, and I moved once more to the bedroom casement.

The twilit sky was a pale silver wash behind the onion domes and the crinkled roofs; already faintly luminous, promising the moon. Darkness descended slowly on the shadowed court, a breathless silence held the back lanes and passages of the old town.

The telephone bell was sharp, almost shocking. I flew to the night table, sweeping up the receiver.

"Constance?" The voice was low, vibrant in the quiet room.

"Guy!" I breathed. "Oh, Guy! I'm *so* glad you're here!"

"Ah, but that's just it. I'm not in Feldkirch, *chérie.*" Then quickly, he added, "Something troubles you?"

"It's Peg. I'm afraid something's wrong, and I——"

"Tell me," he cut in.

"She's gone off with that man I told you about, that Swiss. She should have been here yesterday. I should have *heard* from her, at least."

When he did not answer, I prodded, "Guy?"

"Yes, *chérie?*"

"The trouble is, when she gets here there are more problems——"

"Now, wait a moment." He drew out the words slowly as though to checkrein me. "What problems are we talking about?"

"Those figures. The santo. The mourner. She'd rung me in

Zurich from—from wherever she was. She'd wanted them for some reason. And they're gone."

"I see." After a second he added with what sounded like amusement, "I might worry a little except that you and I know the value, don't we?"

There was some comfort in that thought and reassurance in his admission that the mourner was not as fine a piece as I had originally assumed. I breathed more easily.

"Constance?" His voice seemed far away, an unfamiliar rhythmic whir came between us. "Will you be patient with me a bit longer." I barely heard him now. "My plans have been a little changed. . . ."

"But, everything is changed, don't you see? I'll have to wait for Peg!"

The disturbance in the wire ceased. "That shouldn't be necessary. We can leave messages, you know, for the evening."

"She might *need* me." I did not want to explain about Totallia now, about other things.

His next words were slow again, provocative; they surprised me. "But my dear, are you sure? Are you quite sure she wants you just now?"

I was silenced by his question, by what he implied. Could he be right? Could Peg want to be alone now? Was that what she wanted, what they had planned?

"My dear," Guy dropped into the silence, "A car is en route to the Goldene Krone for you. Soon you will be on your way to a mountain inn, to dine in candlelight, to forget your cares. We *could* keep in touch with the Gasthof by telephone, you know."

"You really think I should leave before I hear from Peg?"

"I think you should. Though even if I am prejudiced because I long to see you, I do think you should consider your friend. Didn't you tell me in London that she was in love?"

He was right, of course. Peg had told me in London, had more than hinted in her communications to Zurich that she was in love. And with or without the santo, she was involved by now in business dealings with that man. What could I do, what could anyone do to halt such a combination?

"I don't think I should go too far away," I said finally.

"You *are* a loyal friend. And you won't be too far away. I am not far now. And when we meet, perhaps we can solve everything. In the meantime," his voice dropped to a teasing note, "don't you want to see me?"

"Yes, yes, I do." Of course I wanted to see him again.

"Then be a good girl. Wear your most mysterious gown and your silver chain for me."

Not minutes after I had replaced the receiver on its cradle—giving me almost no time for the change to my one dark dress—there was another ring. The voice of the relief porter announced that a car was waiting.

Only when I closed the door behind me and faced the brass numeral six on the door of the room opposite did I remember Tony. Tony was due sometime this evening. Tony had planned a memorable reunion.

All the way down the staircase I rationalized that Tony had planned alone, had not consulted me. I had warned him by cable that I had plans with "a friend" in Feldkirch. And after all, I would be back. Guy had sounded busy; he had said his plans had changed.

In the lobby I paused at the porter's lectern, hoping that this new man could take a message for me. I started, "Will you tell Mr. Jenner or Miss Hobart—" I hesitated. How could I tell Tony or Peg anything? I was not sure where I was going, was not certain when I would be back. I ended, "Just tell either one that I have had to leave for—for dinner with a friend."

"Is there any place either one could reach you?" The porter was correct, at least, writing painstakingly on a small pad.

"I only know it's a mountain inn." I stopped, remembering Guy's promises. "I'll try to ring back later."

Outside, at the curb beyond the dimly lighted court, a car was waiting, dark green, the color of the forest, and although it was sleek, it seemed sturdy. A Volvo, I thought.

A woman's gloved hand reached out from the shadowed front seat and released the door for me. "Come along," she said in perfect English. "We have a difficult drive ahead."

While she was manipulating the area of congested traffic in the old quarter of the town, past the centuries-old stone buildings in too-narrow lanes, I became aware of the subtle scent the woman used. An expensive, delicate blend, tantalizingly familiar.

The car glided over the cobbles with no rumbling, little jouncing. We turned out of the arcaded road toward the eerie castle that seemed more than ever in the moon-blue floodlights to be leaning from its cliff in imminent danger of slipping down upon the village at its base.

We rounded the castle, joining the mainstream of traffic that flowed from somewhere behind us toward the heart of Austria; according to the signposts, toward Bludenz, Landeck, Innsbruck.

I glanced at the woman beside me, about to ask our destination, and was instantly aware that she had been glancing at me. Her head moved slightly to the left so that I could see only her profile; rounded forehead, short nose, parted lips, small chin. I would have said she was attractive; indeed except for a recalcitrant thrust of her jawline, she might have been beautiful. Even in the shifting lights of the road I saw the dark glasses and, of course, the turban wrapped smartly about her head concealing her hair. Not a wisp showed, not a tendril. Instead, enormous fragile silver rings hung from her ears, picking up the lights that flowed by or glared ahead of us.

The road wove past handsome villas settled smugly among magnificent pines, small modern factories, straggling cottages, stone farmhouses, fields. We seemed to have emerged into the wide basin of a valley, hills rising dark and remote on either side.

I said, "Where are we going?"

"To an inn," she said. "To dine. A fabulous place."

Her accent was as subtle as the scent that still puzzled me.

"You live here?" It was a natural question. She seemed so familiar with the roads, with the car.

Her answering laugh belied her chic appearance, everything about her. "Not if I can manage to get away."

"What brings you here?"

"Business," she said tersely.

My mind touched briefly on the various possibilities before I decided she might handle rental cars, might be a female chauffeur.

A signpost sped by. "Nenzing," I thought it read. I had no idea where we were although clusters of lights that flung away from the approaching town indicated that the hills rose more steeply now, to our right.

"Shouldn't I know your name?" I asked then. "Especially since we have a mutual friend."

"Friend?" The amusement in her voice was as subtle as her

151

accent. "Yes, of course. It is Náir. My full name is Lori Náir."

I thought about the name for a moment before I asked, "Are you Austrian, Miss Náir?" Her accent still puzzled me.

"*Mrs.*" She corrected me. The pause that followed seemed longer than should have been necessary to answer so simple a question as her nationality. "Austrian?" she answered finally. "Technically, no. I am Italian."

This answered the question of her accent. The fact that she was married no doubt accounted for a name that seemed not to be of Italian origin.

"Why did you ask if I was Austrian?" she said abruptly.

"Your accent. It's charming——"

"Accent?" She cut in sharply. "Do I not speak English well enough?"

I could have said, "Too well," could have explained that Americans would use contractions; "Don't I" and "I'm" and "it's." I said, "You speak beautifully. The trouble is, we don't."

She probed until I explained the little differences, and then she laughed. "I shall remember. No, what should I say? "*I'll* remember?"

I liked her better for the moment, but we were silent for a time, I watching the road as she was. Though the lights of what appeared to be a large town glowed ahead of us, the car slowed abruptly. She switched on powerful headlights and peered at a signpost reading "Schluss," an arrow pointing right.

"There are two roads to—to—" she did not finish the sentence, seemed preoccupied with the turnoff from the smooth tarmac to the lesser road. "I prefer the other route." She was silent again.

Very soon I thought I could guess why. This road was narrow, untended, not well-traveled. We met only a few cars, which was fortunate, for the road was winding steadily upward, the valley falling away at an alarming rate. It must be a very good inn, I thought, to warrant so difficult a night drive.

"Is this a shortcut?" I asked.

"A poor one, is it not? *Isn't* it?" She laughed shortly. "Never mind. With the other route we would have had a very long drive. And two frontiers to cross to reach our destination."

"*Two* frontiers?"

"Liechtenstein and Switzerland. A nuisance. But the roads are better." She swung the wheel right and left on the rising grades, the hairpin curves, expertly shifting gears, applying brakes, controlling directions to avoid mud and sharp rocks.

The road *was* a difficult one. I did not envy Lori Náir, and I was beginning to wish she had taken the longer route to the inn when she said bitterly, without preamble or explanation, "Always to please *his* convenience. Always to satisfy him. I shall be happy when this job is over."

I heard . . . felt . . . the hollow rumble of the car's tires on a bridge the instant before she swung the wheel sharp right up a very steep grade.

A crucifix floated into and out of the car's lights, a signpost read, with embellished capitals: "La Clav." Our headlights glimmered on the gilt-touched wooden plaque, on the chain that linked it to an enormous iron key.

Except for a dim fan of light from above, the drive would barely have been visible. And it tipped up obliquely, adding that hazard to the dense undergrowth, the wet leaves of many seasons that lay thick in our path.

"La Clav?" I spoke the question without thinking.

"Der Schlüssel," she explained. " 'Key,' in English." The car roared to the top, swung in a wide arc onto a terrace where I was surprised to see several cars already parked.

"What language is that—*clav?*" *La* sounded French, but the word for key in French was *clef.*

Lori Náir brought the car to a stop close to the drive and flung her gloves over her shoulder onto the back seat. "It is an old language, Miss Farrar," she said evenly. "One you perhaps have never heard. Ladin."

In that one instant I recognized her scent. The woman who had passed me in the post office, whose long walnut hair had veiled her face.

And, staring past her shoulder into the rear of the car I saw the coat folded there, the shining black coat of the woman who had stood beside me at the Feldkirch station kiosk, with her back to me.

18

For a long moment I stared at the dark glasses, tried in the light from the dashboard to see beyond, to see into the woman's eyes. I was completely aware that Lori Náir was looking into mine, aware too of her defiance. It was evident in the curve of her lips, the tilt of her chin.

I thought: She's been waiting for me, waiting for Guy to send for me. A thought probed further although I attempted to deny it: She's jealous.

Her words cut across my deductions. "I was waiting in Feldkirch for my instructions."

"And now you've done your work." I was surprised that I could be so detached, for beneath the mounting uneasiness I was extremely annoyed. With her.

My reaction to Guy's arrangement was not so much annoyance as hurt that he could place me in this position. He must have known, he could not have helped but absorb something of this woman's involvement with him.

"Only part of my job is done," she said dryly. "We must dine now."

"Not with Mr. Black?"

"Do not fear. He will be with you." She laughed curtly, switched off the car's lights. Waving a hand toward the door beside me, she slipped from the driver's seat and slammed her door behind her.

Outside, I glanced down the long drive to the road we had left; the road that wound erratically to the far-away glimmer of lights in the last village we had skirted, far down in the valley.

Those lights were so far below us, miles away beyond the black damask of leaf and branch. And despite the pale promise of the moon, a black ridge towered above us, around us, impenetrable, untouched by any but the muted glow from La

Clav's windows. The enveloping darkness, full of whispers, of agitated leaves sighing in the night wind, held menace.

I felt something more than annoyance with the woman now, more than hurt with Guy; a disquiet gripped me and I was aware of a tightening of my nerves.

I did not move. I watched Lori Náir cross the flagged terrace of the sprawling fieldstone building. At the first shallow step she turned impatiently. "Come along," she said.

I moved slowly toward her then, watching her. I could see her figure clearly now, the interrupted oval of her face—slashed by the dark glasses—the chic belted suit, a product of London or Paris or Rome; the slender legs in smooth high boots. In the light that shone out from the deep-cut windows her shadow was cast velvety black against the door behind her.

"Where are we?" I said.

"Near the border. The Swiss border." She gestured above us. "That ridge is the Raetikon. The border alps." As she pushed at the wide door, I heard the sound of a car far down in the valley, and I was faintly comforted by the distant purr. I reminded myself that it was early, that this was a public house, that if La Clav was so fabulous, certainly more cars would join those on the terrace behind us.

Below the three steps blurred by moss I stopped, once more diverted. A motor beat in the night sky; its twin lights winked alternately, rhythmically.

"A plane so low? Here?" I watched the lights disappear behind a screen of treetops. "I shouldn't like that."

"I do not like it either." The woman shivered.

That wasn't a jet, I thought. And the sound had drifted as though the engines had been abruptly cut off.

Something bothered me. Peg and I had originally hoped to meet in Innsbruck farther east, but there was no commercial through-flight from London or Zurich; only a private plane connection at Munich.

"Is there an airport near *here?*" I looked up at her.

"There are some private . . ." She paused. "Abandoned military bases from the last war." She held open the door for me, and I followed her into a half-timbered hall that looked like a Shakespearean inn. Over her shoulder I saw the lean and taciturn headwaiter bow to her. He must have been waiting for us. I had not heard him enter the shallow hall.

"*Buna sáira,* Stefan. *La máisa,* you understand."

"*Hei, duǫnna,* the table is ready." There was definitely derision in the lines around the man's lips, which puzzled me; certainly mockery in his voice.

I watched him as we trailed after him into the beamed room, past red-clothed tables, across flickering candlelight. I was listening to the low rush of words, to Lori Náir's answers.

She had been wrong. I had heard that language before. Yesterday, in the Café Goldene Krone. Those men behind me, I realized now, had been talking Ladin, a language not unlike the Romansch of Eastern Switzerland, according to Dominic Regli.

My mind was so absorbed with this coincidence, I was striving so hard to place the man's voice, to decide whether he had been one of the disgruntled pair in the café, that for the moment I forgot the woman. But when we reached the window table midway in the room and Lori Náir pulled off her soft wrapped turban, I drew in my breath sharply.

"What is it?" The smile on her curving lips was as enigmatic as that on the da Vinci painting in the Louvre.

"Your hair." I knew I should have said, "Forgive me for staring," but I could not, for I would not have meant it. The color was as like the natural dark gold of *my* hair as dye could produce.

Removing her dark spectacles, she said quite blatantly, "I liked the color of your hair. It is—*it's* a good match. No?"

Her eyes were a little disappointing, a neutral squirrel-brown, and she had forgotten her brows; they were too dark, too hard against the ivory of her smooth skin.

But I could not look away from the cascade of hair that she was tossing back, lifting away from her collar. She actually clasped it low on her neck as I did, with an amber barrette not unlike mine.

Stefan had left us. I heard the murmur of his voice behind us, but I did not turn to examine the few other diners; I was ensnared by Lori Náir.

"*You* also wear clothes well," she said, implying that she was aware of her own proclivities. "Size thirty-eight perhaps?"

"Twelve," I murmured automatically.

"Ah yes, yes. The British use those sizes also. I must remember. What will you drink?" She leaned past me, raising her hand, and for a moment I thought Guy might have come. I

156

turned quickly to look over my shoulder. Only a round-faced waiter moved toward us.

"*Duǫnna?*" he said.

The woman nodded to me. "A cinzano?"

By now I was resenting everything about this woman, her meddling, her very presence. My flush of annoyance must have been quite apparent, for she smiled slightly.

"Cynar," I said. I could not imagine where the word had come from, why I had asked for the drink Dominic Regli liked.

Her dark brows peaked, her head tipped slightly. "So?" she said. "You have learned French habits?"

"Swiss." She was taunting me about Guy.

"Ah." She dismissed the waiter. "The Swiss drink everything." She shrugged. "Perhaps anything."

I stiffened, infuriated with her, not certain whether I resented her rude statement entirely because of my grandmother's family or because of a newer acquaintance.

But before I assembled a few cutting words of my own, she added what I assumed was meant as an explanation. "You understand, of course; they must import everything, the Swiss. So good for business, for exporters." She lighted a long cigarette from a golden box.

A draft swirled in from the door behind us. I turned again. Only Stefan stood there, a thoughtful look on his thin face. He came toward us.

"You will not wait for the *signúr?*" He was about to pull away the third chair, but I reached out and held it. "I think Herr Black will come," I said. "He expects me."

"We think the *signúr* will come." Lori Náir echoed. "Nevertheless, we shall proceed with that renowned specialty of yours." She moved back as the round-faced waiter edged the tray of *apéritifs* onto the table.

Watching, Stefan asked, "And the wine the *signúr* prefers, *duǫnna?*" Again, scorn in the attitude.

"Naturally."

In London, when Guy had taken charge, had suggested the *apéritifs,* ordered the meals, introduced me to new wines, I had been delighted, felt honored. Even the few incidents with Dominic Regli had, to be truthful, intrigued me, though I had been aware that budgets differed markedly, that Dominic Regli's position was not to be compared with that of a businessman like

Guy. At least I had believed *then* that Dominic Regli had been little more than a salesman working for a possibly nonprofit organization.

Here in this alpine hostelry with a woman I had known for not much longer than an hour I resented her domination.

I said, "What *is* the renowed speciality?"

"You will find veal the principal ingredient," the man said, "an exceptional concoction."

I liked veal well enough. My grandmother's influence had been so strong in our home that my mother had once remarked that it was astonishing that any calves had been permitted to grow old enough in Switzerland to produce milk or the famous cheeses. I did not protest now, especially since Lori Náir had added, "Besides, there is rarely any choice but veal." Nor did I raise my glass to hers as she raised hers toward me. I simply drank the bittersweet blend, avoiding her eyes, as irritated with the situation as I was nervous.

Naturally, I was wondering where Guy could be. By this time I was wondering too, what business could have taken him beyond Zurich, where he would have found me in the flat in the Dolder Weg, or past Feldkirch, where he knew I had been waiting.

The name Genoa rose out of recent memory. Had he been in Genoa, not Geneva, during that last call to London? Was he coming from Genoa now, from business there?

I was growing bolder now, not because of the warming, relaxing spirits; there was a sense of relief in the proof of the inn's popularity. The door across the room behind me had opened and closed several times, and the place was growing noisier with the voices of men, predominantly German-speaking. That and the warmth, the color, the enticing aromas of the place lulled me into a sense of security, false or not.

I said, "Where has Mr. Black been? What has delayed him?"

"You have known him how long? Five weeks? Six weeks?" Lori Náir held out her glass to Stefan, indicated a reorder for two. "Do you not—*don't* you know by now how he moves about? How unpredictable he is? I know him much longer, and I can only *guess* where he is."

The headwaiter stood beside us, long-faced, dour. In one hand he held a slender half-bottle of dark wine.

"*Duónna,* we are ready. The wines have been opened. You will excuse me if I do not suggest the second cinzano."

Although it had not been my little triumph over the will of this dominating woman, I was perversely pleased with Stefan's. But when he poured the ruby wine and held the glass toward her, she shook her head. "Please," she said to me. "*You* must try it. It is for you."

"Perfect with the veal," Stefan murmured.

It was quite good, a trifle heavier than I liked, but I sipped it, not surprised when she snapped at the man. "And what about mine? I won't be cheated out of it tonight. You know I prefer the *Soave,* and never mind whether it is proper with the *Schnitzel.*"

Until now I had paid little attention to the wine Stefan was serving me. But as he had set down the bottle, I had seen part of the label, part of the name on the bottle. One word: *Knabe.*

The entire name was dredged up from my subconscious, from the fear that had been lurking there, growing in my mind during the ride with Lori Náir, during these last moments in La Clav. *Knabe* was one of the words Peg had used to describe the wine she had been "guzzling" at the "super inn."

My voice was strained, almost inaudible. "Would that be *Alte Knabe St. Anton Spezial?*"

The silence, the utterly rigid countenance of the woman, and indeed of the man beside her, lasted only the briefest instant. The man spoke first.

"A specialty of La Clav's cellars, *giúnfra.* You have been here before?"

Instead of answering, I said, my voice as steady as I could manage, "And *Schnitzel Donatal.* Is that another specialty?"

Out of the corner of my eye I saw Lori push away from the table. She was leaving the answer to Stefan, who seemed for the first time to have lost a certain composure that usually accompanied such a position as his.

I wished I could have felt something of a personal triumph now, but when Stefan followed the woman from the room, I felt very different. Something I had been fighting for the past day and night took over my nerves, my mind, my body: stark fear.

159

When a chair scraped behind me, ice went through my veins and into my scalp.

A voice I had not heard for weeks, not since the night I had left Long Island, muttered, "For God's sake, get out of here! *Now!*"

It was Tony Jenner.

19

Tony's fingers circled my wrist. He whispered: *"Quick!"* and slid my coat from the chair, drawing me around toward the door. Walking close to me, leaning over me, he murmured, "Don't act surprised, love. Pretend this is what it's all about."

Heads were turning, though there was no further movement; no one else left his chair as Lori Náir had done. Only the round-faced waiter stared, open-mouthed, from the far end of the room.

In a moment we were past the half-open door and into the hall where Tony glanced around swiftly. Then, with a rough jerk he pulled me along, yanked back the heavy door to the drive, and we were out onto the flagged terrace, streaking toward a small light car that had been parked erratically.

Halfway across I stumbled, and he twisted toward me, hooked his arm around me.

"For God's sake, help me!" He urged.

"Help you?" I gasped. My feet dragged, seemed not quite part of me, but I followed him somehow, half-reluctant, half-relieved. "Where did you come from?"

"The Goldene Krone. I got the message. The inn *had* to be La Clav. I know the place." His voice was hard, bitter.

I stumbled again and raised a hand to brush the mist from my eyes. Something *was* wrong. The leaf-laced sky merged into the towering black ridge above us, into the spangled valley below. I tried to see Tony clearly, but he seemed alternately magnified and reduced. I blinked, trying to focus.

I heard him say, "Hurry! I've got to get you away!" He threw open the car's door. The step was too high, my knees did not respond to my brain.

"Hurry!" Roughly again, Tony thrust me inside, slammed the door.

I swayed in the seat, struck my head against the window as I turned to watch him race around to the driver's door. When he slipped in, I was cooling my forehead against the chilled glass. "I feel dizzy," I said.

"Oh, God! No!" Gears rasped sharply. The car jerked forward, its right mudguard grazing the car beside it, but Tony did not stop.

I heard a commotion behind us now, running footsteps, the clack of a car's door as clear as Tony's had been in the mountain stillness.

Tony's car bounced off the terrace flags and shot down the leaf-molded drive, skidding as it arrowed into the mountain road. "Pray," he said.

Pines, spruce, hemlock, darkness, closed in on us, lighted only by our headlights, which swept low on the hard-packed surface. He drove too fast. Tires protested on the curves. We skidded, rocked, settled onto the short straight strips of road.

At the time I could only hope the effects of that Cynar, that half-glass of red wine, would wear off. I hoped that I *could* help Tony. I braced myself against the hand-hold, tried to straighten up.

"Tell me." I hoped I could hear him through, could concentrate.

"My fault. A mistake. Peg didn't know. Not this year."

"Peg? What do you mean? What has she got to do with this?" I moved in the seat, propped myself against the door. Even to watch him I had to concentrate. His profile swam against the black forest, his skin an unearthly hue in the underglow from the dashboard. "Peg?" I repeated.

"Last year she agreed. She carried something back for me. For kicks, she said." His lips twisted. "Money for *me*. Money I needed." The tires squealed as we took a hairpin curve at shocking speed.

"I don't understand." The trouble was that even through the haze, the mist that was obscuring the rising moon, I was afraid I did.

"You can guess, love. You're not stupid. They'd rigged up the stuff——"

"Stuff?"

"All right. Heroin. Pure heroin. They'd rigged it in Munich last year for us. In one of those wooden figures we'd found over here. That angel she brought back last year, remember. Our pay-off to her. No problem at Kennedy."

My voice came from far away. "And this year?"

"She wouldn't touch the job, wouldn't help. I needed her. I was in debt."

I am not sure where the words came from. "So, you 'planted' something." I was feeling ill, contaminated.

"I told you it was a mistake," he cut in. "Instead of *her* bag, so that it could be picked up in Zurich, where the action is coming up now—" he drew a deep breath, "it landed in *your* bag. God forgive me. One half-kilo. Worth four hundred thousand Swiss francs. More than one hundred thousand dollars."

The dreadful portent of the words he had uttered were penetrating the mist that still seemed to be closing in. And I was thinking that of course he could not have known that we had switched totes, that Peg had taken mine because it was deeper, capacious enough for those figures she had cherished. I managed to ask: "Where did you get the 'stuff?' "

"Coming into the States through Panama, now, through contacts with South American students. Narco agents don't look for it to go *back* to the growing European market now that Marseille is closing down. They haven't caught on to us yet."

His shoulders were hunched, all his strength devoted to the driving. "I've got to get you out of this, Connie. It's—it's a bigger thing, now. They've gone too far."

"They?"

"*Il Cumün,* they call themselves. *Their* language for 'The Village.' It's like the Cosa Nostra. His lips contorted again. "Big business, now. They deal in anything. Everything. Outlet is a slick operation in Liechtenstein."

Totallia, I thought. The exchange point. The staging area. The respectable villa at Malina 10. The ultimate cynicism: *Totallia.* I was beyond speech.

"Big business," he repeated. "And linking up with a resurgence of the Camorra. In Italy. God help me, darling, I got you into this, I'll get you out. This has to be my last job. I'm scared."

162

We were outdistancing the car behind us. I could not even hear it now, but beyond Tony's head when the car tilted at a gradient, twin lights far down in the valley bobbed and straightened, bobbed and straightened on the only road, the hazardous mountain road we drove on.

I blinked again, ran a hand across my eyes again. I was striving to pull my floating thoughts together, striving to comprehend what he had said.

Peg was—had been—involved in something obviously wrong, now obviously dangerous. Or why this race, this chase?

Zurich . . . "where the action is coming up now."

Zurich?

That must be how . . . where . . . Dominic Regli had been involved. The mixed-up luggage must have been the reason Dominic had come to London. He had not found what he wanted in Peg's bag at Dolder Weg 12. He had been forced to retrieve it from Nell Hobart's dressing room. . . for Zurich.

And what about Guy? Where had he been when I had needed him?

It was no good. I could not concentrate. And the twin lights diverted me; they were not so far away now. They blurred, spread. Tony's profile ballooned out of all proportion until I blinked and squinted and focused again.

Il Cumün. I had heard that word before. Where? *Where?* In the café in Feldkirch! The Café Goldene Krone. Those men, those two men speaking that strange language. Ladin—was it Ladin? Not Romansch?

La Clav was Ladin for The Key, Lori Náir had told me.

I wished I could get it all together. Peg. Dominic. La Clav. Lori Náir. Guy. Where *was* Guy?

Our headlights struck a wall of creviced cliff sprayed with wildflowers, swung to emptiness at our right, to the edge of the world where now only the palest moonlight illumined the valley far below.

For a moment I thought we had lost the twin lights altogether, but I was wrong! I was wrong!

Not far enough down the road they swung away, disappeared abruptly. Then, metal gleamed in the only light—the glow of the moon.

"We're going too fast! That's a car!" I cried. "Tony! Tony! Stop!"

163

Even though the brakes, when he applied them, jerked us both off our seats, it was impossible to avoid the car that stood broadside across the road, blocking the way completely. Even my dazed mind could grasp that. Impossible, with the cliff at one side, the blank darkness on the other.

"Jump" Tony yelled. Somehow, I snapped down the latch, instantly felt his hand on my back, felt myself pitch into an empty void, and fall . . . fall. . . .

A head seemed to float out of the edge of the ragged roadside above me: a sharp face framed in black sideburns, black hair, a face sparked with gleaming amber spectacles. The face I had seen in the post-bus to Vaduz. The face I had seen when I had turned on the road to Malina 10.

Then I was tumbling, panting, reaching, grasping at bracken, at scrawny branches, granite, at anything in the darkness. I struck something hard, rough . . . the bark, the trunk of a tree.

The crash, not yards away on the road was stupefyingly loud. And I could see it! Through the mist that was closing in, through the shadowy branches, I could see it. Tony's small light car struck the blocking car at an oblique angle, tore off metal with a ripping, searing crackle. The small car rocked forward, bounced back onto the narrow shoulder for a fraction of a second before it slid sideways, poised on the bank of the road so close that I could see it was not empty. And so close, so horrifyingly close, it plunged from sight.

There was a brief, almost breathless silence, then a lumbering, bumping, splintering tear of metal on woodbark; another and another and another. And the forest was quiet again.

From somewhere there was a rhythmic, rapid beating I had heard before.

Where had I heard it? *Where?* . .

I tried to fight the hands that touched me then. I struggled wildly. I had to get down to Tony. I would crawl. I would find him. But it was too dim in the forest . . . too dark to see. . . .

I grappled with consciousness.

The last I heard was a hoarse curse, a rush of words in German before I blacked out.

Was it my scream that reverberated through the valley after that? Or was that all part of the continuing nightmare? The

164

sounds around me were gleaming knives of panic slashing at the mist I could not conquer. Black shadows clawed and fingered at me, tugged at me.

I could no longer fight. I could not move. The whirling, the beating, was upon me, but I could no longer fight.

I felt curiously alone.

Cold—a dank and penetrating cold—was seeping through my skin, my flesh, my very bones; I ached with it. And a musty smell of animal, old dust, rotting leaves—a reminder not only of forgotten days and nights but of decades, perhaps of centuries— filled my nostrils. I lay still on the cold hard stone beneath me, breathing in the decay; and fearfully, cautiously dared to open my eyes.

Not a glimmer of light shone anywhere in the total darkness, not a stir of life whispered. I reached out my arm and ran stiff fingers over the sweating slatey surface around me. I touched something cool and smooth and recoiled. Slowly, I started once more to explore.

What was that? Leather? Plastic? A metal clamp . . . ring? I fumbled around the bulk of it, the smooth long bulk of it. A tote bag. It had to be a tote bag.

Tote . . . Peg . . . Tony. Everything came back. The horror of everything. The nightmare memory. I started to push myself away from the slick stone. And then I froze. Was that a footstep?

From somewhere beyond whatever filthy walls enclosed me something padded, voices mumbled, grew more distinct. I eased down, waiting with pounding heart as the sounds moved closer.

It was when I flattened myself against the wet stone once more that I realized I no longer wore a dress. Between my aching body and the icy floor was merely my nylon slip covering the scantiest of underclothes.

Dear God! Where was I? *Who was outside?* .

Hinges creaked. I closed my eyes against the ghostlike gloom beyond a widening gap in the blackness, a gap blocked partly by a square bulk. I clamped my lips over chattering teeth.

A flat voice stabbed the silence; a voice I knew, a language I did not understand. That other language, the Ladin, I was sure. It was Stefan. One of the men in the Café Goldene Krone,

165

the man in La Clav. He had made a statement, a harsh demand. A command.

"Now, wait. One's enough." This was the guttural German, the man of the black sideburns. "You want this one to go wrong, too?"

"*Sei still!*" Lori Náir was with them. "Shut up, you two. There's enough trouble. Too much has gone wrong."

Someone slid the tote bag from the floor, was obviously examining it, dropping books, shoes. In the brief silence I thought they must hear my thumping heart. Everything came back. The terrible crash. The terrible silence. Were they talking of Tony? *One's enough. You want this one to go wrong, too?* Sideburns had said. *Too much has gone wrong,* the Náir woman had said. Were they talking of Tony? Of Peg . . .

Had something happened to her, too?

The effort to lie still in the darkness, to act as though I did not hear, was all but superhuman. I longed to scream, to fight, to kick.

"And what about him?" Sideburns said.

Him? My brain did not function until the woman actually spoke his name. Her rapid German was clear enough, too clear.

"That Jenner. Weak, weak, *weak* I tell you. No loss to us, that one. Him and his gambling. Sure, he needed the money, but a link like that could kill us, do you understand? He deserved what he got—what you did. He deserved to die."

The tears that started were hot against my ice-cold cheeks. But tears are silent. The woman did not know that I had heard her dreadful pronouncement. About Tony, who had come to take me away from danger.

"No good to us any more," the Náir woman added.

"Not that one. I don't mean the American," Sideburns burst out. "I mean the boss. You're going to leave this one with him?"

"She's welcome to him." The sneer in the Náir voice was evident.

"She could rot here for all he'll do," Stefan put in.

"So?" The woman's laugh was chilling. "He overplayed his hand with this one. The bastard. And what did he get? Nothing. Nothing in those figures. Nothing in here—" She kicked the bag.

The figures? So it was one of these men who had taken my tote from the Gasthof's cupboard. But, what had been in the

166

santo Peg had wanted; what had been in the mourner? I heard the hollow sound as the woman kicked the tote again.

"Worn shoes," she mumbled. "Books. Ha! All this for nothing!"

"You forget," Sideburns jibed. "I got that packet of stuff from her bag in London. Smart, eh? The way I got the key from the maid, in broad daylight."

"Stop bragging."

"Well, Lori," the man muttered, "you've got that passport you've wanted ever since London. Couldn't manage to get it for yourself, though, could you? Use it in good health. Ha!"

So it was she who had been waiting for me in the lobby at 8 Crown Gardens that morning. That had been her scent. . . .

"Listen," Stefan said. "Did the boss give instructions about the one out there, at—at the bottom?" His tone was as bitter as the woman's, now. "Your *husband*—" he stressed the word "—did he tell you how we handle that?"

"Later," she said. "Both of them."

"You leave us with the job?"

There was a rush of the sibilant Ladin, and Sideburns, the man who did not like the language, cried, "*Halt!*" in German. "You'll speak so I can understand. I do not trust you as it is, you two."

"Listen to who talks," the woman muttered. "You, who could not get rid of this little bitch at Malina. You—you—*Feigling!* I should have stayed at the wheel."

For a coward, I thought, repressing the shudder that threatened me, that dark one had been terribly convincing on the driveway to that lonely villa in Liechtenstein. I wanted to crawl into the floor, under the stone.

"You'll take back that word, Frau Náir," Sideburns said. "Who do you think's been taking risks for you? In London? In Feldkirch? On the road from La Clav?"

"*Hei!* And what have we got? A couple of cheap, empty carvings. Do you realize the value of the contents of one, alone, was worth a quarter of a million Swiss francs on the open market? The market we're finally breaking in Central Europe. The market we're breaking in *Zurich*." Her voice faded as she moved off, gloating almost to herself, "Zurich, the toughest trade-post."

She must have swung around, for her voice was louder, harsh

now. "You could have stolen the stuff yourself and stashed it away. Jewels and drugs in that crummy santo. That Corot rolled up in the phony French mourner——"

"*Me?*" Sideburns shouted. "*Me* cheat the boss? You no-good slut of an actress!"

There was the sound of a scuffle, and Stefan spit out, "Stop it! That's enough from you!"

"You can talk," Lori Náir's voice was a low growl. "Stupid donkey—letting that other one get out to send a message, telling *this* one what *specialité* she was eating, what special wine she was drinking while she was waiting for Guido. Who knows what she might have spilled?"

"Now, you listen to me!" I heard movement, heard the slap, and the woman's shrill cry. "I told you it was risky," Stefan shouted. "This whole business. Passports are enough trouble for the little they bring. All right, I went along with the boss on burglaries. Art brings big money. But, drugs—I've been against it——"

"*Ja, ja,* you're right," the German voice cut in. "*She* can get out now, this sister of yours. She's got the whole package. Including all the American clothes."

"Worth nothing," the woman scoffed. "But, you're right, too. I'm going tonight. You'll fly me down to the car when Guido gets back."

"So, you got your money."

"Enough . . . for now." She was moving away again, her voice diminishing.

"Just what does that mean?" Stefan asked.

"I could spill everything I knew. Figure that out. I'll keep in touch, all right. From America." She must have reached the door, for I heard a latch click and Stefan call softly, "Don't forget your books, sister. As if you'll read them."

He must have thrown the books across the confined space. They struck something hard, wall or door, and fell.

"Bring those along with anything else that belongs in that bag," Lori Náir said calmly. "Come. You'll have to load the bird."

"You're in a hell of a hurry," Sideburns said.

"Nothing to hold me now. Only the photo-switch. My passport reads: 'Constance Farrar, student,' in case you forget."

For a moment I felt they must have heard my indrawn breath, but Stefan's laugh saved me.

168

"And *you* don't forget the English pronounciation!" he could not stop laughing. "I hope Guido's expert can set the birthdate back ten years while he's processing that photo. Student! *Um Gottes Willen!* Lucky for you that women *do* study at all ages in the States."

"Shut up," she said.

The door creaked open, and cold air swirled in with a rattle of dead leaves. Stefan said something I did not hear, and the woman snapped, "Don't be a bloody fool." But the man was persistent. They continued to argue.

"Have it, then," she said at last.

"You can't use it. With *her* luggage, her passport, they'd know it didn't belong. A thousand-franc coat like this."

Footsteps scraped along the stone, returning to me. I stiffened as something cool and smooth rustled down onto my numb, cold skin, and I do not know how I managed not to shrink from the hands that touched me, tucked something around my shoulders and waist.

Sideburns grumbled, "Come along, Vanko. We have to unload the bird when it gets down on the strip. The boss expected another haul tonight."

"Hurry!" Lori Náir called out.

"You hear?" Sideburns goaded Stefan Vanko. "That sister of yours wants to get over the border *fast* now that she's got what *she* wants."

"I'll remember you," the woman threw back as the door creaked. "In the meantime, be sure you lock that girl in now that you've made her cozy. We'll see how cozy *he* makes her." She laughed as the door clicked shut, a laugh I never want to hear again.

I did not wait for the sound of their footsteps to commence or vanish. I had to get out of there. I had to get away before someone came back. "Later," that woman had said. "Both of them." The one "out there" and me.

I pushed myself to my knees and started to crawl in the darkness, knocked against a carton, and edging around it, came against another. It seemed agonizingly long before my exploring fingers touched rougher stone rising vertically, the fieldstone of a wall.

Shivering, I moved as fast as I dared, searching for a window, another door, any opening I might squirm out of. I found a ledge eventually, a deep ledge half the length of my arm, and I reached along it, touched something smoother. My fingers splayed against wood. Wood? Not glass?

I explored the ledge to the end at each side. This must be a deep-set window.

Something came back to me, stories from my childhood related by my grandparents, about the small mountain huts in the high alps and the far-away valleys where there were no glass windows, only wooden shutters to close in the inabhitants against the night or the weather.

The effort to pull myself up to investigate that wooden shutter was almost more than I could manage. But I finally found the rusted hook and tugged at it, pried it up slowly until the catch yielded, and with a gritty *eeek* the shutter sprang outward.

Peering between a straggle of vine and ragged bracken that seemed almost a part of the hut, I adjusted my vision from the blackness to a sky the color of polished steel. The air was cold with the piercing cold of the mountains, hard and clean against my bare arms. I pulled back, shivering again, glanced over my shoulder.

Had those three left me nothing but that shining mass that had rustled down on me, that coat that lay on the floor somewhere behind me?

I turned back, aiming for the gleam that must be the coat. There was nothing else. No handbag. No dark dress. No "all-weather coat" from home. No shoes. No gloves. That woman had indeed absconded with the entire "package."

The coat Stefan had dropped over me was chill to the touch, but it was useful. I swept it up and at the window threw it across the ledge. Though the window was close to the ground, the opening was small and rough. Without the coat I should have suffered more cuts and bruises as I wriggled through. As it was, blood trickled down my legs even before my stockinged feet struck the wild brittle leaves and tangled roots.

But worse—far worse—I teetered literally on the edge of a ravine. Not a yard away from me a landslip fell away sharply, striated and gouged by mountain rains and snows. Moonlight rose from behind a spiked wall of pines, threw back golden glints from mica threads in the rock, made ghostly lace of the leaves, cast black shadows everywhere. Moving shadows behind me, around me. Whispering shadows.

Soft earth beneath my feet, beneath the timeless blanket of leaf mold, gave way. I swayed, and clutching at tall fern fronds fell to my knees.

Quite suddenly the moon was above me, out from behind pines, alps, clouds; its ice-blue radiance fingering down a hundred feet or more, down like a terrible slow-motion nightmare, down into a narrow ravine.

The moon had turned the moss to a silver pool, and now its beams glittered on a figure lying below me, a figure with long black legs—the dark tights she had always worn. The skirt was flung wide; the pale face at a crooked angle upturned to a merciless alpine night.

Peg . . . no. No. *No.*

20

My first thought was that I could not reach her, *I could not reach her!* I needed help . . . help. But, where would I find help? Dear God—where could I go?

I staggered back, away from the ravine's edge, struck the jagged fieldstone of the hut, and lunged away, stumbling over the Náir woman's shining coat, careened around the corner.

There, I stopped, fighting off a sense of unreality. Was this sight ahead of me—all of this—another nightmare? Was the moon playing tricks with its eerie beams?

The glow touched a gathering of vine-laced rooftops, crooked chimney pots, a miniature half-onion dome against the black of velvet, darker than the sky, taller than the pines behind me. Yet, glistening faintly like a chain of moonstones, like a fall of crystal tears, a pencil-slim cascade fell beyond the ghost-village from nowhere to nowhere. There was no sound in the vale, no light; only the moon.

I was on a ridge, a ravine on the one side; on the other, and some distance below, lay a grass clearing bleached to no color by the moon's cold rays.

I could see, on that strip below me, a trio of shadows—that unholy three—straggle across the pool of moonlight, waiting for the "bird' . . .

In my despair I started for the moss-smudged flight of steps that led away, between choking bracken; elusive steps that curved around and up toward the ancient fieldstone cottages of the ancient village that was so dark and silent.

"Oh, God," I prayed over and over. "Dear God, help me! Help me to help Peg!" Without shoes I slipped and fell on the damp stone, clawed and crawled and tore at the wild growth that slapped back at me, sprayed me with dew. Ahead, at last, lay the low sprawling shape of the first cottage.

Beyond the stiff leaves of the monstrous bracken and untended laurel a blood-red door was buried deep in the fieldstone wall, a thorn in the side of the mountain.

I flew toward it and thrust myself at the door. It burst open. From out of the black depths a hand clamped across my lips, a strong hard hand, a man's hand smelling of tobacco, the Turkish tobacco Dominic Regli smoked.

I nearly fainted. For one desperate moment I thought my heart had stopped beating, and then from an aeons-ago past, a forgotten instinct rose, a jungle law prevailed. I fought. I pummeled. I kicked. But he only yanked me away from the door and locked me against him.

"*Still! Still!*" The German was a sibilant ghost of a sound. I felt the jerk as the man sent the door away from us, and just as the latch clicked to leave us in total darkness, I heard a rhythmic whir, the beating of wings or blades I had heard somewhere before. More than once. The helicopter!

Against the cold fingers that still covered my mouth I could utter only fragments of words, and the sound was distorted beyond comprehension. "*Do* something! Get her! You can't leave her out there! It's Peg! Peg! My friend!" The despair was more than I could cope with, more than I could bear. Why did it have to be this man?

I squirmed in his arms, I wriggled, I spat. Of course, he was going to send me out there too, to leave me, too, to leave us both to rot outside this deserted village, down in that forlorn ravine. . . .

The Verlorenen Tal! The valley of lost souls . . . The valley so remote from Feldkirch that "no one goes there, no road goes there." How, then, did these people get here? The Náir woman. Stefan Vanko, Sideburns, Dominic. *The helicopter?* And what was this man doing here, alone?

I struggled wildly, but the muscles that encircled me were like bands of iron around my ribs; the hand that silenced me did not relax.

Outside, the whir dwindled and ceased. Close against me I felt Dominic Regli release a long breath. Then his chest swelled as he filled his lungs again, his body trembled as though an electric current had passed through it.

He had said nothing but the simple: "*Still!*" Now he whispered close to my ear, "Remember, I am with you."

Without a sound from outside or in, not even the normal snick of an electric switch, the room around us was alive with light.

"Remote control." The murmured words above my head held admiration; then for the first time he released his hold on me.

I could not have uttered a sound had he attacked me. I could barely breathe.

The room was magnificent.

"*What a pad!*" Peg had whispered over the wire when she had rung me in Zurich. What a pad, indeed.

I stood staring beyond Dominic Regli's shoulder at the luxurious curtains that rippled to the floor at our right, at exquisite tapestries that hung from mellowed walls, priceless objets d'art. I gaped at what looked like the Turner, the *Piazza at Evening* I had seen not many weeks ago in the flat over the King's Head in London. At Rubens' *Head of a Young Girl,* lost by a prince in Liechtenstein. At a Corot, a Constable, unmistakable techniques. A Bellini painting. Hadn't there been a Bellini sculpture in Guy's London flat?

I closed my eyes against the stunning, dazzling, priceless collection that did not belong there but opened them instantly. I had seen something else.

On the floor beside an antique trestle table lay the broken santo Guy and I had bought in Portobello Road, the mourner— now headless—he had brought me from France to take to Peg.

Nearby, I was aware of swift movement, heard the faint swish of silk. The heavy curtains moved as though stirred by a light

173

breeze and settled again. Dominic Regli had vanished. Only his puzzling words remained: *Remember, I am with you.*

The door swung open, and a man strode into the room. A man in rough gray wools, a black sweater high against his lean brown throat. The man with the silver hair.

For the briefest moment he stood in profile, balanced, wary, quite as though he sensed an alien presence. And then he turned. Every muscle tensed, but he still managed to retain his inestimable poise.

"Ah, Constance." He must have been relieved to see me, for he rocked back on his heels, and smiled faintly. "You have come awake."

"I've come awake." I had come awake in more than one sense, and almost too fast for total comprehension. Something that had nagged at me ever since I had heard Lori Náir utter her name flared clear as a match-flame in tunnel-darkness.

Pan Náir, Dominic had called that mountain *Schwarzbrot,* that black bread he had brought to me in London. The Raeto-Romanisch idiom . . . the Ladin . . .

Pan náir. Pan, for bread. *Náir,* for black.

The name *Guy* of course, was English or French for *Guido,* the man Peg had been waiting for at La Clav while she had drunk the *St. Anton Spezial.* The same wine, containing probably the same drug Stefan had given me.

Guy Black. *Guido Náir.* Náir . . . Lori's husband . . . Peg's betrayer.

The revulsion that swept over me must have been very apparent in my eyes. And I was rigid, trembling, desperately striving to withhold an emotion compounded by fear, by bewilderment at Dominic Regli's desertion, at his inexplicable disappearance.

In my confusion I murmured, "You're not French." A stupid, irrelevant statement.

The amusement flickered, returned to the cool eyes. "My dear, you know all about me. I've told you. French. Italian." He shrugged.

"And what else?"

"What do you mean?"

"They called you 'the boss,' those people who speak the Ladin.

You could be Italian. You could be Austrian." Not Swiss, I thought. I rebelled against that possibility. He and those people at La Clav spoke Ladin, perhaps, but not the Ladin that encompassed any of the Romansch-speaking Swiss . . . I hoped.

Unless he and Dominic Regli were of the same people after all; engaged in a power struggle here on this soil, (their soil?) Austria?

"You could be—be—" I was unnerved, retreating from this vision that had come to me too late. And I was held by the man's eyes now, for they had dropped all pretense and were staring at me with a steady, calculating purposefulness.

"Go on," he said.

It was a desperation stab, but I made it. That name of the servant in London had never rung true. I had nothing to lose now, but I should have welcomed something to lean against, something to support me, someone. "Vanko is not Italian," I said.

He stiffened, eyes narrowed, lips thinned. It was difficult to believe that his man had ever touched me, had ever offered love to me . . . to Peg.

The woman servant Vanko in London had been that "cheap, no-good slut of an actress," as Sideburns had said. The woman at the kiosk at the Feldkirch station. The woman in the telephone box at the Feldkirch post office. The woman in the flat above the King's Head, in the lobby of Number 8 Crown Gardens.

"Lori Vanko Náir," I said. "Mrs. Guido Náir. Mrs. Guy Black."

"Go on."

"Whatever you are—Italian, Austrian, Slavic—you're murderers, liars, thieves, cheats!" I glared into the eyes that glittered like smoked glass now, and I did not move. I was wondering whether I had only sensed the movements around us, the infinitesimal rustling. I was wondering whether I dared hope. "Peg?" I cried. "What about Peg? What have you done to her?"

"You are the one who interests me now," he murmured. "What do *you* know, my little one? What do you know that you have not told me? That's why I have brought you here. To hear from your beautiful lips just what you have done with my treasures."

175

He swept his arm toward the broken figures on the floor.

I repeated: "What about Peg?"

"No longer useful. And she knew too much——"

I cried out, struck out at him, but he caught my wrist, twisted it, showing obvious joy in my pain. "Where is your Swiss *montagnard* now, when you need him, eh?" The smile, the leer that stretched his lips, froze. His head snapped up.

A voice broke the stillness.

"Guido Náir." Tall and straight and steady as he had always been, Dominic Regli stepped from between golden folds of silk.

It was a small thing that he held in his hand, the gleaming blue-black barrel that jutted from fingers that had moments ago held me silent. Such a small thing, but powerful, and the words he spoke were in the language I did not understand. But it was very clear that Guy Black did.

He sprang at Dominic. In an instant the room was alive. From behind doors, tapestries, silken curtains, men converged on the president of Students' Travel (Overseas) Ltd. And first among them, locked against Guido Náir, was Karl Ochsner, the new factotum at the Goldene Krone in Feldkirch.

"Take him, Ochsner," Dominic said. "This is for your Austrian police to handle. Murder on Austrian soil. Smuggling. Illicit traffic in drugs, in art, in jewels."

Through clenched teeth Guy muttered, "How in hell did you get here?"

"Do not underestimate those *montagnards* you sneer at. Some of us are trained by the Swiss Alpine Club. Among other things. Our purpose is to save life, not to extinguish it."

He had removed his jacket while he was talking. Now he draped it around me, buttoned it carefully, avoiding my eyes until the last. "I think we shall go down an easier way, Constance. I think we shall use Signúr Náir's smart little machine, now that it is free."

Down on the landing strip the "bird" Sideburns and Lori Náir and Stefan had been waiting for was poised like a giant dragonfly in the pool of moonlight. Around the machine, just as quiet against the moon-bleached velvet of the grass, were men. Uniformed men holding those three of Guy Black's—Guido Náir's—henchmen.

One officer stepped up to us and greeted Dominic. "I have been waiting, sir, to fly you to Feldkirch," he said. "A replacement craft and crew will arrive for these *Geschöpfe.*" Even in the darkness I could see the scorn on his lips as he spat out the word, "creatures."

"*Guet,*" Dominic murmured in the Swiss I remembered. "And the other matter?"

"The ravine? We have sent men down." The officer glanced away from me.

I felt myself slipping, felt Dominic lift me into the cabin, tuck a blanket around me.

At Feldkirch he must have carried me into the Goldene Krone. I can remember nothing else that night . . .

21

How many hours later was it when we crossed the wide valley I had traveled before, back through the rolling pastures of Liechtenstein, toward Switzerland? Twelve hours? Thirteen? The clock had struck four while I was dressing—the clock I could hear from my room in the Goldene Krone. The sun had already vanished behind the crinkled rooftops and dome outside my window when the telephone rang and Luigi announced: "Herr Regli."

I had not glanced at Dominic since I had found him waiting in the dim lobby of the Gasthof, since he had answered my whispered: "Peg?" with a simple, "All has been arranged. There is nothing further—nothing you can do."

Even then I had avoided that so-typical, so-direct gaze of his. But, staring down at the hand he had offered, accepting his warm clasp, I found I could not control the tears that had been so close for all the hours since I had last seen him. I was grateful when, without words, he offered a folded linen square. Then, nodding quietly toward the dim stairs that led down to the Gasthof's court, he swooped up my two bags.

The court was empty and dark and dank as it had been those

few days ago when I had first entered there. Our footsteps, as mine had been, were barely audible on the damp stone. But outside, between the arches of the medieval arcaded walk, the late afternoon sun slanted down on a sturdy small beige car.

Dominic Regli turned when we reached it. "May I drive you?" he said.

I nodded numbly, not quite trusting my voice, not even to inquire our destination. Those so vividly remembered words of his, uttered high in a moonlit valley, might have belonged to another lifetime, not to a moment a mere night and a day ago.

When the town was behind us and the valley shimmered gold and emerald against the sapphire foothills of the Alps that rose miles ahead, I spoke for the first time. "I must have slept."

"Twelve hours. The doctor said you needed it."

"Doctor?" I relaxed the tight hold on my handbag, attempting to look at him without turning my head.

"You—" he hesitated "—perhaps noticed that there were cuts and bruises."

"Yes." I was well aware that I was patched with gauze and stained with antiseptics; that I ached, that every muscle ached. Since I had awakened, I had wondered about those lost hours after Dominic Regli had lifted me into the "little machine" on the landing field in the Verlorenen Tal. I had wondered who had cleansed my raw flesh, who had patched me.

I said, "I wondered about that."

"You . . . need not have. A doctor and a nurse have been in attendance." There was a hint of laughter in his voice. And I tried again to look at him without moving my head. Out of the corner of my eye I saw his right hand leave the wheel and move toward me, then stop.

We were leaving the last village in Liechtenstein, joining the traffic flowing from Vaduz. In the west, across the Rhine bridge, the snow mountains emerged from purple clouds, their peaks glinting like fresh-mined rose-quartz in the last rays of the sun.

I drew a deep and somewhat uncertain breath. "It's so beautiful."

"Across that bridge is Switzerland," he said. "I like to think of my home country as the most beautiful."

"But this," I made a sweeping gesture, "is still Liechtenstein, isn't it? That place, Totallia—did you—have they done something about it?"

"The villa has been sealed. The operation at Malina 10 was the outlet, the showcase for *Il Cumün,* although some of the business, their 'cover' was in legitimate goods. You see, they bought and sold anything, just as they *stole* and sold anything. The perfect name: Totallia."

I thought about this while the car purred over the bridge and the Rhine flowed sluggishly below us. "The . . . other goods, the stolen art, I suppose that was transported the way mine might have been. By innocent carriers?"

"Some of it. Including passports, which are still marketable at quite high prices."

"And some of this was under cover of Students' Travel?"

"For the last year or so, since Guido Náir took over the offices. He was a busy man."

Yes, I thought, a wave of bitterness silencing me. Kissing hands, making love, preying on human weaknesses, feminine weaknesses, in order to ply his sinister trade.

"In certain situations," Dominic went on, "students were his 'cover.' Transfers of priceless merchandise were often made by them without their knowledge. Drugs hidden in artifacts unearthed by young archaelogists in Southern France. Plastic envelopes not so innocently padding the breasts of some young women who—" he hesitated "—had succumbed to his charms. Paintings ingeniously concealed behind the modest efforts of art students. Jewels like those in your santo——"

"Jewels? Is that what he did with that little figure?"

"We found jewels crammed into it, wrapped in cotton wool. The half-kilo of heroin that you had carried by mistake from New York to London was rolled into a tube with another half-kilo and stuffed *inside* a stolen oil painting by Constable. We found that in the mourner."

"Drugs *from* the States to Europe?"

"Stock-piling against the possibility that European sources dry up."

I shuddered. "And he—his group—did steal important paintings?"

"They trafficked in stolen goods. Inside that fake mourner Náir had brought you from France he had skillfully hidden both painting and drugs. Notice that *he* traveled with cheap souvenir figures like the mourner. *He* could submit to the most rigid custom inspection."

The road was shadowed now, for the day was dying beyond the mountain tops; the sun had drifted into the hovering veil of evening, a silver wash was enveloping the valley. I shivered.

"Are you cold?" Dominic rolled up the window.

I was not cold. My mind had driven me back to that forsaken valley, to that moss and fern-bound ridge outside that miserable hut; to the sight at the bottom of that dark ravine. I said, "It's Peg." And then, protesting although he had not spoken, I added, "She was lost, you know. Her parents were too busy, too rich. Never at home. And her mother couldn't endure Peg's lameness. The sight of her was a constant reminder."

"Reminder of what, Constance?"

"Their favorite child, favorite son, who pushed Peg out of a window of their house when they were children."

His hand did touch mine then with a light brief pressure; that was all. "I think you should know that her parents are coming to claim her . . . body, now," he said.

"Too late, don't you see. It's too late." I did not attempt to suppress the bitterness. "Nobody wanted her."

"*You* did." His voice was low. "She was happy with you, Constance. Happy for you. I remember how her eyes smiled when she told me, 'There's someone in London you'd really dig. You must meet her.' "

I was biting my lip. I could not speak. I dared not speak. The memories crowded back. The first night Dominic had come to London. The first touch of his hand. The tension I had tried so desperately to overcome . . . because, since the beginning, during all of those days, all of those evenings I had thought that Peg was under his spell, that he had won her heart.

I blessed him for his next words. "You had thought perhaps that Mar-gar-ett—that she and I——"

"Yes."

Even above the motor's purr, the swish of passing traffic, I heard him release a long sigh. "I wondered about that. I hoped that was the reason. It was perhaps her enthusiasm. That could mislead." He paused. "I had difficulty with her . . . dialect. No, that is not the word."

For a moment I was so caught up in his complex sentences that I did not supply the word he sought. But when I said finally, "Slang," I rushed on. "You see, it was her way. A kind of protest, a kind of armor. She tried to be tough." I looked down and saw that I was twisting the straps of my handbag. "But she wasn't," I added.

"No," he said. "She was human." Then, quietly, "Constance, you are so loyal."

Large blue and white arrows ahead of us read: "Rapperswil–Zurich."

"Can you wait two hours for dinner?" he asked.

"Are we going to the flat in Dolder Weg?" I was not sure I wanted to hear the answer.

"No."

When he did not go on, I said, "But you know it. You've been there."

"Once. On Thursday when, after that phone call, you left for the station to reserve your seat on the Transalpin. We had to arrange somehow to get you out of the flat while we dismantled the two figures, the santo and the mourner. What we found was proof enough, the proof we needed."

"I see." Something still bothered me. That white packet banded and lettered in bronze, the Turkish cigarettes. "But weren't you there another time? The day before I'd arrived?"

"I had never been there before."

"Your cigarettes—" I stopped. Suddenly, I was back in the lobby of 8 Crown Gardens. I recalled Guy following every movement with a critical eye as Dominic calmly tucked a flat white packet of Turmacs into his pocket. I remembered Guy's comment later. "Odd," he had murmured, "that brand. I should have thought he would prefer something rougher. Gauloises, perhaps."

I could imagine that diabolical mind, now; could believe that Guy had deliberately planted the packet to mislead me.

"I've done everything wrong," I said.

"No. You helped us. From the moment you arrived in Zurich you were under surveillance. Always, in Switzerland."

There was a pause before he went on. "We had problems in Austria. You slipped out of their jurisdiction once. Your sudden decision to go to Vaduz. I have made it quite clear what I thought of that mistake of theirs."

"I think Karl Ochsner tried." I recalled the whirr of the telephone dial as I had sped down the stairs of the Goldene Krone, hurrying to the bus station.

181

"*Try* is not enough." His voice was grim. "As for the second time, I am afraid we all underestimated your friend Jenner."

"Yes." I looked away. I had underestimated Tony, too.

"Only one of us was at La Clav," he went on. "And he could not cope with so many of them when Jenner came. I had left with my Alpine squad from St. Antönien on the Swiss side for our climb to the peak above *Il Cumün*, our descent to the narrow valley. We needed silence, you understand. We could not use any airborne assistance."

"Then, there *is* a Verlorenen Tal?"

"There is. Deserted well over a century ago. After a typhus *Seuche*. You know the word? A serious disease that attacks many."

"Epidemic, I think."

"The valley was doubly doomed. The same winter of its epidemic a gigantic landslide sealed off the village from its neighboring Austrian hamlets in the Montafon and the Swiss side of the Raetikon."

I could almost see the porter, Luigi, at the Gasthof again, could almost hear his stubborn, emphatic, "*No bus goes to the valley of the lost souls. . . .*"

"Everyone said that no one goes to the valley. But *they* got there. Those—those criminals got there." I looked at Dominic. "*He* got there, with Peg."

"By helicopter. Using mufflers and floats. They could drop what I think you call the 'loot' there and at Totallia quite easily. We have seized the Bell–47 and a small plane concealed in a cave at the edge of an abandoned field near La Clav."

Dusk had gathered all around us, lying dark under the pines, closing in on all the farms and villages that seemed to drift in a sea of mist. Lights began slowly to spangle this new valley, a half-timbered farmhouse floated by, its autumn ivy drenched for an instant in the flowing gold of our lights: brilliant, fading, gone. The mountains that so short a time before had glowed jewel-bright in the vanishing sunlight now rose somber, enclosing, almost threatening, funneling toward the dark glitter of a lake.

I glanced at Dominic, and as though I had spoken, he said, "The Walensee. No one knows how deep it is."

Shadowed by steep and rugged mountains, the scene was fjord-like in its splendor. So many changing vistas, so much

182

here in Switzerland; he had so much. I was thinking of him but now I was not suppressing the thoughts, not turning away from them. I said, "You're connected with the law, aren't you?"

"Yes. Swiss Federal police. Liaison with Interpol. This *was* an international band; its only common denominator was the basic language, Ladin. The men were Italian, Austrian." He stopped.

"And the woman, Lori?"

"Lori and Stefan Vanko are technically Jugoslavs, though they pretend to be Italians from Gorizia, on the Jugoslav-Italian border. Stefan was a cook—chef—it was quite natural that he should operate La Clav."

La Clav. For an instant the embellished capitals on the gilt-touched wooden plaque glimmered in last night's moonlight.

"Was it a public inn?" I asked.

"For those who wished to take the trouble to drive there. I think you call it a 'front' but it was, of course, the 'dining room' of *Il Cumün,* though several kilometers over the mountains. Just as Náir and his crew traveled to Totallia when time was short, so they reached La Clav. By helicopter."

"A sort of gangsters' roadhouse . . ." I murmured, thinking that there were such places elsewhere in the world. I turned to him. "You knew about La Clav?"

"At first we thought it might have been the headquarters. We managed to get a man in there to work in the kitchen. It was very difficult."

"Was it the language?"

"Quite. You see, it was a peculiarity of Signúr Náir's that all of his men should speak the Ladin, preferably of the area of the Val Gardena. It was his family's speech, their dialect of the Raeto-Romanisch. They—the men of *Il Cumün*—communicated in this tongue."

"And that's why you were assigned."

"Yes." He hesitated. "I think you should know that I hold the title of professor."

I wondered where the conversation could go after that, what I could say. I tried. "And do you still live in the Engadine? In the Graubünden?" I thought he might live in a center such as Chur, perhaps.

"No. Since I have been alone, since my parents have gone, I have a pied-à-terre in Zurich. I suppose I do not really live anywhere. Or, more accurately, I live wherever I am needed."

I said nothing in answer to that. There was no answer. A tremendous loneliness engulfed me, and I sat quietly in the modest little car moving through the dusk into darkness, past strange town-names . . . Weesen, Näfels, Siebnen. . . .

I was thinking of all of us again, of Peg and her family and. my families, and of Dominic. His words were echoing in the darkness of my mind: "I live wherever I am needed."

My heart yearned toward him. But I turned away and watched the villages appear and vanish around us and below us and over us. I was numb with watching, numb altogether, not caring. I would be leaving this beauty soon, leaving everything. I was going home. Home to what? I did not know.

The lights of the villages were flowing into one long brilliant stream, dancing and flickering across the surface of a wide lake now.

"Welcome to Zurich." I barely heard his next words. "My aunt does a wonderful *Berner Platte* when the weather is colder. Perhaps not quite as good as your grandmother's."

I turned and stared at him. "Your aunt?"

"She's waiting for us, with her quite acceptable *Zürispiessli,* if you don't mind."

"Mind?" I said stupidly. I was attempting to assemble my thoughts, my poise, as I had during our first meeting in Nell Hobart's flat. "The point is," I managed to add, "Will your *aunt* mind? A late dinner. A stranger——"

"You are not a stranger to her."

The shock of the last days must have taken its toll, I thought. Or I was dreaming. I think we were driving through the outskirts of the city, for the glitter of lights had multiplied, reflections swayed and shimmered in the black waters of the lake below us. But I was not quite together, as Peg might have said, not quite with it. Only when Dominic spoke again did I drift back to him.

"There has always been a room for me in her rambling flat. There is one for you, now." I saw him glance in the mirror and signal for a right turn.

"It is not quite home." He was manipulating the car up a long zigzag past sturdy villas and pines, past windowboxes overflowing with geraniums, past vine-webbed stone walls. He made a sharp turn, shifted gears, then almost immediately braked at a dead